Four Seasons of Snarky

of

Snarky

Sherry Kuehl

Book cover design by Sara S. Eskilson

Books by Sherry Kuehl

Snarky in the Suburbs: Back to School
Snarky in the Suburbs: Trouble in Texas
Empty

For more author information go to www.snarkyinthesuburbs.com

For my son Austin Kuehl

Twelve years ago, you explained to me what a blog was, set up my blog, thought up the name Snarky in the Suburbs and then told me to "not embarrass the family." Thank you for getting me started on my Snarky journey and I'm extremely sorry I didn't hold up my whole "don't embarrass the family" part of the bargain.

Foreword

I was an indecisive mess about putting this book together. That's because what you're about to read were all originally blog posts. This fact caused me to hem and haw about publishing a book that contained material that had already been posted on my blog.

But then I got selfish and by that, I mean I worried about dying. What if I die and every single blog post (1,034 and counting) gets purged because I won't be around to pay the annual fee for the website? All that work would just be inhaled into the black hole of things that used to be on the internet.

That thought made me sad and that sadness made me think of the grandkids I don't even have yet. I pondered about how maybe someday they would like to read about their crazy grandma. That right there, my friends, was all it took to encourage me to forge ahead with this book.

Waiting for you are some of my most beloved blog posts that feature my favorite schemes of all times. A few of the stories are almost novellas and writing these posts gave me the confidence that hey, maybe I could write a book. Which led to the beginning of my *Snarky in the Suburbs* book series.

My hope is that in the future this book will become, at the very least, a bedtime story read by grandchildren (when they're tweens because I do use some curse words) and they'll think fondly of their grandmother who might have been just a tad deranged but still thought of herself as a bit of an ass kicker.

WINTER

"Winter forms our character and brings out our best."

— Tom Allen

This is your first introduction to the neighborhood super villain/nemesis Barbara Gray. It's not that I hate her exactly. It's more like I feel an overwhelming need to make sure she keeps her major control issues in check.

Also, right about now you should probably start feeling sorry for me. Imagine moving almost 2,000 miles into a new neighborhood and this was the woman who greeted you.

Suburban Tyranny

MY NEIGHBORHOOD ON the surface looks friendly. Nice enough homes with kids riding bicycles on tree-lined streets, the occasional yapping of a dog and the sound of someone yelling "fore" from the nearby golf course. But a bully lurked on our cul-de-sac. We were plagued with the Cruella De Vil of neighbors.

I got my first taste of Cruella (a.k.a. Barbara Gray) as soon as our moving van pulled up. She "popped over" to say welcome to the neighborhood. There she was oozing faux friendliness and at the same time asking me if I could tell the driver of the moving van to relocate because she didn't want to be looking out of her kitchen window at an 18-wheeler all day. I said I would see what I could do with a big cheerful "hey, I'm the new person on the block please like me smile" and then, of course, did nothing.

As I got acclimated to our new neighborhood, I heard tales of her bullying ways. Although Cruella didn't look like your typical bully. She was in her fifties, tall, attractive-ish and had the glow of a woman who was continually getting chemical peels and facial dermaplaning.

She also dressed like a lady who knew her way around a ballet fundraiser and patrolled the neighborhood like she owned the place and the rest of us were lucky to be in her orbit.

I put up with her attitude - all of it. When she objected to how my son was mowing the grass, I shrugged it off. Cruella wanted everyone in the neighborhood to mow their grass in a crosshatch pattern. "All the lawns must match," she said in a super bitch chipper tone.

I told her my family didn't have the math or horticulture skills to figure out how to make that happen, so we'd be taking a pass on being a part of the matching lawn brigade.

But alas, the comments and commands didn't stop because Cruella was consumed with her yard. It was perfect. I'll give her that. But it probably had enough chemicals on it to qualify as a cancer cluster.

When she objected to my Halloween decorations, I just sucked it up and hoped she would hop on her broom and ride, far, far, away. Cruella loudly exclaimed that they were "gaudy and unseemly."

My favorite quote from her was, "I don't know how you celebrated Halloween in your former neighborhood but here we try to keep tacky out of our little piece of paradise."

I even kept my mouth shut when she suggested to me how to place my trash cans on the curb. It wasn't until she started leaving sticky notes on my door objecting to the way I sorted my recycling that I hit the Cruella wall.

I hate sticky notes. My husband isn't even brave enough to leave me sticky notes so she sure wasn't going to get away with it And it wasn't just a single sticky note. She would plaster my door leaving one for each of my offenses.

Her primary trash objection was that some cereal boxes were being put in the garbage and not in the recycling container. She also mentioned that from the looks of my trash I could be doing a better job of feeding my family.

One sticky note read, "I'm seeing signs of entirely too much processed food." Next to that was a second sticky where she scrawled "You're killing your children."

Excuse me that my kids (and by my kids I mean me) love chocolate Lucky Charms. It really is magically delicious.

I shared my little invasion of privacy story with some of my older neighbors and they began to spout tales of bullying and what I considered down right harassment. These folks were the age of my parents. In fact, one man reminded me very much of my dad and no one on my watch is going to get away messing with senior citizens.

At first, I started yanking her a chain just a teeny-weeny bit. If she wanted to go through my trash, I was going to give her something to find. I went to a restaurant and talked them into giving me lots of empty whisky, vodka, and scotch bottles. So many, that it filled a sixty-gallon trash can, our wheelbarrow and our lawn fertilizer spreader.

Then I bought, shall I say, a few "interesting" magazines including *High Times, Cannabis Culture* and *Naked Magazine* for "the discriminating nudist." (All special orders from Amazon so you can imagine what freaky mailing lists I'm on now.) I put those bad boys right on top of my paper recycling bin and fanned them out so you couldn't miss them.

Cruella went into a tizzy. She banged on my door and demanded that I ask for God's forgiveness and wailed about my family bringing shame to the neighborhood. I acted all confused and asked what she was talking about which just set her off more. Excellent.

Over the winter Cruella got more demanding. If you didn't shovel snow from your driveway (cross hatch pattern preferred) she'd be all up in your business.

Two of our older neighbors were surprised with bills from snow removal crews she had called because she was tired of waiting for them to shovel their driveway. Never mind that they happened to be out-of-town visiting family over the holiday so of course they're not shoveling their driveways.

That was the moment when I realized what I had to do. I would liberate the neighbors from this menace and in a matter of days I had what I thought was a fairly decent plan. The only problem was I needed a team because this plan was black ops all the way. Totally covert and if caught we would have to deny everything. I had two perfect operatives in mind. My children.

Sure, some people would think you shouldn't pull your kids into a plan that at the very least is breaking some local code ordinances. But I thought that would be a waste of talent and I'm all about supporting my children's "gifts."

The main part of my plan involved my son. When I asked him how exactly he would take out a satellite dish and not get caught, he was putty in my hands.

He perked right up. "Military grade, broadcast, or communications?"

I laughed and said, "Just a plain old dish like the neighbors have."

"Oh," he sighed, sounding very disappointed. "Well, the easiest way would be a magnetic accelerator cannon."

Then, I was thinking maybe the child really does need to spend much more time outside. I pressed on with more questions. "What is that? How does it work? How fast can you build it?"

He began to not only explain it but to diagram out on paper how it would work. It was way over my head, and I tried hard not to zone out. In layman's terms he was going to take a bunch of fancy magnets, totally trick out a Nerf gun and fire them into the satellite. The magnets would temporarily mess up the dish's electromagnetic receiver field (whatever that means) but not irrevocably harm it.

I explained to him my mission and he was all for it. I then gave him a code name "My Retirement Fund" and said in tribute to Star Trek fans everywhere, "Make it so, Number One."

Next up was my daughter. She would have the most dangerous part of the mission. I would be sending my almost nine-year-old into the enemy camp. This girl can act, turn on the charm, is a little sneaky and can do a cartwheel. All qualities I needed. Plus, she liked dogs, which was a must for this assignment. She was in immediately. Her code name was Dr. Doolittle.

My husband, a.k.a. Goodie Two Shoes was kept in the dark about the rest of the family's black ops. I didn't have any time on my scheme schedule for dealing with what I'm sure would have been a conniption fit. He was strictly on a need-to-know basis. And as commander of the mission, I decided he needed to know *nothing*.

The kids and I practiced our mission roles for a couple of days, did surveillance, readied our supplies, and watched a couple of *Mission Impossible* movies to get pumped up. Then on Super Bowl Sunday we were ready for action.

Cruella prided herself on throwing a huge Super Bowl party. Not just any Super Bowl, she explained to me, but an elegant "Super Bowl Soiree." Yes, my family was invited. Shocking, I know. I think she wanted us there so she could show me how things are done when you're not a heathen.

The soiree even had a dress code - business attire. Umm, excuse me but who wants to go to a Super Bowl in work clothes? Football needs to be watched in some kind of pants with either an elastic waist or at the very least a thirty percent Lycra blend.

The word around the neighborhood was that if you dared to skip her party she would unleash a year-long reign of holy terror on you. But from what I heard this was a Super Bowl party you most definitely would want to skip.

Let's run down the list of reasons.

Coming in at number one was that the soiree was an alcohol-free zone. Cruella's reasoning was that she didn't want people losing control of their sensibilities in her home and perchance breaking or spilling something on her fancy pants hand-knotted European rugs.

Number two was that this hostess would only be serving a crudité sampler and there would be no queso or even so much as an onion dip because Cruella had a paralyzing fear of people double dipping.

The only good thing about being in Casa Cruella was that she had a T.V. so mammoth it probably affected the gravitational pull of the sun.

My mission was a two parter: Take that party down and take it over.

Our assignments began under the cover of darkness. My husband, clueless to the devastation that lay ahead, went on over to Cruella's house solo. I had told him the kids and I would come over later, maybe for the second quarter. As soon as he left, we synchronized our cell phones. It was now T-30 minutes.

On the top of our to-do list was getting Dr. Doolittle ready and into position. Cruella was the owner of a seriously deranged poodle named Cotswold. She was an angry barking machine just like her owner.

The first part of Dr. Doolittle's mission was to infiltrate the house, subdue the dog so it wouldn't give away our position and then give us the "all clear" to take down the satellite dish. To ensure Dr. Doolittle's success I sprayed her head to toe in bacon flavored Pam. Brushed "Uncle Jeb's Hickory Flavored Liquid Smoke" through her hair and stuffed the pockets of her hoodie with Snausages.

I was afraid I had over done it. The kid smelled so good I wanted to put some honey mustard on her and slap her between two slices of bread. I wiped away my drool, pre-loaded her cell phone with the code GTG (good to go) so all she had to do was hit send, gave her a final warning about what to do if the dog got overly crazed upon smelling her beefy goodness (tuck, drop and roll) and out the door she went.

My son and I were ready to get into position. We were dressed in black and just because I thought it looked cool, had cell phone headsets on. He had sprayed his Nerf N-Strike Raider Rapid Fire CS 35 Blaster turned magnetic accelerator cannon black and we both had painted the magnets that were going to be fired into the satellite dish brown so if found they would look like harmless acorns.

Our job was to get into position, wait for the all clear and then fire. The problem was getting into position. We had to climb a tree to be at the right height to hit the dish. I was there to carry the ladder (also painted black) and assist in hoisting up the cannon. We waited on the edge of our property. Nervous, but excited I whispered to my son, "Are you sure this is going to work?"

He looked at me with disdain and whispered, "Mom, please don't question my knowledge of accelerator ballistics when combined in tandem with magnetic fields."

I'm guessing that was a huge geek put down. So, I shut up and waited for the text message that would send us on our way. Three minutes later we got what we had been waiting for. The letters GTG lit up my phone.

Staying low to the ground we ran over to Cruella's backyard. I set up the ladder and my son began to climb. I was right behind him with the cannon strapped over the back. My heart was racing. I checked for left arm pain to make sure it wasn't the onset of a stroke or heart attack.

Nope, just pure adrenaline. I had a clear view of the "soiree" going on through the windows which led to me fervently pray that no one saw us because it would be most difficult to explain what the hell we were doing up in a tree with a XL Nerf gun.

At last, "My Retirement Fund" got to the right branch and assumed a firing position. I handed him the cannon. Neighborhood Liberation was about to begin. He looked at me and I gave him the signal, the University of Texas Hook 'em Horns sign. He aimed at the dish and released a torrent of magnets.

Damn, I was proud of that boy. We waited, frozen in the tree to see if we had been successful in disabling the dish. Then I got my second text of the night - "bullseye."

We attempted to stealthily climb down from the tree, but my son's big foot stepped on my hand and there was a moment of sheer horror when I thought the cannon was going airborne. Fortunately, my middle-aged cat-like reflexes saved the day, and I was able to secure it.

When we got down, I strapped the cannon to my back, grabbed the ladder, covered up the indentations it made in the ground (I didn't want any trace evidence left behind that could be pointed at us.) and we hauled ass to the safety of our house.

It was Dr. Doolittle's turn to begin part two of her assignment. The party was now in an uproar. No f'ing TV signal! No Super Bowl! Oh my!

This is when my daughter made her move. She said in a very loud voice. "We could have the party at our house couldn't we, Daddy? Mommy just bought something called a pony keg. She told me it's almost eight gallons of beer! "

As predicted, those thirsty, brew starved folks circled my husband like moths to a flame. I knew by this time he would have figured out I was up to something, but I counted on his Achilles' heel - exceptionally good manners - to pull this off.

Unable to say no and sound rude, he did as I predicted and led the party to our house. I was ready. Before we left to fire the cannon, I had preheated the oven and succulent, greasy pigs-in-a-blanket were warming up.

I also got out my hard liquor collection from Costco. Oh yeah, I went top of the line – Kirkland for when you want the very best.

I had to act surprised when my husband came in the door with what had to be forty plus party guests. "What's going on?" I exclaimed. "Oh no, the TV went out at the party. What a shame. Why, yes, I do have a pony keg in the garage. Let me get some chips and dip out and whip together a smoked meat platter."

It took all of five minutes for my house to be transformed into Super Bowl party central. Things were hopping. Unfortunately, my husband was giving me the death glare as he got out cups for the pony keg. He came over and whispered in my ear, "Half bath now."

Oops, a half bath confrontation was not a part of my plan. But I had no choice but to follow him into the bathroom. As he closed the door he whispered, "What did you do now and why is our daughter greasy and reeking of cured pork?"

I stalled, which is my specialty, and said, "Listen, I have been out making memories our children will remember for a lifetime. And about what I did - it's a very long, complex story and I don't have time to get into all the details with a house filled to the brim with guests. Please, I need to get back out there. I'm the hostess."

He did his signature sigh and opened the door.

But my mission wasn't done yet. One more task had yet to be accomplished for the neighborhood liberation to be complete.

As everybody was having a grand time stuffing their faces and draining the pony keg, I walked in front of the TV during a station ID and shouted, "Wow, this has been so much fun. My family really feels a part of the neighborhood. Why don't we make my house the Super Bowl party headquarters every year!"

As cheers erupted, I made eye contact with my kids and winked at them. They nodded back and smiled.

Mission Accomplished. Party Take Down and Take Over was a complete success. I then headed into my kitchen and uh oh there was Cruella waiting. She walked over to me, got uncomfortably close and rasped, "I know somehow that you engineered this and mark my words I will get even."

I offered her a pig-in-a-blanket and replied, "I'd like to see you try."

Looking back, that might not have been the best thing to say because this woman wasn't done with me yet. Not by a long shot.

Lord, help me but I love a good payback scenario. The planning, the timelines, the anticipation - it's like a drug to me. For years I have felt like I have missed my true calling and should have pursued a career in international espionage.

Go ahead and laugh. I'm being ridiculous, right? But I will say that dismantling a PTA board, while not up there with ousting a foreign dictator, was still impressive. Or at least that's what I love, love, love, telling myself.

Undercover at the PTA

I WISH I could mind my own business. Oh, how I dream of being one of those people who make it a point to never listen to gossip and studiously avoid eavesdropping or any kind of behavior that would intrude on someone's personal business. But alas, that is not me and this is why when a friend of mine asked for help breaking up a PTA coven, instead of saying, "What the hell?" I gave an enthusiastic, "Hell yes!"

It all started where any good mom saga begins - sitting on the bleachers watching your kid run after a ball. The friend that asked for my help is Eleanor. We met last year when our children got on the same "club" sports team. The term club denotes that your child has decided to forsake the neighborhood rec team and now seeks to empty your wallet by being on a team that requires "tryouts."

Beware newbie parents of any activity that has a "try out" criteria. It's code for "this is going to cost you a whole bunch of money." I'm not kidding. One of my (many) money-making schemes is starting some kind of competitive league for something or other like the Blue-Ribbon Elite Breathing Society.

All parents (suckers that we are) need to hear is the word elite, select or competitive and we'll pay thousands of dollars for the privilege of our child being one of the chosen ones. It's an awesome business venture. Parents fork out money for the lessons, the league events, the extra training/coaching sessions, the uniforms, travel, registration fees etc. Talk about a cozy little nest egg.

That said there are upsides to club sports. One of them is that your child gets to meet and compete with a lot of kids outside their school district environs.

Which, of course, means you, the parent, also get to meet a lot of new people. That's how Eleanor and I became friends and bonded on the bleachers.

This fall, Eleanor began sharing tales of what life was like at her youngest child's elementary school. Most of the stories focused on the PTA. Which sounded like a very well-groomed domestic terrorist organization. Hello, Homeland Security.

I, with my giving spirit, would offer advice as in: "By God, if my kid went to that school I would do blah, blah and blah."

We've all done it - talked big and braggy about how if we were in someone else's shoes what we would do and how it would be infinitely superior to whatever they were doing.

I find women are most vocal about any kind of husband misbehavior. Brace yourself for the onslaught of righteous indignation flimsily disguised as advice if any friend, colleague, acquaintance, or airplane seat mate confides or confesses that their spouse is a huge jack hole.

We'll get all worked up, offer a slew of "you should do this" guidance and then snuggle up and get cozy in our blanket of "I feel so blessed" (and by that we mean superior) because our husband "would never do that." Really, a good tale of someone's jerk of a husband can make your whole day.

Well, just after the new year Eleanor decided to take me up on some of my esteemed advice. She requested my assistance with her daughter's elementary school PTA. I was all, "Of course, what can I do to help?"

I was assuming she desired more of my sage wisdom. Lord knows hearing myself talk while offering advice are two of most favorite things in the whole wide world right behind Diet Coke and Target. But no, Eleanor wanted a little more from me than my vocal cord calisthenics. She wanted me to get involved, mix it up if you will, with the PTA board. She wanted me to go to their next meeting.

Oh my, this was quite a gift.

It's one thing to go to your own kids' schools and do a little PTA throw down. But you can really only go so far. For the most part, you have to behave yourself because you're forced to interact with these parents every day and there's the principal and usually a few teachers at the meetings. So, you can't go full-out crazy mom. You have to be tactical and a little stealthier.

But just think of the crap you could rain down on a PTA meeting where you would possibly never see or have contact with any of the people again. For me, it was the stuff dreams were made of.

Before I bellowed yes and jumped in the air while doing fist pumps, I told Eleanor she would have to go more in-depth about what problem they wanted resolved. What was their goal? In addition, I would need a little face time with the other moms she kept talking about who also desired my help.

A meet and greet was scheduled for the next day at 4:30 at the community soccer practice fields. I came prepared with my trusty reporter's notebook (Office Depot two for three bucks. You should pick up a few. They're also great for grocery lists.) As I'm talking with Eleanor and freezing my butt off, a white, little bit worse for wear, conversion van pulled up that looked like it could be featured in a *Dateline* episode.

Eleanor waved as a passenger window rolled down and a woman who needed to up her moisturizer game (maybe a night-time serum with some retinol A and a vitamin C chaser) said, "Get in."

For a second I thought, "Get in? Was I being kidnapped? I was doing these ladies a favor. Not that I expected anyone to say, "Welcome, oh great one." (It would have been nice) but, seriously, Get in?

I looked at Eleanor and she whispered, "They're kind of skittish about this whole thing, but it will be okay."

I replied in a very definite non-whisper, "Yeah, well if any of this is going to work these moms need to nut up."

(By the way, what is the female equivalent of nut up? Would it be ovary up? Get your fallopian tubes out of a bunch or unclench your uterus, is that even possible? None of those sound nearly as good to me as the classic "nut up.")

I reluctantly climbed in the van where my olfactory senses were greeted by the reek of boy feet, with a dollop of fermented French fries and finished off with the funk of unidentified lunch box refuse. It was a turbo sinus cleanse.

After my sinus tried valiantly to recover, I noticed that there were four women already seated in the van. The driver was a friendly woman with curly hair and a big smile. She reminded me of Little Orphan Annie - the middle-aged years. I feared that she must suffer from some sort of terminal nasal passage blockage (I'm thinking a tumor - hopefully benign) because I don't know how she drives this van every day without a) passing out or b) taking it to the nearest full-service car wash for a complete detail job.

Then there was the window greeter - Moisturize More. She seemed pretty no-nonsense. I was poised not to like her but then I noticed we had on identical track pants, and I knew I had found a kindred spirit.

In the back row of seats was a very pretty young mom with short blonde hair that accented her wrinkle free face. (I'm thinking - show off.) Next to her was Ms. All Business. This mom had the body language of a woman who could run a Fortune 500 company and the militant bob haircut that would look great in an Ann Taylor suit.

Eleanor and I sat down in the middle row of seats and Moisturize More asked if I wanted a drink and lifted the lid off a cooler filled with Diet Pepsi.

My friends, this is when I began to feel more than a little disrespected - Diet Pepsi in a can from a cooler that I'm certain hadn't been washed since last summer's All Star Little League playoffs. Was this anyway to woo someone to do your bidding?

My first order of business was to class up this group. I suggested, okay, demanded in a chit chatty way to, at the very least, be taken to a McCafe, which is McDonald's attempt to be swanky and yet still serve the same addictive swill. They do though have Diet Coke on tap and even the aromatic stylings of McRib would smell way better than this van.

Orphan Annie looked at Eleanor and said, "Do you think it would be safe?"

I looked around at all of them and said, "There's a McCafe right down the street. Why wouldn't it be safe?"

Eleanor smiled. "No, no, it's not that. We're worried about being seen or overheard talking about the PTA board."

I said, "I'm willing to take that chance. Now are we going or not?"

Orphan Annie tried to disguise her nervousness and said, "Sure, if everyone thinks it's okay," and started driving towards the McCafe.

I sat there thinking while trying not to breathe through my nose, "Holy crap, these women act like a bunch of battered wives. Who the hell is scared of their PTA board? Ovary up, indeed!"

Say What?

I hustled this crew into the McCafe, grabbed a Diet Coke, and herded everyone into a booth in the back. After I took a few calming, curative sips of America's favorite sugar-free beverage I was ready to do a little Q & A with cursing because I was still a smidge peeved about the Diet Pepsi.

My ice breaker was, "What the hell could a PTA board do that has you all so spooked. I'm a little embarrassed that a bunch of freaking grown women could be such damn cowards. Are these women packing heat? Have they threatened you or your children with physical violence?"

More Moisturizer got all frowny-faced. Ms. Business sat up straight and started working her bob like a pendulum by shaking her head at me. (It was a little hypnotic.) Orphan Annie gasped. Cute Blonde just sat there looking about twelve-years-old (still hating her) and Eleanor simultaneously apologized to me about her friends and then apologized to her friends about me.

I held up my hand and said, "Let's not waste our time with good manners. I've got about thirty minutes before I have to start the kid retrieval process. So, someone please tell me what's the damn deal."

It got quiet. I took another sip of my Diet Coke and surprisingly Cute Blonde was the one who spoke up. "These PTA women run the school and if we say or do anything they don't like we're afraid they'll take it out on our kids."

I immediately went for the follow-up question. "Can you give me some examples of how they run the school?"

Ms. Business perked up and I heard her speak for the first time, "Well, they're so bad the principal is afraid to mess with them. Which I don't understand because it's not like they can fire him, but by the way he acts you would sure think they could."

Cute Blonde interjected, "They've gotten two teachers fired!"

Orphan Annie added, "They've taken over things that used to be the job of the principal and teachers. Like they now decide on Student of the Month and do the school awards at the end of the year. You cross them and your kid gets nothing."

Finally Moisturize More with wet eyes said, "I tried, nicely tried, to talk with the President about maybe changing a fundraising policy and my three kids were left out of the Award Ceremony. They were never called up once and her one child got Student of the Month three times last year, three damn times!"

My eyes were now popping out of my head. This went straight from WTH to WTF. "Okay, okay, this is all outrageous and horrible but why do you want me to go to the meeting next week and what do you want me to do? I don't think having me show up and announcing to the whole pack of them that they are on the terrorist watch short list was going to do any good besides the obvious and short-term pleasure of seeing the PTA board get ticked off."

Ms. Business cleared her throat, smoothed her hair, and volunteered more information. "Well, some sneaky stuff happened over the winter break. This group of officers were supposed to be moving off the board because their terms were up. But over Christmas they re-wrote the bylaws in executive session and extended the number of years you can serve as a PTA board member to five years."

"Ugh - bylaws. I don't do bylaw throwdowns. I'm not an attorney," I groaned.

Moisturize More quickly interjected, "You don't understand time is of the essence. At the general meeting next week is when the "new" officers will be voted in. This is the only chance to get these bitches off the board."

I'm not going to lie. I was encouraged to hear swearing. It meant the women were warming up to me and showed they had a fighting spirit after all. "Do you ladies have any ideas of how you would like to go about this?' I asked.

Orphan Annie said, "We were hoping you would show up and introduce another slate of officers to be voted on."

Oh crap, here I was hoping for a smackdown in the cafeteria and these chicks wanted to do revenge by Robert's Rules of Order. So, not my style.

I sat there sipping my Diet Coke saying nothing and thinking. It's obvious these poor women needed my help and at least two of them could use a make-over day at Nordstrom. But I already hated the PTA board of pure evil so my instinct was to jump in and attempt to kick some ass.

I just wasn't quite sure how I was going to approach this one. It wasn't something that could be done by brute force. It needed finesse and a certain level of knowledge about boring crap like parliamentary procedure. Right now, I had no idea how to pull this off.

I looked up at everyone and said, "I'm in, but it's going to take a lot of work.

I'll need deep background on every board member. Most importantly are any of them currently a lawyer, a paralegal, married to a lawyer or the daughter of a lawyer.

"Secondly, I need cover. When I show up at the meeting everyone has to believe for thirty minutes that my kid goes to that school. Get me the most common first name of the boys at your school. Is it Michael? It is Jack? Find out.

"Third, I need to know where the meeting is taking place and a tour of the school. Lastly, I need to observe these mega witches in their natural habitat or lair. I want to see what I'm up against."

I was glad to see Orphan Annie taking notes. Plans were made and assignments were given. It looked like the next day I would be going to Starbucks to spy on my newest nemesis - the board president. (God, that nemesis list of mine is long.) This woman did not disappoint. What do you say about a chick who goes to Starbucks and orders a Venti hot water with lemon?

I say she's one crazy, well hydrated bitch.

Goldilocks

I wonder if the three flannel clad Seattle dudes that opened the coffee-house that led to Starbucks ever thought that their little bean store concept would become the morning hang out for every evil/hot mom and aspiring evil/hot mom in America.

Probably not. But, if you want to observe class wars, mom cliques, boobs that have been, thanks to modern science, hoisted to shoulder-blade height and nostrils that have been hot waxed, cleaned and steamed (Don't tell me you thought you could only do that to your car?) all one needs to do is head to any suburban Starbucks.

That's why the next morning, after last night's meeting with the group of moms I'd code named "Nut Ups," I found myself at an unfamiliar Starbucks casing the joint. I had on my uniform of leggings (yes, how shocking), a fleece Kohl's Tek Gear hoodie, and for privacy reasons, a baseball hat, pulled down low on my forehead. My only salute to fashion was a high ponytail threaded out the back of my hat.

I ordered myself a hot chocolate (my Diet Coke was lovingly waiting for me in the car) and positioned myself so I could watch the door.

Very early that morning I went on social media and checked out the list of names the Nut Ups had given me. I don't mean to slow down this story, but there's always time for a safety lesson. People check your social media privacy settings. None of the six moms whose names I had been given had much, if any, privacy settings.

In fact, I have a theory, the more obnoxiously braggy you are on social media the less privacy settings you have. It's as if you want to shout out to the world, "Look at me! My life is fab! I take amazing vacays! Please track me down and kill me."

So, suffice it to say I already had a lot of intel on these bitches. But I was big game hunting so most of my attention would be focused on Priscilla Davis - PTA President at Waterford Elementary.

I gagged a little on my hot chocolate when Priscilla walked into Starbucks. Instagram did not do her justice. She looked like Goldilocks gone bad. Like if Goldilocks had a really big problem finding the bed that was "just right" so she kept on trying.

Priscilla had faux gold hair that went in ringlets all the way down her back. She also had a heavy hand with the eyeliner and some gold hoop earrings that could double as a towel holder in your downstairs half bath.

It was her outfit that was most telling. It showed a weakness that I would exploit. Priscilla had on a tennis skirt, a tennis warm up jacket, a fur vest, Alo yoga pants under the tennis skirt and of course, freaking mini Uggs.

Many women where I live wear yoga pants under their tennis skirts. I would bet a portion of my 401(k) that most of these moms don't even play tennis. I call this the "active douchey mom on the go" look. What was high value intel about Priscilla's outfit was that it showed a woman who was afraid. Excellent.

I fancy myself a modern-day mom version of Sherlock Holmes. By dissecting Priscilla's appearance from the head down I found out that she had an abnormal attachment to super long hair - signaling a need to hold on to her childhood. This most likely was due to some kind of childhood trauma (parental divorce etc.).

The hair was also her security blanket. She can't let it go. The fact that she couldn't wear just a tennis outfit and had to mix it up with Uggs, yoga pants and that really tacky fur vest suggested she refused to be stripped of any of her physical trappings.

For instance, if she walked into Starbucks in just a tennis skirt, hoodie and tennis shoes with that icky hair pulled out of her face, with no eyeliner she would feel naked, maybe invisible. This chick had a narcissistic need to be the center of attention.

The hideous furry Uggs, the fur vest and full makeup and hair was how she signaled her hot mom pecking order. I had all this figured out before she opened her mouth. It was when the witch ordered a Venti hot water with lemon that I added crazy to my list.

The hot water order says so much. Primarily it's a female power play. Everyone else at the table was drinking some sort of beverage that had a modicum of calories. But Priscilla was showing that she's better than that. She's drinking only hot water which means she wins. By that one simple order she has signaled her superiority. The hot water is the big F U and the lemon was her prop.

She could squeeze it, stir the juice in her cup of hot water, and caress the rind as it laid flaccid on her napkin. These moves kept the group's eyes on her. She had absolute control. It's as if she was saying, "Go ahead you losers at my table drink that crap. I will sit here, sip hot water and make you feel as uncomfortable as I can."

The hot water ploy is also a hundred percent guarantee that at least one person will make the comment, "That's why you're so skinny. Oh, my Gawd, I wish I had your willpower."

Once Priscilla sat down with her flashy flock of PTA board besties, I patted myself on the back for having the perfect spot for eavesdropping. I was right behind her and could hear everything.

This coven talked non-stop about their appearance, dissected other people's appearance with a vengeance, bragged on their children and their bank accounts, and then went deep on their children's school. After thirty minutes I wanted to sever my own auditory nerve just so I wouldn't have to hear their cocky voices and plans for PTA domination.

Practice Makes Perfect

On Monday morning, two days before the Wednesday PTA meeting, I invited the Nut Ups to my house for a rehearsal. I needed to make sure these five women knew exactly what they needed to do. I couldn't have anybody get scared, squeamish, or confused. At exactly 10 a.m. I heard a rumble in my driveway. It was the freaking conversion van. The Nut Ups had carpooled.

I welcomed them into my house and gave extra credit to Eleanor who brought me a fresh Diet Coke, in a thirty-two-ounce Styrofoam cup (my beverage container of choice) with my favorite kind of ice - crushed. I shooed everyone into my dining room where I had muffins and assorted drinks laid out plus paper, pens and a handout.

Also, because I believe in leaving nothing to chance, I had produced a timeline for the takeover of the PTA meeting. I also had given our mission, for fun, a code name, BBG - Bitches Be Gone.

The meeting started out on the wrong foot. Immediately, Orphan Annie objected to the word bitches. Apparently, she was still "reeling" from my "cursing episode" at McDonald's.

I did a swear word inventory in my head and could only come up with three that I probably used - damn, hell and bitches. Those are itsy bitsy, teeny, tiny curse words. It's not like I was spewing F bombs. This made me f'ing mad. To think I baked from scratch for this group.

I said to Orphan Annie, "Seriously, we are about to do battle with a sorority of evil. To do this, you and everyone else at this table are going to have to leave Goody Two Shoe Land where you've allowed, that's right, ALLOWED yourself and YOUR children to be victimized and enter the world of Kick Some Ass.

"If you feel more comfortable just staying with the status quo of "*Oh look at me, I'm so sweet and gentle that cursing hurts my feelings*" then we should just stop right now. I need devious, sneaky, smart women sitting at this table."

I paused to catch my breath and to cool down. I was still super ticked. As I'm exhaling, Moisturize More, bangs her fist on the table and says, "I'm in!" and then to my delight, she shouts so loud my dogs bark, "I want to get those f'ing bitches!"

Oh yeah, that's what I was talking about. A show of spirit and cursing all while shoving a blueberry muffin in your face. That's my kind of girl

Eleanor soon followed with, "Hell yes, we want to do this!"

Ms. Business even stands up and says, "BBG is on."

Cute Blonde responded with, "I'm kind of scared, but I know I'll regret it if I don't do anything so let's go."

All heads turned towards Orphan Annie. I was thinking to myself, come on girl get a backbone when she looked up at all of us and said, "Oh my God, oh my God, I'll do it, but please tell me it will all work out alright?"

I looked her right in the eyes and said with every bit of sincerity I had, "Yes, it will all work out I'm sure of it." Although I wasn't the least bit sure, but I figured it's what she needed to hear.

Orphan Annie then had a moment of conscience and wanted all of us to pray about whether or not we should really do the PTA meeting intervention. That felt weird to me. I'm so over people using prayer as an excuse to never have to make a decisive decision in their life.

It's not that I don't believe in prayer. I was praying right then that the conversion van wasn't leaking oil in my driveway because my husband wouldn't notice me mowing the lawn naked, (to be fair he probably would, but only to tell me to put some shoes on) but oil on his precious driveway well, I'd hear about that as in, "Where did the damn oil leak come from?"

So, I suggested we continue with the meeting then once everyone was home they could pray to their heart's content. That appeased Orphan Annie and I was finally able to get to my timeline.

I walked everyone through exactly what I was going to do at the meeting. Then I had everyone role play about what they were assigned to do. We went over and over it because I wanted everyone to be confident and not timid. When I felt all the Nut Ups had their parts down, I approached the subject of what they should wear to the meeting because it was going to be a no frumps allowed event.

This meant the standard outfit of jeans, generic fleece top and Crocs would not be allowed. I encouraged every woman to dress up, to not be afraid to use concealer and shared that a little eyeliner was good for the soul.

I slyly managed to mention that a new European Wax studio had just opened, and they were doing a first wax for free promotion. As I'm saying this, I make eye contact with Orphan Annie. I told Cute Blonde she needed to channel her inner hottie. We needed her to take her youth (I found out she was twenty-six freaking years old!) and just rub it the face of the peri-menopausal PTA board.

She had what they could never have again - youth. I instructed her to strut her stuff all around the cafeteria that night. It would distract and piss off the PTA bitches and I needed that diversion if we were going to pull this off.

Last on my list for the meeting was a getaway car. I had learned the hard way that if you're going to stir things up you better be sure there's a car waiting to speed you away from the land of hostile moms.

Orphan Annie perked up and said she could drive the getaway car. Hard pass on that. Nowhere in the heist, scheme or covert operation arena would one's first thought be, "Hell yeah, a thirteen-passenger conversion van makes the perfect quick getaway vehicle." Before I could politely say, "We probably need something a little smaller."

She shouted out, "I can use my husband's car. He drives a BMW M3 Coupe."

This totally distracted me. My mind instantly went to a marriage where the wife would be stuck with an aging crap ass van while the husband drives a top-of-the-line sports car. I was thinking Orphan Annie had much bigger problems in her life than a mustache and the PTA board. But I filed that away under thought for another time and said, "Yeah, sounds great. You're my getaway driver."

The meeting lasted almost two hours. The Nut Ups left my house pumped and I was feeling optimistic and excited. The showdown was in T minus fifty-six hours.

Do I Know You?

One of the last things on my to-do list was to pay a visit to the now infamous (to me) Waterford Elementary School.

The morning before the PTA meeting, I was in the school parking lot waiting for Eleanor. My plan was for both of us to walk in together, sign the parent volunteer sheet in the school office, slap on a Waterford Elementary School "visitor" sticker and do some recon.

Eleanor pulled up beside me and we both got out of our cars. I followed her lead as we were buzzed into the school. Just as I thought, it was easy-peasy to sign in at the front desk, (I don't think the school secretary even looked up from her computer as soon as she recognized Eleanor) and walk to the workroom.

Here, like in most schools, are where you find the copy machines, paper, staplers etc. and moms (I know dads volunteer but in my nine years straight of having at least one child in elementary school I have never seen a father collating worksheet packets.) allegedly assisting their child's teacher.

The mothers may be hard at work die cutting hearts for the February bulletin boards, but they're also multi-tasking by gossiping their asses off. This made the workroom ground zero to gauge the mood of the moms. As Eleanor and I were about to enter the workroom she stopped short. I asked her, "What's up?"

Eleanor stepped back and said, "Crap. I hate that mom."

I peeked over her shoulder and said, "Which one are you talking about there's three moms in there."

"The petite one right by the copier with those stupid boots on."

I looked in again and saw a woman in riding boots and freaking breeches or whatever the hell you call those pants that fancy people who ride horses wear. (Oh, pardon me, I mean equestrians) Did she ride her horse to school because I didn't see a hitching post in the parking lot?

I asked Eleanor, "Do you hate her because she wears her horsey pants to volunteer at the elementary school? Because if so, that's enough for me?"

"No, I hate her because we've had kids the same age and in the same class for like five years and she never ever remembers who I am. God, I'm so sick of it. I've probably re-introduced myself to her a hundred times."

"Gag," I said, "One of those. A mom with a bad case of arrogance amnesia. The old 'you're not important enough for me to remember therefore I'll pretend I don't know you as a way to signal my superiority.' Well, what are we waiting for? Let's go in there and mess with her."

Eleanor gave me a pained expression, so I said, "Correction. I'll go in there and mess with her. You pretend you need to make copies."

With that we both walked into the workroom and whatever conversation/gossip the three women were having stopped. Eleanor said hi and I smiled and nodded at everyone. Horsey pants sneered and said, "Do I know you two?"

I gave her an over the shoulder confused look and said, "You're joking right?"

"No, I'm not. Have we ever been introduced? She then gives both of us the snobby once over. "I don't recollect meeting either of you and I certainly don't think you're from the club or the barn."

THE BARN! I'm biting down on my lower lip to keep from howling and suddenly the lyrics to the classic 1950s TV show - *Mr. Ed* popped into my head. No, I'm not that old, but who hasn't heard the *Mr. Ed* song sometime in their childhood? Okay, I'm guessing that's mostly everyone. So, here's the condensed version - Mr. Ed was a snarky talking horse.

What a huge Mr. Ed's ass this woman was. I get it lady, you ride horses. That doesn't make you the Queen of England.

Instead of singing the *Mr. Ed* theme song I said in a very concerned voice, "Okay, now you're scaring me. You do know me from the barn. I'm the dressage champion (points for me pulling that term right out of my butt) and Eleanor and you have had kids in the same class for years."

I then did a long drawn out "Ohhhhhhh" and all of the moms gave me a weird look, including Eleanor.

This is when I stuck the knife in and rotated it counterclockwise, "I am so, so sorry. I should have realized you're going through menopause and having those memory lapse issues my mom's Red Hat Society always talks about. Don't worry, according to my mom it all comes back after your body gets used to the non-estrogen lifestyle. You'll be fine. Circle of life, my friend, circle of life."

As Horsey Pants turned bright red, I grabbed Eleanor's shoulder and turned her towards the door. We both walked out, and Eleanor whispered, "Oh my God."

"I have no doubt she'll remember you now," I said.

Eleanor, still whispering, which was starting to aggravate me, murmured, "Yeah and not in a good way."

"Stop worrying and count your blessings. I'm guessing she'll never even make eye contact with you again. Now, where's the cafeteria?"

Eleanor showed me the cafeteria and how the meeting would be set up. The PTA board members had the custodian set up a dais with microphones and a smart board. When Eleanor told me this, I looked at her and asked, "How many parents come to the meeting that they need a dais and microphones? Most elementary school PTA meetings are lucky to get two dozen parents."

"They really publicize all the meetings, and they take roll. Your kid won't be eligible for any awards if at least one parent or guardian doesn't come to a meeting."

"Shit." I said, "They TAKE roll? (Totally dismissing the just as shocking fact that school awards were based on parental attendance at a PTA meeting.) Why didn't you guys tell me this? I'll need to work around that. Do they take roll at the beginning of the meeting? Is it a verbal roll call or do they just circulate a sign in sheet?"

"They take roll as soon as you walk in. There will be a table and two of the board members will watch you sign in."

"Don't tell me they check I.D.?"

"No. I don't think so. Is this going to be a problem?"

"Maybe, but don't worry about it. I'll improvise. Now show me the exits that will open and not set off an alarm."

A couple of minutes later I felt confident that I knew the school's layout and walked back out, solo, to my car. Oh perfect, there's Horsey Pants in the parking lot. She walked up to me and said, "Not that it's any of your business but I am far too young to be going through menopause."

I was ready to just give her some more grief but then a thought occurred to me. To pull off this scheme the Nut Ups will need parental support. This was an awesome opportunity to turn Horsey Pants into an ally.

"Hey," I said, "You look like you're in your early thirties, (Total lie. She looked forty on a good day.) but Priscilla Davis had been telling everyone you're going through the big M complete with drippy hot flashes. I'm sure she's jealous of you. Seriously, everyone is. You should come to the PTA meeting tomorrow. Did you hear she's trying to be PTA president - again? Like she thinks she's queen of the school or something. You want to get back at her - show up."

"How would going to the PTA meeting get back at her?"

"I don't really know, but I heard a rumor that it's going to be good."

"How good?"

"How about that big, bleached blonde, head of hair of hers is going to be ground zero for a school wide lice epidemic and that's just for starters."

Horsey Pants graced me with a full-mouthed smile and my first thought was wow, those are some bad veneers. If I were her, I might want to cut back on the horsey expenditures for some better cosmetic dentistry. After I got past the slipshod teeth I smiled back and said, "So, I'll see you tomorrow night?"

"Oh, I'll be there," she purrs. "And I'll bring friends."

We both went to get in our cars and as she opened her door she looked back at me, wrinkled her brow, squinted her eyes and asked, "Are you sure I know you?"

"Yes, I've been at this school for years."

Point of Order

It was time. At exactly 6:30 p.m. I was in the safe haven of the Target parking lot. It was our predetermined rendezvous point. I was leaving my car here and Eleanor would be picking me up.

I was ready for battle. I had on full makeup - serum, eyeliner, the works and my arms hurt from using a round brush to blow dry my hair. My flab was tucked away under a double layer of Spanx, well really triple layer, if you count the compression properties of the Spanx black "Tight End" tights. (Black tights are the only way a true cankle sufferer will expose her deformity.)

I wore my "serious" outfit of a black wrap dress, blazer and heels that would put me at a little over six-feet tall. I needed the height. The PTA board would be on a raised dais, and I would be speaking from the floor. I wanted to make sure I wouldn't be easily dismissed.

I also carried my black with navy trim Coach Outlet briefcase/bag. Full disclosure here, I bought it a couple of years ago because I thought it was a briefcase satchel with lots of nifty compartments. Come to find out it was a frigging diaper bag! (What a fitting metaphor for my life.)

My final touch was an upgrade from a spritz of Gain Febreze to the newly released limited edition Febreze Seaside Spring & Escape. (I had a coupon.) The whole hair, makeup, and dressy outfit were doing double duty. I wanted to convey a "I've been doing important things all day" vibe and it was also a disguise.

I don't normally look this way so if I ever ran into anybody that saw me at the meeting, they wouldn't recognize me. I sat in my car checking out my makeup in the rearview mirror when I saw Eleanor pull up.

Wow, she looked good! I think this was the first time either of us had seen each other in something besides jeans. I grabbed my diaper bag/briefcase, took one more glance at myself, hopped out of my car and then almost wiped out because I had forgotten I had heels on.

I got in Eleanor's front seat and asked, "Is everyone in position?"

"Yes, all present and accounted for," she said in a commanding voice.

When we arrived at the school, I went in first. Eleanor followed me about three minutes later with Orphan Annie not far behind her. We did this because I didn't want anybody to know that we were together.

I approached the cafeteria and gasped. Imagine if you will the Kardashians running an elementary school meeting. I'll give you a second to get that image in your head. Got it? Okay, now I'll continue.

As you entered the cafeteria there was a portable smart board set up with pictures of the PTA board members. These aren't images of the board volunteering at the school or chaperoning a second-grade field trip taken with someone's iPhone. Oh no, think professional grade photography with a wind machine.

There were solo shots of each board member and group shots. Each one served up a side of cleavage and some pouty lip action. My favorite was a black and white photo of Priscilla Davis with bare shoulders, her neck extended, her face kind of arching towards the camera, the "wind" blowing her hair back and her glossy lips slightly parted.

In PG-13 terms it looked like she was about to engage in some vigorous amorous activity. While this photo collage was unfolding on the smart board the 2011 hit, *I'm Sexy and I Know It* was being played. I don't know if it was coordinated with the smart board or if the custodian had a radio on, but parents were entering the cafeteria to lyrics that didn't exactly scream – PTA meeting in an elementary school.

I was stopped from entering any further into the cafeteria by the sign in table. Parents were waiting about ten people deep to sign the attendance list. This is not something I wanted to do so I pretended I saw someone I knew and bypassed the table. It was all good until a frisky PTA board member whose whole appearance shouted, "Cougar" stopped me.

"Excuse me, but all parents must sign in before entering the meeting."

"Yes, I know. I'll be right back to sign in, but I must talk to that other mom over there for just a second."

Cougar didn't seem like she was going to let me pass so I did my version of Obi-Wan Kenobi's "These aren't the droids you're looking for" and said, "You have the prettiest skin. I need to talk to you later about what you're doing. Is it a serum or genetics because you look amazing?"

That's all it took to get past Cougs and get the seat I wanted, which was the last row by the exit door to the parking lot. I sat down and smiled when I saw Cute Blonde working the room. She didn't let me down.

This beautiful young woman was in a denim mini skirt with stretch boots that went over her knee. The best part about the outfit was the top. It was a tight long sleeve scoop neck T-shirt and oh God bless her, Cute Blonde appeared to be braless. She didn't have huge boobs. In fact, she was kind of what I would call a small B cup.

But she had young, extremely pert, naturally sag free, one hundred percent organic breasts that showed no signs of stretch marks, breast-feeding wear and tear or any other of the ravages of time that slowly teach our "twins" to head downwards to our belly buttons.

I was impressed and I was pretty sure every woman in the room hated her, which was just what I wanted. The PTA board couldn't keep their eyes off of her. They keep on staring and whispering. It totally distracted them from the storm that was brewing.

Right before seven o'clock Orphan Annie walked over and sat beside me. I wanted her next to me. She was our weak link and I needed to keep an eye on her to make sure she didn't blow it. She was also my ride out of here. I was pleased to see she was mustache free.

Moisturize More was standing by the dais. She looked so good I needed to shorten her name to just More. As I stared at her she tripped, and the contents of her purse dumped out on the dais. Cute Blonde went over to help her tidy up. The air got sucked out of the room when Cute Blonde bent way over and gave everyone in the first couple rows of seats a look down her shirt.

All Business was in the fourth row. She had on a suit and her hair had been given a professional blow out. Eleanor was in an aisle seat seven rows back. The meeting didn't start until 7:05 because that's how long it took for the Real Housewives of Waterford Elementary to strut up on the dais.

Board President Priscilla Davis grabbed the microphone and did the fling and shake with her hair like she was filming a shampoo commercial. My feeling is when you are legally of age to buy alcohol you need to remove "hair flinging" from your repertoire. She then called the meeting to order.

The first ten minutes were all about the pledge of allegiance, the parent and teacher welcome, approving the minutes from the last meeting and then, finally, we got to the good stuff - voting on the slate of officers.

I stood up, walked into the aisle, and raised my hand making it impossible not to notice me, but alas, the board president attempted to do just that. I then used one of two "gifts" the Lord gave me, the ability to amplify my voice without the aid of a microphone. "Pardon me," I said, "Pardon."

Everyone turned around and looked at me (remember I was in the back row) thus forcing Priscilla to acknowledge my presence

She growled, "Yes."

"Hi everyone," I said like I was running for student council president, "I'm Sam's mom."

(Sam being the most common boy's name at the school and, as every woman reading this knows, once you have a kid any introduction of yourself for the next eighteen years will begin with "I'm _____ mom." Also, it's a safe bet if you're trying to infiltrate a school that you pretend to be the mother of a boy.

The mothers of girls know each other better. I think it's because the mom/daughter connection fosters more gossip due to an estrogen fueled "need to know" quest. I also find that generally the moms with a higher daughter to son ratio will be the ones that run the school. I'm not saying it's right. I'm just saying that's the way it is.)

Once that got everyone's attention, I continued in what I thought was a very mom next door attitude and said, "One of my New Year's resolutions was to become more involved in my son's school. (There's a slight chuckle from the audience.) So, here I am!

"I just want to say that I have a Point of Order. I don't believe we can vote on the slate of officers until the entire membership, that's all of us here, vote on the changes that were made to the bylaws that allow officers to serve more than two years. So, what I'm thinking is that the new bylaws need to be voted on first and if that passes then we can vote on the proposed slate of officers."

Priscilla fired back in a bored tone (like how dare the little people annoy me), "But the bylaw changes were already approved in an executive session meeting the board had last month."

"Oh, I'm sorry, I must not have made myself clear, the board cannot approve any bylaw changes without a full vote of the membership. That means it's great that all of you voted it in (as I'm saying this, I use a sweeping arm gesture to indicate the board) but it really means nothing until the membership votes."

All Business stood up and shouted out, "Yes, what she's saying is absolutely correct. We need to vote on the bylaw changes first."

Then a rogue mom jumped up to speak. I was thinking she's the enemy because she's wearing fur. It's not even a faux fur but like a real fur from an animal of indeterminate origins. Who wears a full-length fur with jeans to a school meeting? I wasn't even cold enough for a fur. It went from bad to worse when the first words out of her mouth were, "When I was Junior League President."

Holy mother of God, I now had a furry former Junior League President to deal with. Crap. I had to be careful or Furry would hijack the whole meeting. I didn't want to yield any of my power, so I stayed standing. I gave All Business a look and she also remained standing.

Furry Junior League continued with, "We at the Junior League followed the strictest code of parliamentary procedures in accordance with the Junior League policy on meeting conduct so I must take exception to Sam's mom's statement that the membership has to vote on the bylaw changes. First, we have to vote on voting to have a bylaw change."

Great, I thought death by parliamentary procedure, and really how many times can one woman work Junior League into a sentence, but at least the Furry JL backed me up - kind of. I was pretty sure she was wrong about the vote but what the hell I needed to move this meeting along.

I quickly interjected, "So we need a motion from the floor to vote on whether to vote on the new bylaws."

All Business made the motion, Moisturize More seconded it and it sounded like everyone said, "aye" meaning it was time to move on to the actual vote on the bylaw changes.

Priscilla, clearly aggravated as signaled by her repeated lip gloss applications, kept trying to push everyone to vote on the bylaw changes. She bellowed, "Enough of this let's vote on the bylaws."

I hopped up again, "Sorry, to be such a pain, but I believe before we vote you need to entertain any discussion from the floor about the bylaw changes."

Priscilla sighed, stamped her foot while picking at a cuticle and very quickly said, "Alright, is there any discussion from the floor? I'm thinking no, so let's go to the vote."

Eleanor sprung out of her seat and yelled, "I'd like to discuss it."

I shouted, "Me too, because I'm thinking you ladies are saints to want to be PTA board members AGAIN. Give yourself a much-needed break and let someone else do the heavy lifting."

This gets the crowd talking. Priscilla looked just the slightest bit panicked, and I saw her glancing furtively at the other board members. She then shouted into her microphone, "It's not a problem. We all loooooove volunteering. We're all about the kids."

Orphan Annie jumped up and went totally off script, yelling, "Yeah, it's all about your own kids, not ours!"

Which was all Cute Blonde needed to hear. She said, "Hey, Priscilla, how many times has your daughter gotten Student of the Month? Three times? Is that how you're all about the kids?"

The crowd was now getting into it. Awesomeville! Priscilla was banging her gavel which had crystals glued to it so it looked like something a judge would use if they were holding court in a strip club.

I then went to part two of the plan. Part one was to stir the pot and get things to a boil. Part two was to give the principal a little ass whooping. I signaled to Moisture More by holding up the peace sign. She moved out into the aisle and said, "Let's all speak one at a time so everyone can be heard."

This does the trick and as the crowd gets semi-quiet. I said, "I'm new to this whole volunteering thing, but, and I guess this question goes to the principal. How do these PTA board moms get to pick things like student of month and decide what child gets an award? Isn't that your job and the teachers? Why would you abdicate that responsibility to parents? I mean, talk about a conflict of interest. You can't expect a mom to not think her kid is award-winning." (With that I get my second chuckle of the meeting.)

The principal stood up and walked towards the front of the cafeteria. I know this type of principal very well. He's about twenty months shy of retirement, will do just about anything not to rock the boat and that includes letting (let's use the politically correct term for these moms) "strong willed" parents run roughshod over him as long as they don't go bugging anybody at the district level. He looked right at me and said, "Now who are you?"

I replied with a great, big, proud mommy smile, "Sam's mom and my question is why are you letting the PTA board do this? It's a clear violation of FERPA. The Family Educational Rights and Privacy Act."

He hemmed and hawed a little bit and then said, "Well, seeing how the PTA pays for the awards I didn't see a problem when they approached me about taking over the award process completely."

"That sir," I shouted, "Sucks!"

For a nano second it was total silence and then, led by my team, the crowd broke out in applause.

Not waiting for the applause to die down, I added, "I will be going to the district with this, like, tomorrow. I'm very disappointed in your leadership skills." For the first time in ten minutes, I sat down.

All Business stood up and said, "I think based on what we've heard from other parents that I'm going to make a motion that we do not approve the new bylaws."

Furry JL popped up and said, "I second it, but I think the board should get a chance to speak."

One dad said very sarcastically, "Haven't they done enough?"

All Business took back control and said, "Let's vote first."

The ayes had it. The new bylaws went in the toilet.

Priscilla got to her feet, leered at all of us and croaked out, "Well, without the new bylaw changes approved you don't have a slate of PTA officers. Have you thought of that?"

Eleanor quipped, "Yes, we have." She then reached down into her Whole Foods tote bag and pulled out a bunch of papers and said," I'd like to hand out this proposed slate of officers for everyone to look at and approve.

Orphan Annie, More, Cute Blonde and Eleanor all got up to help pass out the papers. Priscilla had resumed her seat on the dais, and she was whisper-bitching up a storm with her officers. As the last of the papers were being passed out, she stood up, grabbed the microphone, and said, "I make a motion that we wait one month until the next PTA meeting to vote on this proposed slate of officers."

I stood up and said, "No one, I mean not a soul, second this. The last thing you need to do is give these women thirty days (I'm now making jabbing gestures into the air with my fingers) to come up with another way to screw you over, and by that I mean screw your kids over."

God, this was FUN until I saw that Horsey Pants had stood up. She flashed me a smile and my first thought was oh shit here she comes to mess up everything.

Horsey, still in jodhpurs, said, "I make a motion that we vote on the proposed slate of officers right now. A whole out with the old (she says that while staring at Priscilla) and in with the new kind of thing."

Cute Blonde quickly seconded it. All Business said, "All in favor?"

That question was answered with a loud cry of "Aye!"

The PTA board looked ready to cry and then Furry JL stood up and said, "I think this was done incorrectly. The motions from the floor could be invalidated because some of the officers that were on the slate made the motions indicating a conflict of interest."

Which was true. All Business was slated and just voted in as the president. Eleanor was the new treasurer. Cute Blonde was the fundraising chair. Moisturize More was Teacher Liaison and Orphan Annie was recording secretary.

Before Furry JL could ruin all our hard work with her "True Life Adventures of a Junior League President" I initiated the chaos contingency plan to end the meeting fast. We got what we wanted and now everyone needed to vacate the premises - pronto.

I went to the idea I had when I first saw Pricilla's Goldilocks tresses at Starbucks - head lice.

I stood up again, put on my reading glasses and walked towards the dais. I then bent down, jumped back and yelled, "Oh my God, there's head-lice all over this floor under this table.

Moisturize More ran up and said, "Priscilla you have nits on you right now! Lice love chemically processed hair!"

Priscilla screamed bloody murder, the rest of the six Kardashian board members jumped out of their chairs, some crying and because it's human nature when something is "allegedly" on you - vigorously shook their hair.

I yelled, "For God's sakes stop shaking your infested manes. All of you are lice bombs. Everyone clear out!"

In actuality, I had taken tiny white sesame seeds and given them to Moisturize More. When her purse "accidentally" dumped out on the dais before the meeting she and Cute Blonde sprinkled the seeds underneath the table. The seeds looked enough like lice, if someone called attention to them, to cause a freak out, which was all I needed.

Horsey Pants, giddy upped and followed my clear out command with, "God Priscilla isn't this like the third time you've had head lice?"

Well played, Horsey Pants, well played, I thought to myself.

As people rushed to distance themselves from Team Head Lice, I got Orphan Annie and we walked towards the lone back door in the cafeteria and exited. The cold breeze felt good, and I started looking for a BMW sports car. All I saw was the damn conversion van. I looked at Orphan Annie and said, "The van?! I thought we were getting your husband's car?"

"Oh," she said, "He wouldn't let me use it."

Wouldn't let you? This made me think that I needed to release myself from my vow of never offering marital advice sooner than later.

"Whatever," I said, "Let's get out of here."

We both climbed into the beast, it took two tries to get the engine to turn over and after about three minutes we were off school property and headed to the Target parking lot.

I looked over at her, smiled and said, "Say it."

"Say what?" she asked.

"You know what I'm talking about. Just say it. You can do it. It will feel good, and I won't tell a soul."

She laughed and went, "I can't. I really can't."

"Come on. You can do it. Just blurt it out."

"Okay, that was efffffff'ing Awesome!!"

I laughed and said, "Yeah, it sure was."

I don't consider myself a super religious person. If I had to give myself a faith clas-
sification, it would be lazy Methodist. But thanks to being a Baylor grad, I know my
Bible – sort of. And at times it comes in very handy.

Brawling With Bible Verses

I HAD A busy February being evil.

I'm talking going straight to the burning pits of hell kind of evil where you're forced to get a bikini wax every hour whether you need one or not. Of course, it's totally not my fault.

It's my job's fault. My current work assignment is researching and writing a neighborhood safety guide. Talk about a mind-numbing snoozer. And who needs a freaking guide? The whole thing can be summed up in two sentences: *Hey, you fools in the burbs practice some common sense. Don't leave your keys in your car and lock your wrought iron, faux French country, mahogany enriched front door.*

Oh, if only it were that simple. But no, I have to drag that information out to create a guide. This dull, boresville task led me to fall back on my greatest talent - the ability to waste time. Before anyone who works in human resources gets all high and mighty about my "goofing off" during company hours. Relax your ass. I get paid by assignment, not how many hours I work. So, the only one I'm hurting is myself.

That said, I would sit down at my computer with the best of intentions, but ultimately would get sidetracked by Satan's earth-bound assistant – social media. It was while I was simultaneously checking my newsfeed and looking at shoes on Zappos that I noticed a decided upswing in the number of Bible verses being posted by my "friends."

Now, I'm from the South and went to Baylor so as you can imagine my newsfeed is thick with Bible verses. Some days it's like I'm on the Christian Mingle version of Instagram. But, upon further research I discovered that it was two women, who each live in the same town, that were posting a Bible verse approximately every two hours.

This made me curious, so I dug deeper and started lining up their Bible verses. That's when I got a snarky tingle that started at the base of my spine and worked its way to the *"Oh no you didn't"* part of my brain because holy crap from the looks of it these two middle-aged moms were bitch-slapping each other with the Bible.

Hallelujah!

To confirm my theory, I went deep into the social media archives. I sorted through these women's homepages and discovered what I believed to be the source of the friction. As with most mothers, the falling out seemed to be over children.

Facebook pictures told the story. Each mother had a fifteen-year-old daughter. The girls both went to the same high school. Back in April both moms had posted about being "So excited for cheerleader tryouts!"

Scroll down to July and one mother's page was filled with photos of her daughter at summer cheer camp. The other mom's page was not AND right about the time the cheer camp photos started popping up was when the non-cheer mom began the first barrage of Bible verses.

She went Old Testament, and it was brutal. Each verse was accompanied by a cryptic personal message.

So proud of my daughter and her values! She would never cheat to get ahead. That's something for this mom to c-h-e-e-r about.

Proverbs 20:10 *"The Lord hates both these things: dishonest weights and dishonest measures."*

Right after that the cheer mom Proverbs right back.

Proverbs 12:22, KJV *Lying lips are abominations to the LORD: but they that deal truly are His delight.*

And then it was off to the races. Each mom would volley back a Bible verse that in some way was a put down to the other mother and her family. From reading between the Bible verses, I surmised that the non-cheer mom thought that the cheer mom's daughter cheated to make cheerleader and that the mom helped her daughter cheat.

At first Proverbs got a nice little workout. It seemed to be the non-cheer mom's favorite go to book of the Bible. She even made this verse her Facebook cover photo.

Proverbs 29:27 *"An unjust man is an abomination to the just: and he that is upright in the way is abomination to the wicked."*

The cheer mom though was no slacker. She didn't fear going to that scary place - Revelation.

Rev 21:8 *All liars—their place will be in the fiery lake of burning sulfur. This is the second death.*

I couldn't help myself. I had to get involved. Wouldn't you? It's just too delicious and way better than writing about McGruff the Crime Dog home safety tips.

So, I used my time when I should have been working to invent Bible verses and then I took those fake verses and shared them on each woman's Facebook page. My thought process was that the women would then use my faux verses in their status updates skirmishes.

Why did I do this?

No, it's not because I'm mentally unbalanced, well, truth be told that could be some of the reason. But the real reason is I did it as an act of evangelism.

Yeah, that's right I did it for God. Because, although I'm not a biblical scholar, I don't think the Lord Almighty meant for his Good Book to be used in a Bible verse, bitch-slapping, battle between two bitter moms.

Now, you might think it's hard to invent Bible verses, but I found that if you put a "thou" or some old-fashioned word in a sentence you were pretty much good to go. I also started out attributing my Bible verses to the Book of Zephaniah because I googled "least quoted book of the Bible" and that's what popped up.

This was one of my made-up favorites and the non-cheer mom loved it! Even better when she put it as her status update it got fifty-seven likes.

Zephaniah 1:19 *A mother who lies passes thou sin to the daughter who the almighty will curse a thousand times over till hell becomes the descendant's burial grounds.*

Then I started feeling guilty, like God might smite me or something for incorrectly using the book of Zephaniah. So, I began making up my own books of the Bible.

I thought I would get busted for this as soon as I posted it on Facebook. As

I said I went to Baylor and you have to take a semester each of Old and New Testament religion that are ridiculously hard. So hard I took my religion classes at McLennan County Community College because I didn't want the Bible to make me cry or lower my GPA.

Plus, if you judge my Facebook associates by their posts a lot of my "friends" consider themselves very devout and righteous individuals. I assumed they would know their Bible.

They did not.

I was going on week three of posting gems like this:

Hermesian 4:29 *"A daughter's reflection should be of the Lord and not of her mother who is rife with deceit."*

FYI - It got more than one hundred likes. (Yeah me!)

It took my husband of all people to out me. Which is just mind blowing because he went to the University of Texas, so we all know that makes him ninety-seven percent heathen. I was stunned he knew even one book of the Bible. He rarely gets on Facebook, but just happened to be scrolling down his newsfeed and saw one of my "Bible" verses being shared by the non-cheer mom.

The key here is I never posted the verses as my status update. I only took turns sharing them on the two bickering mom's pages. Most of the time they would copy/paste them as their own verse of the hour. It was when the non-cheer mom gave me a shout out that I knew I was doomed.

My husband, taking the Lord's name in vain repeatedly, asked me, "What the hell are you up to? And "What the hell is the book of Hermersian?" Adding "Isn't that a beach in Southern California?"

While cooking dinner I quickly blurted out, "That's Hermosa beach, you idiot."

I then did the whole Bible verse debrief. I knew in my heart my husband would see how I had God's back and was a virtuous woman. Unfortunately, he was filled with the very unholy spirit of unforgiveness and insisted that I cease and desist.

"Whatever," I said, "I'm kind of getting tapped out creating Bible verses."

"Here's a bible verse for you," he announced all pious like while drinking his vodka on the rocks. "Do unto others as you would have them do unto you."

"That's not even original to the Bible," I scoffed, feeling superior. "It's a philosophy found in every major religion."

"Doesn't matter where it's from. Try following it."

I rolled my eyes right in his face and said, "Well, Mr. Vacation Bible School Drop Out, I hope if I'm ever a passive aggressive jackass that uses the Bible to go one-on-one with another mom on Facebook that someone will do exactly what I did."

He got silent for a moment, took a sip of his drink, and sighed, "Well, you do have a point."

And then as if God agreed with him a beatific glow of light filled my kitchen. It was that or someone had left the refrigerator door open. I prefer the hand of God theory myself and that's what I'm sticking with.

SPRING

Spring is nature's way of saying, 'Let's Party!'

Robin Williams

There are so many times in my life when I thought that if only women would quit making each other feel bad about themselves we could change the world. I tried to take a small step in that direction by giving a juice party (a.k.a. Hey chubby, you need to go on a liquid diet and buy this outrageously expensive blender.) my version of the middle finger.

March Fatness

WHY DO WOMEN hate themselves? That's the question my husband asked me as I stood in my kitchen chopping Granny Smith apples as he dipped his seventy-third blue corn tortilla chip in guacamole and chased it with a beer.

Yes, indeed I was counting those chips and congratulating myself on the genius decision I made years ago to marry this man. He met all my spouse criteria. He was cankle free (as a cankle suffer I've always been keen to not want to pass that affliction on to my children) and very smart.

I hear wives all the time talk about how their husbands are idiots. This perplexes me because who would willingly marry a person who was lacking in any intellectual gifts?

Also, I didn't have the luxury of going in that direction because I desperately needed to upgrade my gene pool to dilute the big dumb ass DNA that runs rampant in my family. This meant I needed to marry pretty high on the old I.Q. scale.

Okay, wow, that was some sidebar - sorry. Now back to what made my husband ask the question *"Why do women hate themselves?"*

Well, I had just finished a tale of woe about being invited to a "cleanse" party. In the starvation hierarchy a cleanse gets a gold star and I thought receiving an invite to a cleanse was code for "Come Join Us for a Body Shaming Celebration."

My neighbor, Yvonne, was hosting the "cleanse" party and had sent out an evite. From the look of the email list, it was directed at any women over the age of eighteen who lived in the neighborhood and was ambulatory. I had clicked the "Oh, so sorry to miss the party" box and blissfully thought that would be the end of thinking about something called a cleanse get together.

I was wrong.

Yvonne was a petite woman who on warm days would do yoga in her front yard. Not her side yard or her backyard mind you, but her front. This irritated me for a variety of reasons.

One would think the main one would be because I was jealous. Yvonne looked damn good, and she knew it. I'll admit that a part of me was eternally envious. But my feelings about her were more complicated.

You see Yvonne was also a two-fer of pushy and preachy and I've never been a fan of being on the receiving end of unsolicited weight loss advice. One time while I was walking my dogs, she yelled at me that I "needed more cardio than dog walking."

Then there was a neighborhood cocktail party where in front of a group of people she told me that "Spanx can't do everything" and that I "needed to back away from the buffet."

She wasn't helping matters on the "I hate you" front with her non-stop campaign to get me to come to her cleanse party. She repeatedly sent me emails harassing me about why I wasn't attending, barked at me from her lotus pose when I passed her house and sent me a barrage of texts about how she "just knew, KNEW, this could change my life."

"What makes her think I want to change my life?" I asked my husband. "Doesn't it take a lot of hubris . . ."

As soon as I said hubris my son yelled downstairs, "Exaggerated pride or self-confidence."

My husband looked at me and asked, "ACT vocab word?"

"Yes, and if I knew taking a prep class would make him interrupt almost every conversation to show off his mastery of word definitions, I probably wouldn't have signed him up. Now where was I? Oh yeah, isn't it exceedingly presumptuous to assume that someone is unhappy with their life?

"I don't wear a T-shirt that says 'Looking to Change. Please Help Me'. Maybe I have the most wonderful, joyous life in the world and would die, really die a quick death, if anything were to happen to alter my perfect existence. Or maybe I'm change-a-phobic or better yet maybe she's a change-aholic and needs to be under twenty-four hour supervised medical care.

"But seriously, why do you think my presence is so desperately needed? Was

I going to be the mascot for the party? The token size fourteen? I'm telling you Yvonne really needs to back off."

That's when my multi-tasking eating, drinking husband stopped mid chip to mouth and asked the question, "Why do women hate themselves?"

I was offended as soon as those words came out of his mouth. "What do you mean?" I asked, sounding very hostile, "I don't hate myself."

He gave me a guilty look and said, "I'm talking about women in general. Admit it, some, but not all, women must harbor a level of self-hatred. Because there is no way in hell a guy would have any kind of party whose sole purpose would be to make you feel bad about yourself. Guys have parties where you drink, talk about sports, lie about money and how great you are."

I tried to interrupt him to make a point and defend Team Female, but he was on a roll.

"Furthermore, if some guy tried to have a party whose main purpose was to make you feel like crap and then attempt to sell you something because in their estimation you look like crap. He'd get a beat down."

"Okay, okay, you might be onto something." I admitted. "But some women, note I didn't say all, may at times, not like themselves very much. But speaking for women everywhere, we, as a general rule, do not hate ourselves."

"Wrong," he said, taking a swig of beer. "If women liked themselves then something called a cleanse event would never be considered a party."

Later that night as I unloaded the dishwasher, I had to admit that my husband had a point. How else could a person send out an evite with the words "bowel refresh" and get women to click on the box that says, "Thanks! I'd love to come."

The next morning, I brought up this topic with some friends as we walked our dogs. I told them what my husband said and was waiting for their moral outrage. You know what I got? Agreement. Instead of women shouting, "What a bunch of crap!" I got, "Yeah, we do kind of hate ourselves."

"Really," I asked, ``We do? Why?"

My friend Kelly sighed. "I don't know, blame our parents, blame society, blame men, but not many of us are in love with who we are."

"Are you serious?" I asked. "I think we should blame ourselves. Just look at what we - the female species - have done to something as fundamental as being a mother. We've made it into a competition, and it sucks."

This was when I saw my walking companions give each other the "look."

"Yeah, just stop with that," I growled. "I see it and I know what that look means. That's the 'Oh dear God, she's going off on a rant' look. Well, this is a good one so settle in."

"We'll settle in, if you'll settle down," said Allison. "We love your rants. We promise. They make us all walk faster but don't worry it's not because we're trying to get away from you."

I ignored my best friend and began my rant prep. It started with a deep breath to ensure an optimum supply of oxygen. Really, you don't want to have to slow down your rant to breathe. It messes up the whole rhythm or much worse gives someone a chance to pull *a rantus interruptus,* which is the height of bad manners. Once I had ensured my lungs were in scuba tank mode I began.

"Becoming a mom means time traveling. No, I take that back. Becoming a mom and entering an elementary school means time traveling. When I worked full-time, I was judged on my ability, which meant how much money I could make for the company. If I was making money, I could look like the love child of a troglodyte and Sasquatch and no one would care.

"I mean I'd have to smell decent and address any unsightly facial hair issues, but really my appearance wouldn't be a deal breaker. But enter a freaking elementary school holding the hand of the love of your life - your child - and it's junior high 2.0. It's all about the pretty, the skinny, your clothes, your handbag, your daughter's backpack and that backpack better not be from the Target clearance rack.

"There's also the posturing, the cliques, the feeling that the group of moms you just walked by were talking about you. And God forbid if you dare to admit to eating and sleeping. Yes, the two very things essential for our species survival are frowned upon.

"Eating is bad unless you're subsisting only on, I don't know Whole Foods Fair Trade organic eucalyptus leaves. What are we koala bears? And sleeping means you're a lazy slob. Do you realize how many moms brag about how little sleep they get? We're not mothers of infants anymore. We're allowed to sleep - right? Even worse to prove they're not sleeping, moms use social media to give their not sleeping a shout out with their "look at me I'm not sleeping" updates.

"You know I'm right about this. How many times have you gone on social media in the morning and seen the moms that posted at 3:35 a.m.? 'Still working on my volunteer project.' Or 'I can't sleep. Going to the gym.' It's hell and we do it to ourselves.

"As much as we'd like to, we can't blame men or our mothers. It's twenty-first century Momming. I tell you years from now cultural anthropologists are going to look back on this and it will be like the stonings in biblical times. We're killing each other and that's why someone can throw a cleanse party and we'll all come."

And then I had to shut up because I felt like my lungs were going to explode.

Allison spoke first, "I have nothing to say, but that you're right, I'm hungry and I slept eight hours last night."

Then Kelly gasped, "Oh God, you're planning a scheme, aren't you?"

"I can honestly say, I currently have nothing planned, (pause) at this juncture but as we all know that could change."

The next day things did change. I was running errands at the mall and just happened to walk by a Mrs. Fields' cookie store. In the display case was a large round cookie cake decorated to look like a basketball and in big letters March Madness was spelled out in black frosting.

As soon as I saw that cookie, I got an idea. I asked the young woman behind the counter if she could replace the M in madness with a F and the D with a T? She said, "No problem. Just give me a minute."

She took the cookie cake to the back and then came out a couple of minutes later and said in a perplexed voice, "You do realize your cookie cake now reads March Fatness?"

Smiling, I said, "Yes, I do." I then paid for the cookie and literally skipped out of the mall. I was going to go to the "Cleanse Event" this evening after all and my cookie cake was going with me.

When I got to my car, I called Allison and told her I needed her to go to the cleanse party. She said, "Hell no." Then I mentioned the cookie.

"Is it from Mrs. Fields or the Cookie Company? Because if it's Mrs. Fields I'll go, that buttercream icing is the best, and you better make sure I get a big piece with lots of icing."

"Yes, it's Mrs. Fields and yes I promise you'll get the biggest piece with the most icing."

"Then I guess I'm going to a cleanse."

I announced to my family during dinner that I would be gone for about an hour to attend a party. My husband gave me a worried look and said, "The cleanse party. You're actually going? I'm afraid to ask why?"

My daughter then overshares that I bought a cookie cake for the party. Big mouth.

"You're taking a cake to something called a cleanse party? Yeah, like this is going to end well. Tell me again which neighbor it is so I can be sure to avoid them for the next six months."

I just rolled my eyes and then my son whipped out his phone and showed his dad how he had taken some map app and put little flags in all the locations of people I've ticked off. When he told my husband he named them "Zones of Exclusion" my only thought was that I deserved a better family. How dare they not appreciate my gifts for truth and justice?

Whatever. I had a party to attend. The cleanse event started at seven and I had decided to arrive thirty minutes late. I took my cookie cake and headed outside to walk across the golf course to Yvonne's house.

There are two reasons for this. One, it was faster and two it gave me a terrific vantage point to spy on the party before I entered. Yvonne's house backed up to the 12th hole and there was a nice cluster of maple trees I could stand behind and engage in a little Peeping Tom action.

As I walked across the course some random golf Karen ran out of her backyard and began scolding me for being on the golf course. I was mystified by the outrage. No one was playing golf. It was nighttime and I was walking on freaking grass, not the Shroud of Turin.

I pretended not to hear her and started jogging which isn't that easy with a cookie cake the size of a large pizza. I got to the maple trees and took in the bird's eye view into the back of Yvonne's house.

The family room looked pretty full, and I noticed different glass containers of what looked to be colored water. That was my cue that it was time to liberate the cleanse. Just then my phone rang. It was Allison.

"Why aren't you here?" she asked, sounding very unhappy.

"I am here. I'm hiding behind some trees on the golf course and looking right into the French doors of Yvonne's house."

"Wave at me."

"Why would I wave? You can't see me. It's almost dark."

"Just wave."

"I'm waving. Do you see me?"

"Maybe. Where's the cookie cake?"

"I had to put it on the ground because I can't hold the box and my phone."

"Get my cake off the ground," Allison demanded. "That's gross, think about the ants. Hold on a minute I'm going to walk to the bathroom so I can talk. So, guess what? Yvonne, the hostess without the mostess is basically holding us all hostage here until we buy some sorry ass looking witches brew she's calling bowel broth for $8 a bottle and she's also trying to sell us $350 blenders so we can make our own broths."

"No way," I shouted, "$350 for a blender. I seriously would have more respect for her if she announced that she's a raging shopaholic and needs money for a Louis Vuitton handbag so, 'bitches you better buy my broth.'"

"Really, you would respect her more if she actually confessed that?"

"Well, at least it would be honest, and she wouldn't be trying to lower her neighbors' self-esteem so she can shake them down for cash. You know what really makes me mad? She's trying to get us to buy a $350 juicer and not once, not one time, has she so much as bought a roll of gift wrap or a box of Girl Scout cookies from my kids."

"Okay, calm yourself and get over here. I want my cookie cake."

I did the sprint/walk to Yvonne's front door and didn't even bother to ring the doorbell. I just sauntered in and placed the cookie cake on the dining room table right next to a punch bowl filled with a greenish liquid that looked like slime my daughter would make from a kit she got for her birthday. It didn't exactly scream "yummy!"

My cookie cake though did, and it attracted quite a crowd. This made Yvonne super ticked off. She trotted into her dining room, made a beeline for the cake and announced in a voice that didn't exactly give you the warm fuzzies, "WHO brought this CRAP?"

"I did," I said smiling. "See how cute it is? It says March Fatness. Isn't that kind of darling?"

("Darling" being my "go to" word to disguise when I'm being an ass.)

Yvonne bellowed, "It most certainly is not darling. Nothing in that cake, cookie, whatever it is - is on the cleanse list. It's all about the broths and you can't make the broths without the juicer!"

"Oh, sorry. I didn't know we were starting the cleanse right at this moment. You know what? I bet all the grease in the buttercream icing will act as an awesome colon lube for the upcoming cleanse."

"You can't be serious about that," she said in a pissy voice, "And I'll have you know this evening is the kickoff party to start your cleanse." Now her voice got a little breathy and high-pitched like she's just seen Jesus and she cooed, "You can buy this juicer tonight and tomorrow wake up and start your brand-new life."

"What if I like my life the way it is?" I asked. "I happen to think I have a great life."

As soon as I finished that sentence someone I had never seen before walked into the dining room and went, "That looks delish. When can I have some of that?"

"Right now," said Allison and she used her hands to rip off two pieces of cookie cake. She gave one to the woman next to her and then shoved the other piece in her mouth.

Yvonne looked me up and down and said, "Don't tell me there isn't room in your life for improvement. I mean have you looked at yourself in the mirror lately?"

Allison, while chewing her cake and with orange icing on her nose went into best friend mode.

"Yeah, she's looked in the mirror and she's happy with what she sees. In fact, I think she has a perfect life. Having her life was my number one New Year's resolution - three years in a row now. Number two, in case anyone cares, was having more sex. Well, really any sex."

I looked at Allison and blew her a kiss. It was then that I noticed Yvonne was about to lose her shit which really fitted in with her cleanse theme. She came over, grabbed my arm, and sneered, "I'm going to have to ask you to remove that cake and yourself from my home."

"Umm, okay, I just bought it as a hostess gift, but no problem I'll take my cake and go."

As I began to close the lid on the cookie cake a couple of women asked me what I was doing.

"Yvonne wants me and my cake and clear out. I think I offended her with my food offering."

A youngish woman who I knew from the soccer fields asked, "Where are you going with it?"

"I don't know, I was thinking of taking it out to the 12th tee box and finishing it off."

Another mom laughed and said, "Can we come with you? I don't have $350 to blow on a juicer and I want to leave before she starts the aggressive sales pitch. Yvonne has already told me I need to lose at the minimum fifteen pounds so I can't get out of here soon enough."

"Sure, in fact, let me make an announcement. Excuse me, excuse me, everyone. I'm going to be taking my cookie cake out to the golf course. I then plan to eat it until there's not one crumb left. If you care to join me, I'd love to have you."

Yvonne squealed as Allison and four other moms followed me out of her house with the cookie cake. When we got to the golf course, everyone plopped down, and I put the cookie cake box in the middle of our impromptu friendship circle. We then began eating and bitching about $350 juicers, the slime punch and bottled broth that looked like the remnants of a colonoscopy. Allison, taking the last slice of cookie cake, looked at me and asked, "Did everything go like you planned?"

I grinned. "Oh, I think it went better than planned. Once this gets out there's not a magically melt the pounds away shake, diet cookie, cleanse, detox, juice fast, weight loss party that anyone in a fifty-mile radius will invite me to and that means my work here is done."

And then I took a really big bite of cookie.

Oh goody, Barbara Gray is back (said no one ever) and this time she really pushed all my buttons. Not that my buttons need that big of a push. I'm always looking for a reason to rumble with the neighborhood pain in the ass and this time it, umm, might have gotten a bit out of hand.

Yard Wars
An Eight Part Saga

I DO A lot of things I'm not very proud of. The good news is I have what I consider to be a gift of being able to justify my bad behavior.

Earlier this month I went on what could be called a HOA crime spree. I dampened neighborhood property without verbal permission or written permit. I trespassed. I illegally parked a three-ton vehicle with an attached trailer, and I committed larceny with intent to permanently deprive. Am I a bad person? No.

Here's my defense. The weather made me do it. If I was given the opportunity to plead my case to a jury of my peers which would be any female over the age of eighteen afflicted with terminal frizzy hair and water retention issues, I would be assured a speedy acquittal.

The extreme and almost unprecedented early spring humidity was playing havoc with my mental health and grooming. My hair was out of control even though I had upgraded to salon strength de-frizz balm and the excess moisture in the air was causing my body to experience acute bloating bordering on head-to-toe edema.

Seriously, even my XL leggings were snug and my boobage was swelling out of my Champion athletic bra. What's with humidity and boob swelling? Ladies forget the breast augmentation and just move to a humid climate.

All of these factors combined to not make me responsible for my actions due to a psychotic break brought on by acute water vapor coupled with bipolar barometric pressure.

I know right now you have to be thinking, "Oh my God, why isn't she an attorney? Clearly this woman is one of the great legal minds of this millennium."

Well, here's the crappy deal - that stupid LSAT and of course, my college GPA kept me out of any kind of law school, even ones in Puerto Rico. Law schools really need to upgrade their admittance process and base their acceptance on the craftiness of your mind, not your ability to memorize something like Pollock vs. The Farmers' Loan and Trust Co.

But enough about all that let's get to my crime spree. It started on the morning of April 2 when I was doing my most favorite things in the whole wide world, minding my own business, while doing a series of meditative prayers as I practiced my Kegels and hosed off my deck. (Spoiler alert - I was only doing one of those things and I'll let you guess which one.)

As I braved the humidity to clean my deck, I was blissfully unaware that evil was lurking. But then yard terrorist, Barbara Gray, looking Downey fresh and spring like in one of those so simple but costs a fortune linen shift dresses that say, "I take a vacation that's not based on how many Marriott points I have" (damn her), emerged from her faux Tudor house and began verbally bitch-slapping me with complaints that I had "gotten her grass MOIST."

Any other day I probably would have just taken her insults and moved on. Because we all know that's what I'm about - forgiveness and adhering to the Golden Rule. But that day, due to a humidity level last felt in hell (BTW - Hell, not a dry heat.), I was not in the best of moods and her harangue set me off for many reasons.

First, I knew for a fact that I did not get her grass "moist." I share just the tiniest sliver of a property line with her. So, I felt duty bound to inform Barbara that "my hose did not have superpowers nor was I Elasti-Girl from *The Incredibles* thus making the feat of getting her yard wet most unlikely."

Secondly and perhaps most important was her use of the word "moist." Ugh.

But to be a good neighbor I gave Barbara a chance to explain herself and asked, "Did you have some kind of yard work done where your lawn can't get wet?"

She looked down her very regal (I'm guessing a tip rhinoplasty or at the very least a cartilage reshaping) nose at me and barked, "No, I just don't want *your* water on *my* yard."

"R-e-a-l-l-y," I said, using my best you are such a dumb ass voice, "You do know that all of our water comes from the same place?"

"I don't care. I just don't want YOUR water on MY grass. Got it?"

"Oh, I've got it alright." I said, trying to sound like a tough chick. Then I aimed my hose in her general direction as she sprinted off. You could hear her cloven hoofs going clippity-clop. I was hoping she'd wipe out and her designer nose would get a big ole whiff of grass. Unfortunately, she made it safely back to her yard - for now.

I immediately went inside for a restorative burst of air conditioning and tried to compose myself. It took one large Diet Coke with a twist of lime and a cold shower to get the job done. While I was in the shower, I had an epiphany probably brought by the sudsy power of my husband's Irish Spring body wash and my Suave shampoo.

As I lathered, rinsed and repeated I thought about the conundrum that was Barbara Gray. You would think she would have learned not to irritate me by now. I had brought down some major schemes on her and yet she always comes back for more.

I think she has some freaky control issues that need addressing by a tag team of mental health professionals. But until that happens there is nothing I can do except continue with a course of corrective behavior training.

Any good parent knows the key to success in disciplining your child or dog is consistency. I need to be consistent with Barbara. It's obvious her "moist" yard comment was a sign of her acting out. To do nothing would just reward her negative behavior.

This meant I had no choice but to strike back which meant I was going to throw an impromptu Water Carnival. This party would be fifty percent Pinterest goodness and fifty percent hillbilly which if I'm doing the math correctly equals one hundred percent awesome.

The Trebuchet for the Win

Once I picked up my kids from school and fully briefed them on what their responsibilities were, it was almost party time. I got a box of wine out of the fridge and siphoned it into a carafe because I'm classy like that.

My daughter put on her swimsuit and headed to the backyard to turn on the hoses. And my son was instructed to break out the trebuchet. That command got him interested. "My trebuchet," he said excitedly. "We still have the trebuchet. I wonder if it works? Where is it?"

"I dug it out of the deepest corner of the basement, and it looks to be in pretty decent shape. I wheeled it out into the yard. So go and make sure it can still catapult."

A trebuchet in its simplest term is a geeky kid's best friend. It's loosely related to a catapult and was used in the Middle Ages to fling projectiles over enemy fortifications. My son had built a mini-trebuchet in seventh grade using a Radio Flyer wagon, scrap wood and my gently used Spanx. His trebuchet had amazing accuracy in flinging water balloons and seemed to me to be just the thing for a successful water carnival.

As soon as I got the Franzia into a carafe, help arrived. My friends Kelly, Nikki and Allison all walked in with screaming kids that immediately descended into the backyard. I told the not yet thirty and gorgeous Nikki, "You're on kid patrol and I think you know why?"

"I'm guessing it's because I have the youngest kids," she said while smiling.

"No, it's because you walked into my kitchen wearing cutoffs and a bikini top. You're being punished for being young and beautiful with no visible sign of cellulite or spider veins."

Nikki laughed and said, "Should I wrap a beach towel around myself to make you feel better?"

"No, I'm afraid the damage is already done. My self-esteem will now require a Franzia I.V."

"And I know how much you'll hate that," she said and still laughing walked outside and started running through the *Dora the Explorer* sprinkler with her two kids.

Kelly looked at me and said, "I better not get 'Annoying Mom' hostess duty again. I always get that."

I gave Kelly a guilty look and then launched into a pep talk. "It's because you're so good at it. You can stand there and converse with annoying people without saying things like "Shut up, please just shut up?" I can't do that, and we all know Allison sure as hell can't. Really, you have a talent. It would be rude of me not to let you use it."

"Let me get this straight. You're telling me I have a talent for chatting up obnoxious moms?"

"Yes, you're a diplomat. An ambassador. An envoy bridging the gap between the awesome (I said pointing to the three of us left in the kitchen) and the icky."

"Great," she said with zero enthusiasm. "It looks like the icky are arriving so it's off to the backyard for me."

Allison then quickly volunteered to be the "wine hostess."

"Just exactly what does one do as a wine hostess?" I inquired.

"Easy, I keep the Franzia flowing."

"How do you know it's Franzia in the carafe? It could be something fancy?"

"Seriously, I could smell the Franzia from your driveway?"

"My driveway says boxed wine?"

"No, your driveway says boxed wine with a coupon."

I smiled and said, "You got that right!" and gave her a high-five. Allison grabbed the carafe while I got the plastic wine glasses and the fruit tray and we both headed outside.

It took only about twenty minutes for the water carnival to be in full swing. So many things were in my favor for a successful event. It was an unusually hot and humid day, and it was way too early for any of the local pools to be open so running around in the backyard was still considered not that "uncool" for the older kids.

It was also a Monday. The one day of the week my children didn't have any after school obligations and from the turnout it looked like a lot of families had similar schedules.

The sprinkler and hose created a soggy paradise. Because my neighborhood has a golf course that runs through it, fences are not allowed for any home that backs up to a fairway. If you do have a fence, it must be no taller than four feet and have spacing between the slates to "ensure a seamless neighborhood vista."

What this means is that while I have a fence, (A white picket one. Yes, the irony.) Barbara does not and my fence offers no protection from keeping water out of her yard. To further ensure that her lawn would be a soaking mess, I told all the kids that under no circumstances should they let water get in "that" yard because the lady that lived there would get super angry if her yard got wet.

Of course, that little statement was like waving a red flag in a bull's face. Most of the kids made it their mission to, ahem, moisten Barbara's yard.

As I stood watching the moist mayhem, I was forced to play gracious hostess and converse with the three annoying moms I had invited, Organica, Zillow and TBTT. They were here because I had been blowing them off for almost a year with one of those, "Yeah, we do really need to get our kids together soon."

They also had children who were holy terrors that I knew would deliver a huge water mess. So, I told myself I was killing two birds with one stone. I was coming through on my "let's get the kids together" promise and I would also have some water "helpers."

I had just broken out the Otter pops and was beginning to circulate them to the kids when "Organica" just couldn't help herself and had to ask me if the Otter Pops were homemade. I said, "Um no." She then questioned if they were naturally free of additives and part of the Rainforest Alliance Pact?" It took all the etiquette training my mother had forced upon me and that includes two years participating in Cotillion to not holler, "Are you shitting me?"

Instead, I sweetly smiled at her and said, "Oh yes, these Otter Pops are made with amniotic fluid from free range wood nymphs that live in the fair-trade enchanted forest and are sweetened with localvoire pixie dust."

You could see Organica trying to process what I had just said. All the buzz phrases she longed to hear were there - free range, localvoire, fair trade. It took a couple of seconds before she said a bewildered, "Huh?"

"I'm just teasing you," I said. "No worries, this brand of Otter Pops is from Whole Foods."

She smiled and I smiled because the water, high fructose corn syrup and red dye #2 ice pops were from Costco. But I've learned when a mom questions me about food the simplest way to shut them up is to just say, "Whole Foods."

The next mom to irritate me was Zillow. Zillow is a realtor who goes around telling everyone what their home is currently worth. Zillow greeted me with a chirpy, "You'll never sell this house until you do a total gut job on this kitchen."

"Good to know," I said in a curt attempt to shut her up.

It didn't work. She continued on with, "I don't even know how you can cook in a kitchen without marble. It's so 1980s."

Not wanting to engage, I tried to quell my craving to throw her some side eye and said, "Gee, I've probably made thousands of meals in this kitchen without marble countertops. I guess I'm kicking it old school."

"I'm just saying it's a shame you can't go more upscale."

I thanked her for her concern and immediately walked back into my non-marble kitchen while texting my son who was in the backyard and instructed him to trebuchet the woman in the yellow top on the deck with at least two water balloons ASAP. I then took a great big sip of Franzia and counted to ten. By the time I had gotten to nine I heard screams from Zillow. The trebuchet had made a direct hit.

I laid low after that happened and busied myself with filling up more water balloons. Unfortunately, TBTT found me. The TBTT stands for "Too Busy Too Tinkle." This woman's goal is to be the busiest mom in the forty-eight contiguous states. She validates her self-worth by being so incredibly, extraordinarily busy (in her own mind) that she has zero time to empty her bladder.

Every conversation I've ever had with her starts with some version, "Oh my God. I'm about to wet my pants. I've been so busy I haven't gone to the bathroom since 6:15 this morning."

I've called her out on this a few times. I mentioned how it's not really a good thing to not answer nature's call and that it's a tad awkward to start every conversation with an overshare of your bodily functions. She's yet to take the hint.

That afternoon she greeted me with, "Girl, where's your bathroom I've got to pee like a racehorse. I've had four coffees, three meetings and no time to go potty."

I directed her to my half bath and when she came out, I began my version of *"Word Problems They Didn't Teach You in School."* I said to TBTT, "I just timed how long you peed. It was exactly forty-six seconds. The entire time you were in the bathroom was one minute and thirty-six seconds. That includes pants down and up, toilet flush and hand washing. You mean to tell me that in the, I'm guessing ten hours you've been up, you didn't have one minute and thirty-six seconds to void your bladder?"

"Oh my God, you timed my pee? That's so gross."

"No grosser than you telling me you have to pee like a racehorse. I'm just trying to help, to illustrate that you do, indeed, have time to use the bathroom."

"I don't expect someone like you to get it. I mean you'd have to be a really busy person to understand what it's like to constantly be doing stuff all the time. It's not just that I don't have time to pee. It's that I'm so busy I forget that I have to pee."

I didn't see myself winning this to pee or not to pee argument, so I agreed with TBTT and said, "Yes, you're right. I could never grasp being so devoid of time management skills that I couldn't take a couple of minutes to go to the bathroom. "

She smiled at me and said, "I know, I know, I need to slow down, but it's who I am. I'll sleep when I'm dead."

"Well," I said, "here's hoping a bladder infection doesn't kill you." And off I went to deliver the water balloons to the kids lined up at the trebuchet.

I then walked over to where Nikki, Allison and Kelly (who had escaped the trio of annoyance) were standing and surveyed my yard. I felt like Francis Scott Key observing the battle of Fort McHenry.

Over the ramparts I watched sprinklers gallantly streaming. There was the rockets wet glare as kids shot each other in the eye with super soakers and the mini trebuchet, courtesy of my XL "booty booster mid-thigh shaper" Spanx, was brilliantly delivering water balloons bursting not just in the air, but Barbara Gray's yard.

It was a H2o dream come true. Kids were slipping and sliding, blowing bubbles as they sat in wheelbarrows and plastic wading pools filled with water and running through sprinklers while they screamed, "It's so cold!"

The only thing missing was Barbara Gray but just as a flock of clouds obscured the sun she emerged out on her back deck, took inventory of the chaos and gave me a look that, I fear, would have killed a weaker woman.

I looked right back at her and returned her glare. I was reveling in the moment until my husband pulled into the driveway. Crap, he was home early. When he got out of his car he stared into the backyard and shook his head. Then as Barbara made a beeline for him, the big chicken raced into the house.

This didn't deter Barbara. She just pivoted to my backyard and yelled at me demanding that my party needed to "cease and desist."

I offered up a cheery, "No problem, the party is almost over. I told the kids repeatedly to not get your yard wet. Please accept my sincere apologies," and then I offered her an Otter Pop.

She waved her hand at the Otter Pop like it was a turd on a stick and squished her way through my very wet grass to her almost as wet backyard. Then right as she's plopping herself in a fancy chaise lounge on her deck the trebuchet launched three balloons. They hit her, not in the face, but right at her feet. The balloons exploded, the water splashed up and soaked her linen dress and then to make it even more perfect, she cursed like a sailor trapped on a ship during shore leave.

I answered back with an "Oops, sorry!"

It was good to be me right up until ten o'clock the next morning when the shit hit the fan - literally.

Oh Crap

I woke up the day after my water carnival show down all zippity-damn-doo-dah. I was confident that Barbara Gray had been vanquished for at least a couple of months. I held on to that happy thought until mid-morning when I smelled something God awful. I followed my nose and it took me right to Barbara's house.

She had a landscape crew literally shoveling shit all over her lawn. They were spreading manure in the flower beds, around her trees and shrubs, even raking it through her grass. Yes, I know it's super environmentally friendly to fertilize with manure, but Barbara wasn't just fertilizing she was carpeting her entire yard with bovine feces.

As I stood in her lawn breathing through my nose a neighbor walked over and said, "This is just horrible!"

"I don't know how Barbara can stand this," I said while gagging. "Who wants cow poop all over their yard?"

"Oh, didn't you know? She's at her lake house. I'm supposed to keep an eye on things for her until she gets back."

"Are you telling me Barbara took off and left the neighborhood in a state of crapapalooza?" I moaned.

"I guess I am," the neighbor winced and then hurried back into her house so she could breathe.

This whole landscaping with nature's number two got my snarky senses tingling. Something besides the crap didn't smell right. I walked over to what seemed to be the head landscape guy and asked if he knew when the order was placed for the manure spectacular.

"I think we got the call late yesterday afternoon from Mrs. Gray. She requested that every inch of her yard be spread with cow manure because she was going green and wanted to experiment with manure as a lawn fertilizer. I told her it was going to smell something awful, but she didn't seem to care."

I stood there and thought, well, well, Barbara, you think you can one up my water carnival with a strategic shit bomb. We'll just see about that.

I thanked the yard guy, sprinted inside my house and then took a couple of minutes to enjoy breathing again. Once I was no longer light-headed from a lack of oxygen, I got on the phone to do some research.

My first call was to the landscaping service Barbara uses. I identified myself as a writer for the website *I Want Yard of the Month*. The nice lady that answered the phone seemed thrilled to be talking to a "journalist." I shared with her that I was a neighbor of Barbara Gray's and was fascinated by her use of cow manure as a fertilizer. I asked if this was a new trend in suburban landscaping.

"Oh no, we do use cow manure in flower beds, but this is the first time someone has asked if we could do their whole yard. It usually isn't done on the entire yard because of the smell and the neighbor's complaints. There are some HOA's that don't allow it."

"Really? Some HOA's have a problem with it - interesting. Now, I haven't noticed my neighbor using cow manure before. Do you know why she suddenly wanted cow manure?"

"You know I really can't say. I do know that her phone call yesterday afternoon took us all by a complete surprise. It was so, how do I say this, so un-Mrs. Gray. We even tried to talk her out doing manure over her entire yard, but she insisted."

"She just decided to do it yesterday. Wow, you guys work fast! What time did she call?"

"Oh, it was right after five o'clock, but Mrs. Gray is one of our best clients, so we try to keep her happy."

"Hmm, I bet you do. Now, is there a downside to using cow manure besides the odor?"

"Well, if you're not careful about the quality of the manure you can get what is called weed seed transfer. That's when the vegetation the cow eats ends up in its poop and those seeds can then end up in your yard."

Upon hearing this my heart skipped a beat and I experienced the thrilling rush of retaliation. I tried to contain my joy and say in a voice that's as normal as possible, "How devastating. You mean if you're not careful you could end up with a yard full of weeds?"

"Yes, there's a chance that might happen but then most people don't use cow manure all over their yard."

I thanked the landscape lady profusely for her time and promised to send her a link to my article just as soon as I posted it online. I then quickly called my neighbor who was keeping an eye on Barbara's house for her and asked if she knew exactly when Barbara would be back. I found out she's gone for an entire week. Excellent.

I then changed into my navy-blue capri track pants, threw on a t-shirt, shoved my size eleven feet into men's flip flops (They're way cheaper people.) and headed to our city's one and only organic nursery. I was off to buy some seeds.

Why organic, you ask? Because I wanted to buy dandelion seeds and I knew the organic nursery stocked them for the deluxe crunchy set who make their own home-grown dandelion wine. (Yuck.) I was planning on liberating some dandelion seeds right into Barbara's yard and this was just the beginning.

Field of Dreams

I was greeted by a very attentive garden employee - Saffron Luna. I told her she had a lovely name and she laughed and said it was an upgrade from her real name which was Sue. I agreed about the upgrade and then told her I was helping my daughter with a school project that involved discovering which kind of weeds would grow fastest in a manure-based soil.

Saffron was full of great suggestions. While dandelions were a no-brainer, she also suggested thistles, something that was a cousin to crabgrass, clover, chickweed and various nut and onion grasses. Unfortunately, all they sold were the dandelion seeds, but she knew the local Ag Extension office (for you big city types the Ag office in the simplest terms is a cooperative education outreach for farmers) would have some, if not all of, the weed seeds.

Mother Nature had my back because not only was the extension office more than happy to load me up on "lawn combatants" they also didn't charge me a thing. The gentleman there said, "He was pleased to help any youngster with a scientific endeavor."

Yeah, I know I should have at least blushed or hung my head in shame for fibbing, but I had bigger issues at stake than the truth - revenge.

The trip out to the country and back took up most of my afternoon and I barely was on time picking up my kids from school. I warned them as they exited the car to use their backpacks to cover their face and not to commence breathing until they were inside the sealed pod that is our home.

Of course, they didn't obey me and I was serenaded with my daughter screaming, "My eyes are bleeding!" and my son moaning, "It's the Killing Fields!" My daughter even had the nerve to announce, "Mom, this is all your fault! If you hadn't made Mrs. Gray so mad with the water carnival we could all breathe outside."

My son added, "Yeah, Mrs. Gray showed you up because not being able to go outside or open your windows trumps water balloons."

I shook my head in disgust and said, "Really, this is what you two are all about - giving up, quitting, hugging defeat. I'm seriously doubting that you two are my children. There must have been some kind of switched at birth scenario because anyone with my DNA surging through them would not be this lazy! This isn't the time to quit. This is the time to shine. To let your opponent know just what they're dealing with. I'm telling you two, I've got this."

Then I misquoted Winston Churchill (big time) and made, what I thought was a stirring closing argument.

"We shall fight her in her yard, We shall fight her in the HOA, We shall fight her in the fields and in the streets, We will outlive the menace of tyranny, if necessary for years, if necessary alone."

As usual they were not impressed, but I tell you, I gave myself chill bumps.

Before the Dawn's Early Light

At approximately 3:45 a.m. my alarm went off and I got out of bed ready to be-gin phase one of my retribution campaign. Because I had slept in my super sexy nighty which is an XXL men's black Hanes T-shirt, I already had on most of my camouflage outfit. All I needed to do was pull on pants, tie my tennis shoes, leash up our black dog and I was good to go.

I slipped out of the house with a dog poop bag filled to the brim with the lawn combatants. Then using my elderly bichon with bladder control issues as an excuse to be roaming the neighborhood at such an early hour I set out for Barbara's yard.

Once I got there, I began pouring seed from the poop bag into nice little rows. I felt like a real Johnny Appleseed. Everything was going great until something touched my shoulder.

"Holy Crap!" I whisper-screamed. "Who sneaks up on a woman in the middle of the night?"

"Sorry" my older neighbor who lived down the street, whispered back. He was smoking and I guess that's why he was up. I knew his wife didn't allow him to smoke in the house. "I was just so curious about what you were up to I had to come and take a look-see."

Hmm, what to do, what to do. Should I confess the truth or try to cover up my actions? My neighbor, Bob Olson, was retired and had a cool, aging hippie vibe. He and his wife do things like travel the world watching sunsets while doing yoga on top of a mountain. I decided to go with confessing because I knew Barbara had given him plenty of grief over his xeriscape yard. So, the odds were in my favor that he might want to be on team retribution. This meant I spilled the beans/seeds.

As soon as I was done, he started laughing his ass off. He was so loud I was sure he was waking up the neighborhood. After he calmed down Bob bent down to pet my dog and said, "I think I can help you in this little plan you've got going on."

"Oh, you're going to help spread the weed seeds?"

"Nay, I can do better than that. What would you say if I planted some weed?"

I gave him a confused look and said, "Well, I'm already planting weed. I have clover and chickweed and..."

He interrupted me with, "No, I mean real weed."

I looked at him again, still confused and then I got it, my eyes bigger than the full moon. "Ohhhh, you mean weed, weed, marijuana! I gasped and said, "You want to plant pot in Barbara's yard?"

At this point I was experiencing a wide range of emotions from giddy delight to having Mrs. Stick Up Her Butt growing pot in her yard to the fear of being busted. I can see it now, "Local Mother of Two Arrested in Pot Sting - Feet Too Big for Women's Prison Slippers."

My delight overtook my fear, so I went for the follow-up question. "Just how would you do that?"

"Easy, I might possibly have access to a couple of marijuana plants that perhaps I could put in those front flower beds right over there."

"Like full size, already grown plants?"

"Yes, full size plants."

"Okay, I can't tell you how happy this is making me, but I can't have any part in being anywhere near marijuana. If you do this, I cannot help you. I'm going to have to go all *Mission Impossible* and disavow any knowledge of your actions."

"No problem. Give me the rest of your seed bag and take your dog inside. I'll take care of the rest."

I felt like I was right in the middle of a drug deal or something and my heart was thumping furiously. "Okay," I said, very cautiously, "I'll just drop my bag here and go back to my house. It was good talking to you. Tell your wife hi for me" and then I turned tail and ran home.

I was extremely worried that I may have crossed a line, so I woke up my husband and told him my story. He looked at me with sleepy, pissed off eyes and said, "You were out in the middle of the night with seeds in a dog poop bag spilling them on a neighbor's yard with our dog as your co-conspirator?"

"Yes."

"Then you accidentally meet up with Bob and he volunteered to plant pot in Barbara's yard.?"

I thought his grasp of the story was remarkable for someone who just woke up and answered, "Yes."

"Did you ask him to do it? Did you see the plants? Did you see him plant the plants?"

I answered, "No, no and no."

"Then go to sleep. For all you know he was just yanking your chain and P.S. you might need to go on some kind of medication"

"Not going to happen. I don't think there's a medication for making someone un-awesome."

He yawned and said, "You do know your awesomeness is probably a textbook case of crazy?" and then he rolled over and went back to sleep.

I was too wired from my nighttime excursion to even close my eyes, so I barely got any sleep. It didn't matter because when my alarm went off, I bounced out of bed, took my dogs on an earlier than normal morning walk and when I saw about half-dozen pot plants standing tall and proud in Barbara's front flower beds, I was one hundred percent all aboard the happy train.

Good lord, he had done it! Barbara Gray was now a pot farmer.

Pace Yourself

Not one to rest on my laurels, I was all over another opportunity that presented itself to me later in the day. I volunteer at a non-profit that takes people's used cars as donations and then sells the, usually very crapped out, cars to a dealer for cash. I was working the phones for them when a call came in from a woman who wanted to donate her recently deceased father-in-law's car.

She sounded very embarrassed about the condition of the vehicle, and I assured her we had gotten cars donated that a good junk yard would have turned away. Her problem was they were about to put her father-in-law's house on the market, and they needed the car out of the driveway as soon as possible.

"The car can't be that bad," I said.

"Oh, trust me it is," the woman replied, "It's a 1975 rusted out, dented, moldy AMC Pacer with the roof caving in and raccoons got into it a couple of years ago and shredded most of the interior."

I hope right now you're thinking what I was thinking because I was thinking I've got to get my hands on that car. She had me at AMC Pacer.

"That does sound bad," I said, "But we still would love the donation."

"Well, there's one more thing. The Pacer has one of those tin can travel trailers attached to it. The trailer is in worse shape than the Pacer. It even has a couple of bullet holes in it,"

I gasped in delight, but the woman thought I was gasping about the violence of bullet holes, so she quickly said, 'Oh no, it's not what you think. The bullet holes are from a hunting trip when a bunch of men got drunk and used the trailer for target practice."

I'm thinking to myself, "Awesome!" But I said to her in a voice of sweet innocence, "It's okay. I was just taken aback for a minute."

In a very relieved tone she responded, "I was worried you were going to back out and you still might because the problem is you have to take both the car and the trailer. You see the tow hitch on the back of the Pacer is so rusted out we can't get the trailer off."

"Oh no worries, no worries at all - we'll take both," I said as I'm rubbing my hands together in unfettered joy. "Let me ask you something - can you still drive the Pacer?"

"Barely."

"Well, here's the deal, our parking area where we store the cars before the dealer we sell them to shows up to haul them off is full right now. But if you could manage to drive the car and the trailer to my house, I could store it for you and then when there's room in our lot, we can move it there."

"Oh, bless you! You're an angel. I'll get with my husband as soon as I hang up the phone and see about moving the car today."

I gave her Barbara Gray's address and told her to make sure to pull the car and the trailer into the driveway as far as it will go. I also shared that I was going to be gone all day, so she just needed to leave the key to the Pacer in the front seat of the car since I was pretty sure no one was going to steal it.

By 3:30 that afternoon Barbara had not only six pot plants in her front yard, but the world's most disgusting AMC Pacer that was being upstaged by a vintage trailer that probably housed meth chefs in a former life and was decorated with bullet holes. I did exactly what you would have done. I took pictures, lots of them. Then I called the HOA and requested an emergency meeting.

The Devil's Minions - The HOA

Our HOA board is composed mostly of retired people in very bad moods with control freak tendencies boarding on the psychotic, which is why Barbara, as the recording secretary, fits in so nicely. These folks also love, love, love meetings. To request an emergency one, I have no doubt, makes their day.

My meeting inquiry was quickly approved and scheduled for 10 a.m. the next day. I suggested we all meet in Barbara's yard and added that it wouldn't be awkward because I knew she would be out-of-town.

As befitting such an important and solemn occasion as an emergency HOA meeting in a neighbor's manure laden lawn, I showed up the next morning dressed in my finest casual wear. Jeans, a T.J. Maxx cashmere twin set with pearls and my hair in a headband. I looked like Hillary Clinton, circa 1992. I carried a basket of mini muffins that I passed around and I also had handouts.

Nothing says I'm a serious person who once worked at an important job a decade ago as color handouts. My handouts, in extra-large type, thank you very much, for the mature set, listed the HOA "crimes" Barbara had committed.

It was a long list. There was the use of unapproved lawn fertilizer resulting in endangerment of the health of other homeowners, possible growing of illegal vegetation, violation of the parking rules and having a vehicle or lawn ornament that reflects negatively on the beauty of the neighborhood. I also noted that as a HOA board member she should know better.

The board, four retired dudes, two ladies who lunch and also do hard time as sustaining members of the Junior League and garden club, and my friend Kelly (board treasurer who very kindly left work so she could be there for me.) were "aghast," "taken aback" and "saddened" by Barbara's "egregious" and "blatant disrespect of the covenants of the HOA."

Kelly was getting me off my game a little bit because she was trying not to laugh, and the effort was making her entire body shake. I couldn't make eye contact with her for fear I would start howling.

To try to regain my composure I proposed a moment of silence where we could all reflect or pray, depending on your religious affiliation or lack thereof, for Barbara's soul. One gentleman requested we form a prayer circle and hold hands.

That pushed Kelly right over the edge. She got the hiccups from excessive laughter suppression and had to excuse herself to go and get a drink of water. I told everyone the manure smell was most likely causing a partial larynx paralysis.

After the moment of silence, the HOA board president opened the meeting up for discussion. I thought the two garden club groupies would try to have Barbara's back and might defend her. I was wrong - kind of.

They did have her back, but it was to stick a garden trowel in it. They also aimed for her jugular by making a motion for the HOA death penalty. This meant that Barbara would be ineligible to participate in the *Yard of the Month* for two years! They had a quorum and took a vote. It was unanimous - Barbara got the death penalty.

One of the women wanted to call Barbara and inform her immediately of their decision. No, no and no, this can't happen I thought. I don't want Barbara to rush home. I need a couple of days for my damn seeds to germinate and those pot plants to take root. This is when being prepared and forcing yourself to read thirteen pages of HOA rules pays off big.

"I don't think that's a good idea," I said, "According to the covenant you have to send the rule violations in writing via registered mail. It would be a flagrant violation of our own policy and might render the charges against Barbara null and void."

They all agreed, and the meeting was adjourned with the president vowing to get the letter written and mailed today. I waited until everyone left, checked on the pot plants, gave them a little water and then did a happy dance.

Slight Detour to Annoying Neighbor #2

I spent the remainder of the week counting the days until Barbara got home. According to the neighbor "keeping an eye" (and just between us she was doing a mighty poor job) on Barbara's house she was scheduled to be back in town on Monday. I hadn't been this excited since I found six sleeves of Girl Scout Thin Mint cookies hidden in the back of my freezer under a five-pound bag of Trader Joe's Chicken Wontons.

On Barbara Eve, or as some of you may call it Easter, I woke up, pilfered candy from my kids' Peter Cottontail Hopping Down the Bunny Trail baskets and got major attitude from my husband about his Easter present.

He was ticked off that I got him what I dubbed a "Bitch Basket." It was seventy-two rolls of toilet paper from Costco which I used as the base for the basket and then added ten chip clips, two fingernail clipper sets, scissors and a lint roller.

This is all the stuff he's always bitching about as in; "Where's the toilet paper?" "Why can't I ever find a chip clip in this house?" And "Who took the scissors?"

I thought it was inspired. Who wouldn't like seventy-two rolls of toilet paper? And it was Charmin Ultra Soft. It's not like I went Walmart house brand on him.

To escape his negative vibe I took my dogs for a walk before I got dressed for church. As I turned the corner with my hounds I was greeted by a banner on my neighbors fence. It proclaimed *"The Kendell Family Easter Egg Hunt. Who Will Find the Golden Egg?!"*

Just gag! Thanks to Kevin Kendell (a petite, hairless man who resembles a turkey baster and is always dressed in bike shorts and a spandex tank top with his erect man nipples in a constant state of thrust) four years ago our neck of the burbs chose to abandon its forty-three-year Easter egg hunt tradition.

This is because Kevin went on a search and destroy mission to guarantee his kids Kelsey, Kaleb and Kacey found the most eggs. Due to his aggressive "take no prisoners" special forces tactics a couple of kids were trampled and that escalated to five dads getting into a shoving match that some off duty firemen had to break up.

After that incident and the subsequent cancellation of the local egg hunt, the Kendells have hosted their own private, invitation only, Easter Eggstravaganza where the eggs are not filled with anything as bourgeoisie as candy. No, these eggs are stuffed with cash.

The Golden Egg is the one with five $100 bills. As you may have guessed the Snarky family has yet to receive an invitation to this Easter egg hunt. After I passed the obnoxious sign, I saw Kevin's bike short butt bending over as he hid eggs in preparation for the hunt. I picked up my walking pace, so I didn't have to make eye contact with him.

Twenty minutes later I got home from walking the dogs and as I was unleashing my part beagle, part basset hound mutt (Oreo) I got a present. Oreo opened her mouth and dropped a plastic yellow Easter Egg at my feet. This dog loves to pick up items on our walks, specifically golf balls, and surprise you with her treasure when she gets home.

When I saw the plastic yellow Easter egg my only thought was does it have candy and if so I wonder if any dog slobber has managed to permeate the candy's wrapper? As I opened the egg five $100 bills fell out. Oreo had found the Golden Egg! Good dog Oreo. Good dog.

I know what you might be thinking. That I should march right over to the Super Family and return their egg. It is after all one of the holiest days in the Christian faith.

Well, I decided on another course of action. I went finders keepers losers weepers. Oh, calm down, I didn't keep the cash and put it in my emergency Diet

Coke and hair highlight fund. I took the five crisp hundreds and placed them in the church offering plate when they were doing a special Easter collection for the food bank.

My husband raised his eyebrows when he saw me peel off the cash, but he didn't say anything. He saved that for five hours later.

That's because four hours later I had a policeman knocking on my front door. You can imagine how excited this made my entire family. I told everyone to calm down. It's not like we haven't trained for this.

"Everyone," I snapped, "Man your battle stations. This is not a drill."

By that I meant for my husband to get his phone and prepare to speed dial our attorney and for my kids to take their positions at the upstairs windows to record what was going down with their phones. I may need it for my trial.

"Remember," I told my kids, "I want one of you getting the close-ups and one of you keeping steady on the wide shot. Don't go all fancy camera moves on me."

I was in luck when I opened the door and saw it was the SRO (School Resource Officer) as the cop of the day. Officer Matt did the DARE and Safety programs at the elementary and middle school. He must have drawn the short straw by getting Easter Sunday duty.

The good news for me was that over the years I had developed a congenial relationship with the young police officer. I'm about to give you newbie parents some great advice here so get ready to take notes. When your kids start school, you will, of course, give the teachers gifts, but it's even more crucial to gift the support staff.

School secretary, librarian, custodial staff and the SRO were recipients of my gratitude for all they did. This is why as soon as I got my door opened, I gave Officer Matt a great big hug, asked about his mother and offered him a piece of pie and then inquired about why he was paying me a visit.

Blushing and slightly stammering he said, "Your neighbor thinks you may have stolen $500 from him."

"Do you mean my neighbor who is trying to hide himself behind my oak tree, that one?"

Officer Matt looked over his shoulder and said, "Yes, that one."

"Do you know why he would think that I've stolen five-hundred bucks?"

"Sir," he shouted to Mr. Super Family, "Please come here."

Mr. Super Family strutted over in his spandex and said, "All I know is that I'm missing my golden egg and the only person I saw when I was hiding my eggs was you and your mutts."

I looked at Officer Matt and could see that he was having trouble keeping a straight face. So, I say, "Wow, the case of the missing golden egg. It's like *Encyclopedia Brown* meets *Mother Goose*. How exciting. "

Mr. Super Family takes that jab as an opportunity to get all up in my face and screech, "It doesn't matter what you say. I know you did it."

"Golly Kevin," I purred, "anybody or even an animal could have picked up an egg. You have your great big fence sign and I also believe you blasted it all over social media that there was a golden egg stuffed with $500. Then there was your TikTok Easter rap that, full disclosure, I found a little unsettling."

"What a minute," Officer Matt said to Mr. Super Family, "It's common knowledge that you hide eggs with money in them all over your yard."

"Yes"

"When did you post on social media that you had eggs stuffed with money in your yard?"

"I don't know about seven hours ago. "

And then I jumped into the interrogation with, "How do you even know your golden egg is missing?"

"Because the egg hunt is over and no one found the golden egg."

"Well, did you consider that one of your children or guests found the egg and took the cash and didn't want to tell anyone. Maybe they were afraid they would have to share it. Seriously, I can think of about a thousand scenarios on how that egg could have gone missing. Perhaps, the dad of one of those kids you trampled four years ago in the city Easter Egg hunt might have taken it."

Officer Matt's face turned angry, and he said, "That was you four years ago? Not cool man, not cool."

While I looked at Mr. Super Family I asked Officer Matt, "Is there any kind of legal recourse I can take for having a neighbor call the cops and accuse me of stealing on Easter no less?"

Officer Matt smiled. "I'm sure there's at the very least some kind of harassment charge you could file."

I beamed at him and said, "I'll consider taking that under advisement with my legal counsel."

Officer Matt then glared at Mr. Super Family and announced, "Sir, I'm afraid you have no complaint here. The egg could still be in your yard or one of your teenagers could have 'borrowed' it."

That was enough for Mr. Super Family to do the walk of shame back to his yard with his tail between his bike shorts.

Before Officer Matt could turn and leave, I reached out, touched his elbow and asked if he could answer a question for me.

"Sure, What is it?"

"Well, it's about something growing in my neighbor's yard. I think it might be cannabis sativa."

Now that got his attention.

The Freak Out

Finally, the day came for Barbara to return home. I'm sure she thought the manure smell would have dissipated and she would pull into her driveway secure in the knowledge that she bested me and all was right in her well-ordered lawn dominatrix world.

Sadly, for Barbara as she turned the corner and veered into the winding road that would lead to her cul-de-sac, she was greeted with a yard covered in tiny little seedlings of clover and dandelion proudly peeking out of the cow crap.

Next up was the driveway surprise of a raccoon condo better known as the 1975 AMC Pacer mating with the rusted, bullet bedazzled tin trailer.

The piece de la resistance was five strong stalks of a dioecious flowering cannabis herb gently swaying in the late afternoon spring breeze. The sixth stalk had been removed by a law enforcement officer on Easter Sunday.

In preparation for this moment, I had stayed home all day and had my ears on high alert for screams of anguish. As luck, or the fact that I spent most of my day outside scanning the street for Barbara's car, would have it, I was able to witness the moment when she arrived back to her lair.

Due to the AMC Pacer and trailer taking up her entire driveway she had to park on the side of the street. As she threw open her car door, her wedge heeled sandal feet raced up the sidewalk and she started screaming, "Whose car is this! Whose car is this!"

She stuck her head inside the windowless Pacer as if she was hoping to find a clue and then bolted across the street to the neighbor who had been put in charge of watching her home. The neighbor raced out to her front porch just in time to be treated to Barbara bellowing questions.

"Who owns that damn car? Why the hell is it in my driveway? How long has the car been parked here?"

When Barbara stopped to catch her breath, she noticed her lawn had been infiltrated with grasses that didn't answer to the name of Kentucky Blue or Rye.

This led Barbara to scream some more and in between her tantrum she whipped out her cell phone and called the police. It took all of five minutes for the cops to arrive. It took six minutes before a crowd gathered and only eight before the president of the HOA walked by. I entered the fray at about nine minutes in. The police had a problem calming her down especially after they pointed out she had marijuana growing in her flower beds.

All I can say is that for a woman who prides herself on thinking that she is superior to all other lifeforms Barbara certainly wasn't very refined. She was a cursing tornado belching the F word like a drunken frat boy. After I soaked up the spectacle for a few minutes I felt the need to step in.

I said, "Excuse me officers, but if she really doesn't know where the Pacer and trailer came from I could call a tow service for her, but it might be a couple of hours before they could get there. I didn't want the non-profit I volunteered for to lose out on a donation, so I had always planned after I tweaked Barbara with the car visual to have the two junk heaps hauled off.

"Also, I'm sure that weed is just pure nonsense. This woman, although she's currently swearing like she's just given birth to a fourteen-pound baby without an epidural and recovering from an episiotomy that was done with a spork, is nevertheless a pillar of the community and co-chair of the Lyric Opera Guild Gala 2022 - An Enchanted Evening."

One of the police officers looked at me and smiled, "We figured the weed wasn't hers. It's not something you would usually grow in the front of your house and it's hard to prove who planted the pot. Was it the original owner of the home? Was it airborne seed? We just need it eradicated. Oh, and thanks for the offer of the tow truck."

He then paused and glanced at Barbara who was now sitting in her manure yard with her head between her legs taking deep breaths, and said, "You know lady you're mighty lucky to have such a great neighbor."

Barbara lifted up her sweaty, make-up-stained face, scowled and then gave me not one, but two middle fingers. I grinned and cooed, "Oh, officer, I would do just about anything for her."

Epilogue

By dinner time the Pacer and trailer had been towed off to the junk dealer's lot and the weed was history. Last weekend Barbara began the process of having her entire lawn ripped out and re-sodded in an attempt to rescue her virgin grass from the virulent soil combatants that the manure had "released." She's currently in the process of appealing her HOA death sentence and has secured an attorney in her quest to reclaim Yard of the Month privileges.

All of this has left her with no time to mess with me or anyone else in the neighborhood. We're all enjoying leaving our garage doors open, not mowing our grass in a crosshatch pattern and using yard decor that is not from Barbara's sanctioned places like Frontgate, Serena and Lily or Pottery Barn.

On occasion, when Mr. Super Family is out in his yard, I especially like to play fetch with my dogs by throwing yellow plastic eggs for them to retrieve. I'm sure he loves to hear me say, "Good doggies, now go get that golden egg."

Just what the hell is wrong with parents today? How did so many of us become delusional about our children's intellectual gifts? On top of that when and why did the oversharing about said "gifts" become the norm? Hmm, maybe I should do some research and get on the Ted Talk circuit.

Yes, Your Kid is a Genius Now Leave Me Alone

APPARENTLY, THE TEST scores are wrong. Grievously wrong. American children when compared with students in other countries continually score in the medio-cre range in math and science and are perched pretty low on the reading totem pole, as well.

But that can't be right. Just ask almost any parent and you'll discover that their kids are all super geniuses.

Yes, I once lived under the delusion that my children were brainiacs of the highest order. Then, when they were each about nineteen days old, I realized I might be wrong.

Sure, if crying were a sign of intelligence, then, why yes, back in the infant days they were geniuses, veritable Einsteins at bawling their brains out. But alas, I have learned to lower my expectations.

The whole kid competition thing starts immediately after your precious infant is born. The first salvo fired is when another new mom asks the dreaded question, "Is your baby sleeping through the night?"

Um, no, you think to yourself, because aren't you supposed to feed your newborn like every three hours?

Well, of course, the new mom that asked the sleep question, can't wait to share that her little angel requires no night-time nutrients and has been blissfully racking out for ten hours a night since being shot out of her lady loins.

I know deep in my heart that there is a special place in hell for these kinds of parents. The people who take a scared, sleep deprived, first-time mom and begin to torture her with tales of their super baby and then look at you like you must be doing something wrong because your baby isn't as awesome as their baby.

After the sleeping through the night marathon there's the rolling over, sitting and standing Olympics. Followed by my personal favorite - sign language.

Yes, if sucking on your fingers was a sign that one of my babies was hungry then yes, they could sign. No, they could not sign their take on the nation's healthcare conundrum or that they thought I was having a good hair day.

That competition checklist is quickly followed by the triathlon of walking, talking and potty training. God give you strength if your mommy/baby play dates turn into a parenting throw down.

Kids grab the pacifiers because it's time for "Who's the Better Baby!" What this, of course, really means is "Who's the Better Mommy?"

I never won. Not once. I didn't even medal. Although, one time I thought, for sure, I would get a bronze.

Fast forward to elementary school and the stakes are even higher. Who's reading before kindergarten, who's already doing addition and subtraction. Then, there's always the mom that thinks her little piece of heaven is too advanced for kindergarten and needs to leap-frog directly to first grade.

The absolute worst in the game of parenting is people who like to share their children's achievements with total strangers. I call them "Peacock Parents." And as luck would have it, one descended on me during a spring break vacation. I'm telling you it's like I'm a peacock parent magnet.

Right before this peacock marred my spring break vibes, I was lounging by a hotel pool while my children frolicked in the water, blessedly far, far, away from me. I was using that quiet time to peruse the "spa menu" and contemplating why anyone would want to ruin a good massage, by sharing it with their spouse. Couples massage - yuck.

That deep thought and my mojito buzz was disrupted by a pesky mom - "Mrs. Two Lawn Chairs Down From Me." She perkily asked me the age of my children.

I shared the information and that's all it took for her to launch into a forty-seven-minute monologue about her brood of geniuses. Apparently, her hometown of Lufkin, Texas was a genius hotspot. Attention top-tier colleges, go to Lufkin for the best and brightest students.

Goodness, her thirteen-year-old had already taken the SAT, her eight-year-old was going to an invitation only gifted and talented camp this summer and her five-year-old was so advanced it's baffling the school where to put the little lamb-chop.

Kindergarten would be abhorrently easy, and first grade would probably be a waste of time. But if they put her in second grade it would be precedent setting for the school district, groundbreaking even. It was absolutely keeping her awake at night.

Really? Because it was putting me to sleep. Like I care. Like anyone besides her spouse and the grandparents would give a hoot about this laundry list of accomplishments. I'm guessing even nana and papa were probably getting pretty sick of it by now.

Seriously, what drives people to proselytize about their kids to strangers? Was she hoping I worked in college admissions at an Ivy League? What about stranger danger? Maybe I'm a kidnapper who targets gifted children. She probably would have gone on longer, but mercifully one of my non-geniuses showed up begging for money for a snack.

I gave my fourteen-year-old son a ten-dollar bill and told him he had to split it with his sister. He stares at me - bewildered. So, I spoke very, very slowly and said, "Take the ten dollars, buy yourself a snack that does not exceed five dollars so your sister will also have five dollars to spend on her snack."

He acted all huffy and groaned, "Duh, I know how to split a ten, Mom, I thought you meant I had to share my snack with her." He then stomped off and gave me an over the shoulder, "Whatever."

Mojito buzz diluted further.

Spawner of geniuses upon hearing this discourse with my son piped up and asked, "How old did you say he was again?"

I replied, "He's four years away from college, that's how old."

"Oh my," she said.

And this "Oh my" was long and drawn out with an overture of superiority, an undercurrent of "ha, ha, my kid is better than your kid" and just a wee bit of pity.

I sighed and went deep on thinking bad thoughts about this mom. Can't she leave me alone? I'm a woman in need of solitude and I'm having to pay a daily resort fee on top of the hotel room rate so back off.

Adding insult to injury or maybe injury to insult. Yeah, that sounds right because I was insulted first. This brag bag was wearing a two piece for crap's sake? Not a tankini but a legit bikini and she looked good in it. Had she no mercy?

Meanwhile, I'm wrapped up in a one piece with a full-length sarong covering my thighs. On top of that I have strategically draped a beach towel over my stomach. It's not that I'm ashamed of my body, I just like to have some time to work up to descending into the pool.

Just as I was thinking about getting into the water this woman took a big breath and launched into phase two of her assault - her children's gifted and talented aptitude scores and how they relate in correlation to their IQ tests. At this point I wanted to strangle her with my beach towel.

Was it too much to ask to be left alone? It was spring break and I just wanted to escape my children for a few minutes, suck on my overpriced mojito that I was seriously questioning, at that point, if it had any rum in it at all. "Mrs. Two Lawn Chairs Down From Me" was cutting into that alone time.

Yes, If I were a better person, I would have done the smile and nod and just let her drone on while I went to "my happy place" (which was cakes and cobblers), but I am not a better person. So, I launched my counterattack – Shut the Hell Up.

"Oh my," I blurted out. "I don't want to alarm you, but I work with a consortium that is doing long-term research on gifted children and their transition into adulthood and the findings have been rather surprising."

"What do you mean?" she gasped as she leaned over her chaise lounge to hear me better.

"Well, we've found that most gifted children peak at a very young age. For instance, your eldest child may have already seen her intellectual heyday and your five-year-old could be a victim of "over peaking" where her brain stimulus core - to put in layman's terms - just shuts down. (Nice touch I thought with the whole stimulus core. Maybe I'm *the* genius.) It simply doesn't want to process more information."

"So, what seems like a high IQ now could in a few years mean your kids will be average. Much, like when infants learn to walk and talk. Some begin doing so earlier than others but eventually everyone learns how.

My advice to you is what I tell every parent I see in my practice (now, in my most syrupy, patronizing tone I added this kicker) just love your kids (dramatic pause) no matter what their IQ."

"You're a doctor," she asked?"

"No, I'm not a M.D. I'm a research scientist," I replied. I said that because I'm thinking there's laws against being a poolside faux physician and with my luck as soon as I pretended to be a M.D. someone was going to need CPR or a baby delivered. Although, twice I have pretended to be a cop and once a F.B.I. agent. Good times.

Then I brought out the heavy artillery. "My son, who you just met."

She quietly said, "Yes, yes, the fourteen-year-old."

"Well, once upon a time everyone thought he was a child prodigy. He talked in complete sentences when he was barely six months old - off the charts developmentally. Then, all of a sudden there was a complete slowdown in all mental growth. He's what inspired my research."

I grabbed at the edge of the beach towel stacked on my stomach, lifted up my sunglasses and dabbed at my eyes for a final touch.

"Mrs. Two Lawn Chairs Down" was silent. I rendered her speechless. Mission accomplished! Slowly she got up and gathered her belongings.

"Where are you going?" I asked. "A couple's massage?"

"Umm, Umm," she stammered, "I think I need some time to process everything you shared with me."

As she walked away, I hollered, "If you need more information just google - IQ backslash brain stimulus core."

Then I ordered another mojito, felt a little guilty for about three seconds for my festival of fibs, rearranged the towel on my stomach and began once again to soak up the sun and the silence.

SUMMER

"You are so much sunshine in every square inch."

Walt Whitman

My personal philosophy regarding children's sports is that if your ego is so fragile that your kid's win/loss record, team placement, or playing time dictates your personal happiness then perhaps you need therapy or an intervention. I considered what happened in this story to be an intervention of sorts.

Batter Up

I HAD NEVER been so glad that I had a ball free son. Wait, that sounded really wrong and anatomically incorrect. Let me start over, my son is ball-less. Okay, that sounded worse.

Here's what I was trying to say - my son has never been into sports. Although, we tried. Lord, did we try. But he always had zero interest in catching a ball, chasing a ball, throwing a ball, kicking or hitting a ball. He wouldn't even hunt for Easter eggs.

I remember when he was three and wearing the cutest smocked, seersucker Easter suit with little bunnies on it. We were at our church's annual Easter egg hunt and my son looked up at me with his big brown eyes.

No, they're better than brown. My husband has brown eyes but my son, my beautiful son, has eyes the color of brown sugar, butter and heavy cream mixed together in a saucepan on the stove right as those three simple ingredients hit the magical boiling point and transform into a rich, frothy caramel.

So, make that he looked at me with his beautiful caramel eyes and asked, "Why do I have to run and look for eggs? Can't we just go to the store and buy candy?"

I tried to explain that an Easter egg hunt was fun and that he would enjoy it. He didn't believe me, and no amount of persuasion was enough to make him leave my side and sprint around the church playground looking for eggs.

I will admit that having a son who doesn't embrace sports puts you into a parenting wilderness. You feel left out, bereft at times and are without a common denominator that allows you to freely communicate with other parents.

This lack of mother/son sporting experience is why last week I was sitting at a Shipley Do-Nuts in an undisclosed town in Texas with my mouth very unattractively hanging open, making me glad that I had at least stepped-up my teeth whitening regime. (Thank you, Optic toothpaste.) I was listening to a horror story about something called the Little League Draft.

At first, I was all, "Wait, they draft kids? WTH?" And then it got worse. My two friends from my childhood hometown (I was visiting my parents) began throwing out alphabet categories like AA and AAA, majors and minors. Were they talking about batteries, college degree plans? Had they gone all adult ADHD on me and were having issues with staying focused on one subject? Worse, had they been drinking? It was only 10 a.m.

I finally had to ask them to please shut up and to slowly explain to me what they were talking about. They both looked at me like I was mentally flawed, like how could a mom not know about the inner workings of Little League. I smiled and said one word - "Clay." (That's my son's name.)

They smiled back, nodded their heads and then my friend Lisa said, "Oh yeah, that's right. You've never been a boy sport's mom."

"Nope, never."

I couldn't tell if they felt sorry for me or were maybe a little bit jealous. I'm going with jealous. It made me feel better. So, following my instructions they gave me a quick course in Little League for moms who have sons that don't play sports.

If you have a child who plays Little League, you may want to skip ahead. If you don't, stay with me. Here's the deal as I remember it. I could have gotten some of the finer points wrong. I'm not saying this is the gospel people so please don't email me a lengthy treatise on where I made a baseball error or left out a salient point in the history of youth sports - subsection Little League. The important thing to remember for the benefit of this story are two words – baseball draft. And apparently it's a big freaking deal.

Tryouts precede the draft and parents, most especially dads, get into it. I'm talking about special outfits, clipboards and filming stuff with their iPhones and having assistants (who usually answer to the name "mom") that take down notes. It's huge.

The tryouts are so the kids can get seeded for the draft. What all parents are hoping for is that if their son is ten or older, he gets drafted to the Majors. That's the big time. Second best would be the AAA, then AA and so on.

In this neck of the Texas suburbs the draft was held in private at the Country Cup & Kettle restaurant three days after tryouts. Only coaches, Little League staff (which are all volunteers) and the commissioner are allowed into the draft room. What goes on was top-secret. I'm guessing it's kind of like fight club as in the first rule of the Little League draft is no one talks about the draft.

This was the point in my lesson where when I heard the word "commissioner" of the Little League I thought my friends were joking. Really, a commissioner of Little League? You've got to be kidding me?

When did we, as parents, drink this special brand of crazy Kool Aid? It can't just be the head volunteer or manager? It has to be a commissioner. I was howling. Like I was seriously squeezing my legs together and kegeling to prevent any unsightly leakage.

I abruptly stopped laughing and immediately forgot about my pelvic floor muscles when my friend Nancy said, "And the commissioner is Martha Barnett."

Ugh! Martha was my introduction to a female taking bitch and making it a long-term lifestyle choice. I have no memory of her ever being nice. No, correction, I have no memory of Martha ever being genuinely nice.

Even in grade school she was the queen of the backhanded compliment. One of those girls who would say things like, "Oh, you look pretty today (pause, wait for it, it's coming) you know, for you. Did your mom buy that outfit at Sears?"

Being a pre-adolescent girl, you are, at first all smiles because of the "you look pretty" comment and then your feel-good moment comes crashing down and gets stomped on like a bear dancing the polka at a post hibernation cotillion with the "for you" dig and to really make sure you got the insult Martha always had a follow-up insult in the form of a question i.e. - "Did you get your outfit at Sears?"

As I got older, I avoided Martha to the best of my ability. If I did come in contact with her, I was locked and loaded with an arsenal of quick retorts. For example, sophomore geometry, she told me I looked "decent" and followed up with "for a big girl" and then did her zinger. "Can you shop at regular people stores?"

I fired back, "If by regular people stores who mean where there are clothes for people with good taste, then yes, I can shop there. So, I guess that means we will never be seen at the same stores."

Martha chose not to leave her hometown. As far as I can tell she's had the same friend set since preschool at the First Baptist Church. I know I digress, but I feel duty bound to share this with all the women out there who have a BIG issue with making new friends. So, here I go.

The problem with having ONLY long-standing friendships is the inbreeding. No one being allowed to move in or out of a group creates personality mutations where the worst character traits of each person slowly merge to create defective friendships.

There I said it and you know I'm right.

So, back to hating on Martha. My last encounter with her was when I was home over Christmas. It was at the HEB grocery store, and she did a surprise attack. Before I even knew she was in my vicinity she had rustled her cart right up to me and with a big old, fakey smile she did the four-second y'all which is when someone purrs out the greeting.

I y'all-ed her right back as she gave me the once over and then said, "You look the same as you did in high school. I thought maybe you might slim down one day."

I curtly replied by telling her she sounded exactly the same as she did in high school and then I "accidentally" rolled my cart over both her feet.

As soon as Nancy and Lisa saw my eyes roll at the mention of Martha Barnett, they started bitch-slapping me with stories of, "when Martha made three moms in the bleachers cry." And "when Martha told so and so's son he shouldn't be allowed to play baseball because he was an insult to the sport.'"

I tell ya they were both turning me right off my bullseye which is a mighty feat.

The bullseye, for you poor souls who have never encountered its greatness, is a doughnut (without its signature hole) impregnated with the richest vanilla buttercream/Crisco-esque frosting you'll find anywhere in the South. Its yumminess continues with a light coating of chocolate icing, sprinkles (whose colors change according to the holidays) and a jaunty flourish of the already mentioned vanilla buttercream that adorns the center of the doughnut like the world's most darling "going to church" bonnet.

When they got to the part about Martha stalking the Little League fields with a monogrammed baseball radar gun and holding court, I got queasy. When they told me about all the moms and dads in town kowtowing to Martha because of her "power" I went full on CVS - Could Vomit Soon.

It took a fresh thirty-two-ounce fountain Diet Coke in a Styrofoam cup to clear my digestive track of the nausea. As I slowly sipped my D.C. I discovered that the draft was that evening, which explained why Nancy and Lisa's emotions were running so high.

Apparently, for the past three years Martha's twin boys, Belton and Beaumont, always got on the best team. Well, if I believe everything I've been told, it's more of a super team that trounces every other team in the league, which was not supposed to happen.

The draft was set up to allow each team to draft an A player and then a B player and on down the alphabet so no one team could get all the good players. Somehow Nancy says the team Martha's boys are on always get front loaded with the most talent every year.

I sat there and listened to this thinking well, nobody ever said Martha Barnett was dumb. But I was also a little confused and asked, "Why haven't the other parents called bullshit on this? Isn't there something in the, I don't know, the Little League Constitution about this?"

"Who knows and we don't do anything because we're scared," confessed Lisa.

"Umm, scared of what? It's baseball, not a terrorist organization."

This got Lisa worked up. "She has the power to put our boys on crappy teams. To ruin their Little League experience, the whole summer even. Little League determines a lot of things like if they'll make the high school baseball team or have a chance at division one college ball."

This made me laugh. "Lisa isn't your kid eleven? I don't think Little League is going to make or break his athletic career."

Both Lisa and Nancy gave me looks that said, "Woman, you do not know what you're talking about." And they could be right, so I shut up for a good ten seconds and then asked, "Why don't you crash the draft and find out what's really going on?"

They both sighed and then Lisa said, "How? The draft is top-secret."

"How top secret can it be? Didn't you say it's held at the party room at the Country Cup and Kettle?"

"Yeah, but they close the whole restaurant."

This was when I got a little ashamed of both my friends. For the love of God, they are both born and bred Texas girls. Where was their ass kicking spirit? Their ingenuity? Hell, the three of us spent one summer inseminating cattle. If you can survive that you can pretty much take on the world.

I shook my head in shame for them and asked, "Does the Country Cup have free Wi-Fi?"

Nancy said, "Yes, but why does that matter?"

"Do the coaches bring in laptops or iPads?"

Lisa volunteered, "Yeah, they would have to. I know a lot of coaches keep stats on the boys on Excel spreadsheets. I'm guessing they would want to consult their spreadsheets and update them as the draft goes on."

"Well, then problem solved. Give me a minute."

I took my phone out of my pants pocket and texted my son telling him to call me ASAP. I would never dream of calling him directly because being a child of the twenty-first century he doesn't believe in answering his phone. Apparently only losers or old people do that.

Clay called me back and I asked him if I was right in assuming that if an establishment had free Wi-Fi that I could maybe tap into it from the parking lot and somehow get eyes on what was going on inside?

He was very quiet. For a couple of seconds, I could only hear him breathing on the other end of the phone. Then he said, "For security reasons I will not have this conversation on an unsecured line. We'll talk when you get back to grandma's. Oh, and bring me two bullseyes. No, make that three."

I hung up my phone and asked, "What time is the draft?"

Nancy looked worried and said, "Seven."

"Do you want a front row seat to the action?"

They both smiled and in unison said, "Yes." And then Nancy added, "I think."

"Okay then, we need a car no one will recognize, and we can't use mine since it has out-of-state plates."

Both Nancy and Lisa confessed that their cars were out because they were covered in Little League stickers.

I thought for a moment and then said, "We can use my mom's. She drives a white 2006 Camry. You don't get more nondescript than that."

After that proclamation I told my friends I would pick them up at 6:30 and then we would be off to the draft.

"Wait a minute. That's it, just like that, one phone call to your son and now we're going to be able to see what's going on?" asked Nancy, sounding very confused.

"Yeah, just like that. Don't you trust me?"

"Well, it's not really a matter of trust. It's more of a matter of being in a state of disbelief that one phone call gets us into the draft, so to speak. But it's not like I have a lot of options so I'm hitching my wagon to your star."

I winked at Nancy and Lisa and they both laughed. "You do know you're a little crazy," Lisa said.

"Well, I like to think of myself as crazy with swagger. I find it an upgrade from just plain old crazy."

⇥⇒ ⇐⇤

Nothing irritated me more than when my son treated me like I'm an idiot. I mean if you want to talk idiots then perhaps, he needed to examine why he had yet to figure out that dirty clothes go into something called a hamper not the floor.

But alas I needed my son's help, so I put up with the condescending tone he was using on me as I received a lecture on the finer points on cloning and remotely controlling someone's laptop.

As he talked, I was mentally making a to-do list and starting to panic. From what my son was telling me it sounded like I was going to need a man on the inside.

Basically, if I understood correctly what he was saying, someone was going to need to go into the County Cup, insert a flash drive into Martha's laptop for approximately fifteen seconds so my son could clone it, then remove the flash drive and exit the premises, all without being seen. Unfortunately, I had no ninjas in my family or friend circle so I seriously doubted I could pull this off.

My mom, who was listening to my son, piped up and volunteered to do the deed. I attempted to shut that down - fast. "That's a big no can do mom. You don't even know how to send an email that's not in all caps. I'm guessing the flash drive would stroke you out. Plus, everyone in town knows you. How are you going to waltz into the Country Cup and pull this off without being seen?"

She petted her large and in charge blonde hair helmet, gave me a searing look that made me feel like I was back in high school and said, "That's why I'm just the person to do this. Everyone knows me. There's not a room the good Lord has made that I don't know how to work. I'll just meander right into the back, ask if anybody has seen my purse because I think I left it there at lunch, and then distract that common as cornbread Martha Barnett and do that flash drive doohickey thing."

"Got to hand it to you mom, that's a good plan. The whole old lady lost my purse thing - genius. And I had totally forgotten that you can't stand Martha."

My mom quickly interrupted with, "She's as bad as her mother, maybe worse. Going around putting on airs. You'd think she lived in Dallas or something."

Before my mother could go off on one of her tangents about the growing number of people being all gurgle and no guts (translation: boastful with nothing to back it up) I refocused the conversation to the flash drive. "Mom, it doesn't matter if you can work a room. There's still the problem of you and the doohickey."

At this point Clay gallantly jumped in to defend his grandmother, "Mom, if Grandma can plug in a toaster. She can insert a flash drive. I'll even have her practice."

My mom grinned and said, "So it sounds like we've got ourselves a little fun this evening."

This was when my dad's ears perked up. He had been silently reading the newspaper up to this point. "Am I hearing this correctly? Are you planning on using your mother to illegally insert some sort of software that will allow you to remotely control another person's computer? I can tell you right now that's not going to happen. Your mother is not going to go to jail."

I said nothing and just smiled. My dad doesn't have a chance of stopping my mom from doing anything. She knows just how to manipulate my father to get her own way. It took under ninety seconds for her to convince him that she needed to do this for the betterment of society. Hell, she even made it sound like she'd even get a Citizen of the Year award for it.

I think what really won him over was her assertion that no one would want to send an old lady to jail and that she would use a dementia defense. My dad backed down after that and then announced that he was going with us.

"You can't, Dad," I whined. "We're taking mom's Camry and I've already got me, Clay, Mom, Nancy and Lisa going. That's five people. You won't fit."

"Well, then I'll just follow you in my truck and take the dogs with me. You never know when a dog is going to come in handy."

I sighed and tried to not get aggravated, "Gee Dad, why don't we just put lawn chairs in the back of your pickup and have a hillbilly jamboree outside the Country Cup. It's not like that won't attract attention."

My mom, a little slow to pick up on the sarcasm, joined in with, "Let's pack snacks and make a night out of it!"

"Mom, no on the snacks. Well, maybe some snacks. What were you thinking?"

"I've got some of my homemade jalapeno puffs and they go great with lemonade."

This distracted me. Usually, I'm not easily distracted unless you introduce food into the conversation and then I'm a goner. I forced myself back to the topic at hand and because I'm a dutiful daughter and I knew there was no other way my dad would let my mom go, I said having him as back up would be just grand.

It was now 6:50 p.m. I was stuffed in the back of my mom's car, between Nancy and Lisa. Clay was in the front seat and my mom was driving. God help us all. How this woman has never had an accident in her fifty plus years of being behind the wheel of a car was proof that there is a higher power, and an angel was riding shotgun in her Camry.

From my peripheral vision it looked like Nancy was giving herself last rites. Clay yelled over my mother, who was simultaneously flooring her car and honking, that he was going to be riding back with grandpa.

When we mercifully arrived at the Country Cup, Nancy and Lisa started counting cars in the parking lot and announced that it looked like everyone that was affiliated with the draft was present and accounted for. I told my mom she was good to go and reminded her that Martha's laptop was in a paisley monogrammed case.

My mom put the flash drive in her skirt pocket, checked her coral lipstick in the rearview mirror, smiled, gracefully exited the car and began to saunter up to the Country Cup. As she opened the door of the Cup my dad got out of his pickup and followed her in. I just shook my head. Of course, I should have known he was going to do that. Always the gentleman, he would never let my mom head into alleged danger without his assistance.

Clay, still in the front seat, had his laptop out and joined the Cup's wifi. He was doing some rather aggressive clicking on his keyboard and in less than five minutes he announced, "Grandma's done it. I've got control of that woman's computer."

Nancy and Lisa were all smiles. But I was concerned that my mom and dad hadn't left the Cup. What the hell were they doing in there? Then I heard Clay laugh. "Look Mom," he said, gesturing at his computer screen. "Grandma and Grandpa really do know how to work a room. Grandma's even giving baseball advice."

Sure enough, there was my mother, holding court and wishing everyone in the room "the best draft ever." I could see my dad pat guys on the back as he very discreetly maneuvered my mom out of the party room.

A couple of minutes later they were back in the parking lot, and you would think my mom had just won the Powerball. I had to tell her to act natural. This prompted my dad to deadpan, "This is natural for your mother."

He was kind of right. So instead, I told her to shut up and get in the car. My dad insisted on also getting in the car. He was downright adamant about it. This meant Nancy was forced to sit on my lap so my dad could squeeze in the back. Could we be any more conspicuous? Six people crammed in an aging Camry, with one woman sitting on another woman's lap. We looked like a package of Jet Puffed marshmallows shoved into a Dixie Cup.

Lisa told Clay to raise up his laptop, just a smidge, so we could see what was going on from the backseat. The draft contingent was making a prayer circle. They had all joined hands and had bowed their heads. This made me laugh. Really, praying that everyone has a good Little League draft? They should be praying that Martha doesn't screw up the draft - again.

Martha began beseeching "our heavenly father to smile down and lift up those who will be making difficult decisions this evening, to use his wisdom from above to direct everyone in making purposeful and meaningful selections that will glorify his name and to bless everyone in the room for the work they do to spread Jesus's love through baseball."

Where's a thunderbolt when you need one? I'm not the most religious person you'll ever meet, but holy crap this sounded blasphemous. How did Little League draft picks glorify God? My mom, who considered herself highly religious, smirked, "Well, with that prayer she had the devil snickering and getting her room ready in perdition. I think we all need to say a prayer to cancel that prayer."

"Later, Mom, let's pray later," I pleaded.

"No, we're going to do one quick prayer."

"You know, Mom, I don't think that's how prayer is supposed to work. This whole prayer one-upmanship thing sounds wrong, like unholy and I don't think you can cancel out someone else's prayer with another prayer."

My mother rolled her eyes and said, "I don't know what prayer one-upmanship even means but I have it on good authority (she was now looking towards the heavens like she's Facebook friends with Jesus) that you most certainly can pray over a prayer. So, everyone, let's join hands."

Knowing it was easier and faster to just go along with my mom than try to insert logic into the conversation I followed her instructions and we all joined hands, to the best of our ability, and my mom rattled off, "Dear Father, please forgive those fools who waste your time praying about baby boys' baseball and distract you from the bigger picture of caring for the sick, those suffering and the needy. Amen."

As soon as the last amen was murmured, Clay eagerly shared, "Mom, Mom, it's started they're doing that draft thing."

At first it all seemed a little humdrum as every coach took turns picking their A and B players. It wasn't until they got to the C players that things got interesting. Martha's boys Belton and Beaumont had yet to be taken in the draft. I'm going to guess that she figured one of her twins would be an A, the other a B and they would be drafted onto the same team.

I checked my hypothesis with Lisa and Nancy and they both agreed. Nancy added, "It doesn't matter if they're A, B or Z players, you just wait, Martha's twins will both end up on the super team."

Shortly after Nancy said this, we saw Martha's huge head fill up the laptop screen. Lisa screamed and that made my mom scream. "Calm down everyone," Clay scolded. We're using her laptop camera and she's now sitting at her laptop that's why all we see is her face."

"Do you know what she's doing?" I asked.

"Give me a second and I'll tell you. She seems to be in an Excel spreadsheet of some kind and is reassigning letters of the alphabet to different names."

This information got Nancy all excited. "I knew it! I knew it! I knew it! She's manipulating the draft by messing with the seeding. That's how she makes sure her kids' team always gets the best players."

Boring was what I was thinking while I started to get concerned that I was numb from the waist down due to having a grown woman sitting on my lap. Then a cute guy walked over to Martha and asked her a question about the seeding.

My dad said, "Uh oh, that's the new youth minister at St. Paul's and he played college ball. The real deal. I'm talking NCAA Division One. I think he's figured out she's cheating."

The nice, youngish man said in the kindest of tones, "Hey, how is Ian Vansickle an E player and how did he get on your children's team? That kid should have been at least a B. He's got an amazing arm."

Martha stood up and was trying to use her commissioner mumbo jumbo on him, but he wasn't backing down. No matter what lame excuses Martha gave him he politely told her that none of what she said made sense.

That sent Martha into full crazed mama bear mode. Like she was in his face with her chest pumped out. This prompted me to tell Clay to prepare the live stream.

"Like put it up?"

"No, just be ready."

I then told Nancy and Lisa to get out their phones, pull up their social media links and be prepared to type.

And then it happened. I had my justification for sharing Martha Barnett's special brand of icky with the world. I have standards when it comes to revenge. For me to engage in any sort of payback a person has to greatly exceed the limits of everyday douchery.

Garden variety unkindness I tolerate. Sadly, it's part of the human condition.

But when someone crosses that line into vicious with a side of vile, I feel it's my responsibility to act for the greater good.

When Martha went off on the youth pastor I still wasn't prepared to engage. It took her launching into a tirade about how this was "The Major League Little League not the Special Olympics."

She then went deep into a rant about how only the best kids should be able to play and that "funds were being wasted on the less talented which meant the good kids weren't given the resources to get even better."

When that happened, I said three words, "Ready, set, go!"

Martha and her dumbassery were being live streamed from her own computer and Nancy and Lisa were sharing the video on social media. With the status update "OMG have you seen Martha Barnett at the Little League draft - shocking and so sad."

Oh, and what a tantrum Martha was having! A real three alarm hissy fit about someone having the gall to question her power as commissioner. Karma was on our side because she was perched perfectly in front of her laptop for the optimum camera angle.

I let her go on for about four minutes, then told my son to drop the live feed and turn those last couple of minutes into a continuous loop. Just in case there was ever any question that Martha shouldn't be commissioner Nancy and Lisa would have evidence of why she should be banned for life. I then told my mom to get us the hell out of the Country Cup.

It took longer than I would have liked because I thought we were going to need the jaws of life to extract my dad from the Camry's backseat. As soon as he was out my mom floored it and we hauled back to my parent's house.

Nancy and Lisa camped out in the dining room and worked all their social media contacts. I told them they had one hour to get the word out and then they should delete the video. I also told Clay to make sure he had erased or whatever you do so no one will figure out that Martha's laptop had been cloned.

My mom walked around feeding everyone and said things like, "If I do end up serving hard time, promise me you'll bring me my Clairol." She was talking about her hair dye, affectionately referred to around these parts as Lone Star Blonde.

This story had a happy ending because my team of family and friends hit a home freaking run with the bases loaded. Martha is now the ex-commissioner, my mother did not end up in jail, a rather sizeable donation was made to the Special Olympics and Nancy and Lisa's boys enjoyed a terrific baseball season. Although Lisa continued to insist "that the teams still didn't seem all that fair."

Sigh.

I started my parent journey as an AMA. No, that doesn't mean I'm in the American Medical Association because frankly I washed out of science in the tenth grade. What AMA means in my case was that each time I was pregnant I was of Advanced Maternal Age (ouch).

This little three letter designation was all over my medical charts. When I was pregnant with my daughter, I joked with my husband that maybe Ama would be a lovely name for a girl. (We went with Isabella instead.) But being an older mom has proven to be useful in many situations. This was one of them.

The Aggressive Aqua Mom

I'VE BEEN DOING my summer due diligence - spending vast amounts of time at the city pool. It amazes and amuses me what information one can pick up simply by donning sunglasses and stretching out on a lawn chair. It's like you become invisible and people feel that they have no need to edit their conversations.

Hello, I'm almost sitting in your lap, so I can hear everything you're saying to your lawn chair friend on the other side. Of course, having the eavesdropping skills of a super spy also helps. Three weeks into summer, I'd heard about a suburban swingers' club and a mom who had hooked up with her daughter's "much older" boyfriend. A great big yuck to all of the above.

I had also been busy teaching some young mothers how to tame what I'm calling an "Aggressive Aqua Mom."

It was the first day of diving lessons for my daughter who was in a beginner class. She was with a group of fellow elementary school kids who seemed very enthused to heave-ho themselves off the board. Their teacher was a beautiful, sun-kissed college student who first wowed the kids with some amazing dives.

As the kids oohed and aahed at their teacher's diving prowess the moms brought their pool chairs closer to the boards. We were all equally excited to see our kids master something besides the cannonball.

Everything seemed to be going well. The kids were happy and all the moms were impressed at how fast our children were learning to do a forward dive with decent form. But with twenty minutes left in the lesson trouble showed up wearing only a Speedo and camo Crocs.

Uh, oh.

The Speedo tank suit on a lot of advanced middle-aged women is a big fashion no. Okay, correction. A lot of women my age look amazing in a Speedo – me not so much. Primarily because the tank suit doesn't exactly have a lot of breast support. It's nylon with a very inadequate lining that encourages my boobs to swing to-and-fro like Tarzan's rope during a tsunami.

This Speedo mother exhibited none of my swimsuit insecurities and with her Croc clad feet confidently marched into the lesson while exuding a vibe that said, "Back off. I have business to attend to."

And indeed, she did. Mrs. Speedo, with her two kids following her, interrupted the dive teacher and hijacked the lesson.

It started with her introducing her children to the teacher (not a problem) but then she segued into a dissertation about her kids' strengths and weaknesses and the areas of improvement she'd like to see the teacher focus on. (Did I mention this was a beginner's dive class?) As this continued on for seven minutes (yes, I was timing) the other wet kids stood by the diving boards and shivered.

At some point you would hope that the dive teacher would take control of the conversation and get back to instructing the kids. In her defense she was young and I'm sure was a little overwhelmed by this mother. You can bet Mrs. Speedo counted on this because she continued to drone on.

I could feel the anger seething out of the other moms. At last, a boy got sick of waiting and jumped off the board which started the domino effect of other kids diving off the boards and the teacher had to quit giving her full attention to Mrs. Speedo to take back control of the class.

Problem solved, I think. The kids were diving. The teacher was no longer being monopolized by Mrs. Speedo – it was all good. Right?

Not exactly.

Mrs. Speedo, stood at the side of the pool, shouting instructions to her children. Then she hoisted herself up on the medium high diving board (eschewing the ladder because it was blocked with other kids) to further yell at them. (Excuse me, I meant she offered motherly suggestions given in the spirit of love.)

As she hoisted her body, which required a kind of straddle with a jump to get up to the board, she did a full flash of her lady business to the moms seated poolside. (Alas, beware of aging swim wear with chlorine distressed nylon fibers.)

Once she'd claimed the diving board as her throne, she used her body as a barricade effectively blocking any other kids beside her own from using the board and kept the diving teacher preoccupied with her two spawns as they attempted to refine their belly flops.

By then, all the moms were enraged. They were bitch whispering and planning what they should do to stop this mother. I listened to them but pretended to be engrossed in making a shopping list.

I, of course, could solve the problem of Mrs. Speedo in a matter of minutes. I have, at least, ten years on most of these moms and the adult bully battle scars to prove it. But these younger parents had to learn by doing. I felt I must give them wings and let them fly.

The decision among the moms was to confront Mrs. Speedo. (Bad idea.) They decided to wait until after the lesson and go in a group to tell her off. They thought was it's better for all of them to go because, you know, safety in numbers.

Right after the kids took their last dive the six moms, two with babies on their hips (I'm thinking human shields), went up to Mrs. Speedo and tried to "sweetly" tell her that they "didn't appreciate her interfering in the diving lessons" and that she was a "deterrent to the other students learning."

Like putting a match to the gasoline can by your lawnmower, Mrs. Speedo burst into flames. She got right in the moms' faces and bellowed, "Don't you dare tell me how I can interact with my own children."

The tirade continued for about two minutes (yes, once again, I was timing) the younger moms backed away from Mrs. Speedo, one of the two babies started to cry and then a mother with her hair in pigtails who looked like she was in a touring production of *Pippi Longstocking* (I kid you not.) burst into tears.

I sighed, shook my head, stood up and entered into the fray. I'm nothing, if not a sucker for tears. I used my age, girth and height and assumed an alpha dog status. I separated Mrs. Speedo from the shell-shocked moms and showed the early thirty something mothers how it's done.

Watch and learn my young ones. Watch and learn.

This group's first mistake was going on the offensive. Any chick strutting around in a Speedo and Crocs who flashes her follicle rich privates without even a "begging your pardon" was not someone you could confront.

Her bossy behavior at the dive lesson all pointed to the fact that she likes, and I would guess, even looks forward to confrontation. So, you don't go that route. You'll lose. This kind of woman responds to flattery. I laid it on thick.

Step one: I introduced myself as a great admirer of her instruction technique. "Did she use to be on a dive team or a coach? Really, never. You sure wouldn't think that after watching. Gosh, you were really great."

Step two: Compliment her children. "Your kids were awesome. Do they have some kind of gymnastic training? They seem athletically gifted. I bet they play select sports."

Step three: Go in for the kill. "Don't you think your kids are too advanced for this class? Wow, if my daughter was that talented, I would take her to the Dive Academy. That's where all the real athletes are. You don't know about it? On the off chance you didn't, I wrote it down for you. I got the number off my phone. Here, take this. I'd give them a call now and see about starting tomorrow. Your kids are too good to waste any more time here. I mean really, just look around, it's a pretty talent free environment."

Mrs. Speedo was now preening and actually scratched her crotch while I was talking. She agreed with everything I said, (shocking - not) and hurried to get her phone to make that call.

Crisis averted.

Mrs. Speedo and her progeny had been hustled off to another diving class where she could soon become some other parents' problem. Sorry, not sorry.

When I was done patting myself on the back, I turned to see the young moms watching me. One of them said, "We couldn't really hear you. What did you tell her to get her to leave?"

Another mom fearfully asked, "Do you think she's gone for real?"

I told this group of young hero worshippers that I would be glad to expound on my knowledge. My price? An icy Diet Coke from the snack bar.

When I received the drink, the moms huddled around me. A reverent hush took over the covered snack bar area and I began to share my tips for taking down the dreaded, but multiplying in frightening numbers, mom bully.

Ahh, it felt so good to be needed.

There's something terrifying about sending your first child off to college. Even more terrifying is finding that college. As a mother you just want your kid to be happy and to thrive in their new environment.

The whole time I was looking at colleges with my son I felt like freaking Goldilocks. This one was too small. The next one was too big and so on and so on. Finally, I just had to let go and tell myself that it was all going to be okay. My son would survive without me and the college he picked would be fine.

He ended up staying in state and loved his university. All was well until four years later when I had to go through the college tour 2.0 with my daughter.

The College Tour

MY SUMMER VACATION wasn't spent hiking in the mountains or lollygagging on a beach. Oh no, there was zero time for that kind of nonsense. This was because I was a mom on a mission.

It was time to start the college tour death march and I was all in. My son and I would be touring five different college campuses in five days, and it was time to get this party started.

My 16-year-old, almost junior in high school, son was ready (although he didn't seem as eager as me) to embark on his first round of college visits. Our plan was to look at colleges he was curious about, had highly rated business schools and that had also been actively recruiting him by email, texts or sending him enough letters, color brochures, reports, and student magazines that I'm certain resulted in at least one acre of deforestation in the Pacific Northwest.

Here's a tip to all seven thousand and counting institutions of higher learning - cut back on the four-color, 8 1/2 X 11 heavy card stock recruitment crap. It will save you a bundle and you can pass that on to the student by decreasing college tuition by at least one-third.

Now for a parental pointer. Once your child takes the PreACT and PSAT their freshman or sophomore year go out and get another recycling trash can or bin.

You'll need it because that's when your mailbox will start seeing some major activity. I don't care if your kid makes a two out of a possible 1520 on the PSAT there will still be at least two thousand colleges that think your child "shows academic promise," "demonstrates leadership" and would be a "great fit" for their university.

Our college tour would be of the mother and son road trip variety. My husband very wisely was taking our daughter to Lake Tahoe because I couldn't think of anything more painful than dragging her from college to college and hearing her moan, "This is the worst summer vacation ever." Or her classic and most used refrain, "Is this ever going to end?"

I hit the road with high hopes. We were off to get this college adventure started. As soon as I got on I-35 I found my favorite SiriusXM station and lo and behold the *Dixie Chicks* version of *Landslide* came on and I started singing along.

God, I sounded good! Where's the *American Idol* for the middle-aged mom set? I'd so try-out for that.

Never mind that as a teenager I was not so gently asked to drop out of the Richfield High School Concert Chorale due to what the choir teacher termed "the worst case of tone deafness he'd ever heard in his twenty-one-year teaching career."

I also was told I had a "gift of shouting rather than singing the lyrics." Whatever, apparently some people don't know talent even when it's screaming in their ear.

I was really getting into the song. I mean how could I not? It's about things changing and here I was taking my first-born to look at colleges. Where did the time go? It doesn't seem fair. One blink and my baby was a teenager. And yet here I am still carrying around my postpartum poundage. But that's a deep thought for another time.

I channeled those intense emotions into creating a superb vocal performance. That was until my son took off his headphones, looked at me and said, "Even with noise canceling headphones on, I think you caused my ears to start spontaneously hemorrhaging. Seriously Mom, stop it. I can't take this thing you call singing."

Jerk, who just then sounded just like his father. To keep the peace, I turned on NPR and drove five-hundred miles south to College A.

We spent the night in an adequate Fairfield Inn using Marriott points, of course. My husband is a hotel and airline point hoarder. Where's that reality TV show? I can see a long, slow camera move that zooms in on a man, just beginning to go gray, hunched over his laptop calculating the best airline route to take to maximize his frequent flier miles. His brow furrowed and his lip spotted with sweat from the agony of deciphering the optimum flight choice.

Last year I stayed at a Hyatt and forgot to give the front desk my Hyatt Gold Passport number. When my husband found out you would have thought I had just told him I had a lover, and it was a chipmunk named Bruiser who was very gifted with his bushy tail.

Good lord, he was pissed. I think his exact quote was ``I might as well have taken his wallet and thrown it out a window."

What a freaking drama queen.

The next morning, we got up early-ish because we had to be at the university visitors center at 7:45. I was dressed in casual mom attire of my sort of dressy jeans, last summer's wedge sandals, and a super cute blouse I had just gotten from the Boden catalog. Trust me, a Peter Pan collar is flattering no matter what your age. I was also having an exceptionally good hair day. I felt, dare I say, co-eddy.

My only early morning downer was when I took a hard pass on the Fairfield Inn free breakfast. This was because when I saw the line at the waffle maker, I had an anxious moment followed by some acid reflux due to an unfortunate event last year.

What's that? You want to hear the story behind that event. Okay, flashback time it is.

Well, last summer, at the Fairfield Inn in Sacramento (near the Roseville Mall, home of the Louis Vuitton store that I got kicked out of because I dared to bring my Diet Coke into the land of Louis.) I had to break up a waffle maker oligarchy.

There was a dad with his, I'm guessing, middle-school aged son that was barring anyone else from making a waffle.

Here's the weird part - besides the fact they were dressed in matching Nike orange nylon shorts, tank tops and white knee-high sports socks with those awful looking shower shoes - they weren't making waffles.

Instead, they were holding the waffle maker hostage until the rest of their family came down to breakfast. How bizarre is that?

Even more bizarro world was that no one was doing anything about it. Sure, people were standing in line complaining, but no one was going all "excuse me" on them. I couldn't believe it.

My husband suggested I let it go and get myself some Frosted Flakes. I suggested he take his complimentary *USA Today*, banana and vanilla yogurt back to our room because I was getting myself a waffle.

He urged the kids to go with him, but they declined his kind offer. I gave my son my room key and told him to have it at the ready in case things got really bad and he needed to take his sister and make a run for it.

Then I sweetly approached the waffle oligarchy and told them I was going to make myself a waffle. The dad, as he had told everyone else who approached the waffle maker, barked at me that he was "saving it for his family"

"Where is your family?" I ever so politely asked.

"Umm, they're still in the room, but I know they'll be coming down soon and we all want waffles, so I guess you could say I'm tagged in on the waffle maker."

"Hmm," I cooed, "Let me get this straight. You're keeping everyone else here from making a waffle because you think your family, who is not even here yet, is more important than any other person currently in this room." (I said the last part quite loudly with a dramatic emphasis on the words "more important.")

Yippee, that got the crowd agitated. Toast was dropped and one man was holding a banana in his hand like he was ready to use it as a weapon.

And really how could folks not get upset? Because how dare anyone think that their family is superior to your family. One very XL dad (I'm talking huge because I actually felt petite and that almost never happens) got up from his table, stomped over and said, "Hey, what's this about your family being better than mine?"

"Yeah," I said. "All of our precious (precious is such a great word it totally disguises the fact that you think someone is a mega idiot) families are actually here, like in this room, right now and we would so loooove to make some waffles."

Then the big dude lifted up his stomach (it took two hands) and got right in the other dad's face. It was getting tense. I looked over my shoulder at my kids and gave them the mom face that said, "Get ready to haul ass."

It took about thirty seconds before the waffle oligarchy sensed defeat, surrendered the waffle maker and beat a quick retreat back to their room. The big dad was such a sweetheart. He told me to "please make my waffle first." Chivalry is not dead, my friends.

So, that's my saga on why I didn't want to partake of the "free" breakfast at the Fairfield Inn. Fortunately, I had two protein bars in the car, so I was calling that breakfast. As my son ate both bars, I drove to the campus visitors' center where my claim to fame was that I only got lost three times.

When I found a parking space, I fluffed my still incredible looking hair and then turned to my son as he was getting out of the car and said, "Wait get back in the car."

He rolled his eyes and slid back in. "What?" he moaned.

"I think we need a safe word," I said.

"Huh?"

"Just look at this itinerary," I scowled, pointing at the lengthy schedule the university admissions department had emailed us. "There's a lot of stuff on this. If you hate the school or something we need a word that's the signal that one of us wants to bail. So, let's pick a word, but it has to be something that won't give us away and fits into the context of the visit."

I said all of this while I was lovingly gazing at my hair in the car's rearview mirror. I'm not kidding it had never looked better. The humidity had to be historically low. I was even thinking that maybe I could pull off the whole side swept bang look. It would totally camo my forehead wrinkles.

My son thought for a moment and said, "Okay how about SAT score? If one of us says SAT score that means initiate the bailing sequence."

"Oh, that's a good one." I said smiling and still touching my hair. "Now let's go in there and see what this college has to offer!" I put my hand on the car door to open it and noticed my son wasn't getting out of the car.

Poor baby, I bet he's scared, I thought. And why shouldn't he be. His life was about to take a giant step into adulthood. I reached out, patted his arm and said, "Oh sweetie, don't be nervous. This is going to be fun."

"I'm not nervous," he said. "Well, I'll take that back. I am nervous. Nervous that you're not going to be able to keep your mouth shut. I'm not kidding, Mom, don't talk. I mean you can talk, but don't go off on some tangent."

Now, I rolled my eyes. When did he turn into his father? I also didn't like his tone. It was a little sassy, but I just sighed and said, "I'm here as your silent partner. I won't even raise my hand to ask a question. Alright? This is all about you."

"Okay," he sighed, like he didn't believe me for a hot minute and we both got out of the car.

Meet Your Competition

As we entered the university visitors' center, I gasped. Sweet halls of knowledge, it was like I had walked into a P.T.A. meeting in hell. Hot moms, boastful, windbag dads, "I'm footing the bill for this" assertive grandmothers, parents with notebook binders or worse notebook binders and their laptops, smug couples whose body language seemed to be saying "I know something you don't know" sprinkled with parents standing in the back of the room like they're literally doing their best to blend in with the wall.

My son leaned in and muttered, "Remember your promise."

After doing a visual of the cornucopia of parents filling up the foyer of the university visitors' center, I decided I needed to work the room. It was time for some intel and there's no better way to get that than doing the smile and shine.

For those of you poor souls not from the South that means you smile really big (as in you have to show some teeth), then you give some random person who you have never seen before in your life a compliment, thus quickly gaining their trust and then you proceed to pump them mercilessly for information. I looked at my son and informed him of my plan.

"You and your work the room thing." He said in an irritated whisper, "Mom your problem is you think you're Homeland Security when really you're more like the T.S.A. guy checking if people have their shoes off."

I recoiled at that low blow but didn't even have a chance to threaten him with a punishment before he asked. "And why do you think you're so good at working the room?"

"Please, there's not a room that's been made that I can't work, and as for why I'm so good at it? Just think of who MY mother is and there's your answer to that question. Now watch and learn here's a life skill lesson coming your way."

And with that I turned my head so my hair swung to and fro creating what I just knew was a vision of middle-aged follicle majesty.

Unfortunately, my son's idea of watching was to do what every other teenager in the room was doing, staring at their iPhone. Not one kid was even attempting to make conservation with another fellow junior in high school.

I decided as a "smile and shine" warm up I would start with something easy - the family, in what I will kindly describe as being dressed in wrinkled "leisure apparel," hogging all the seats in the foyer with a pack of bored kids.

I don't get families that have to do everything together. What's the reason for it? Do the husband and wife not trust each other? Are they afraid to let their spouse out of their sight? Do they each think the other one is not intelligent enough to do anything solo with the kids?

I know this type of family very well. These are the couples that bring their crying babies and toddlers to any and every adult function or event. I dread them most at the movies. Why can't some parents grasp the concept of taking turns, tag team parenting, if you will, as in one person stays home with kid(s) while the other one sees the movie then when that person gets home the other gets to go.

Don't you dare tell me it's because the couple wants to spend time together. Seeing a movie is all about shutting up and looking straight ahead. There is no "time spent together," only time sitting next to each other, and you can do that in the car.

Now, I do see the value in bringing your entire freaking family to the big city, but while mother and son or dad and daughter are doing the college tour thing the other parent could be taking the remaining six kids, grandma and grandpa and the aunts and uncles to the zoo or a museum in their twelve-person passenger van.

Why this wasn't done was a conundrum to me. Seriously, I need insight into why anyone would descend on a college tour with this many kinfolk.

Because I knew I would never see this large family contingent again I indulged my curiosity and asked the father of the clan that very question. Well, of course I asked the question fluffed up with layers of sweetness as in "Hi there, you've sure got a lot of family with you today. That's just so great that y'all are here to do this together."

The dad puffed out his chest and said, "This is the sixth college we've seen so far, and we have ten more to go on our list."

"And all of you have gone on every college visit?" I inquired trying to keep the shock out of my voice.

Grandma perked up with a very firm, "Yes, going to college is a family decision and we all need to be very involved, especially me."

Oh lord, suddenly I felt an overwhelming sorrow for the mother of the soon to be college student. I'd bet a forty-two-ounce Diet Coke with crushed ice that when this woman gave birth to each of her kids there was so much family in the delivery room it was standing room only.

I just knew a grandma this pushy pushed her way right into the birthing process. To check my hunch, I smiled and asked the grandma, "I bet you've been involved since the day your granddaughter was born?"

"You would be right on that count. I was the first one to hold her."

"Before her dad or mom?" I asked.

"Why yes, I was in the delivery room and took her right from the doctor."

More like grabbed her from the doctor, I thought.

"Now, who here is the soon to be college freshman?" I asked.

A tired looking girl with long, somewhat greasy hair tied back in a ponytail (Not that it's her fault. Call me a hair whisperer because her sloppy, oily ponytail was talking to me and it said, "I don't get enough quality, uninterrupted time in the shower to adequately rinse out all the conditioner.") and sweatpants with her high school's name down the side looked at me and said, "It's me."

"Do you have a favorite college yet?"

She mumbled, "Yeah, the one the farthest away from home."

I winked at her, bid her clan goodbye, and walked over to the power couple standing right by a massive pillar that looked like it was imported from the coliseum in Rome or the Caesars' Palace shopping mall in Vegas.

These two fascinated me because when they weren't texting or talking on their phones they were smirking. Like they knew something the rest of us didn't. Hmm, what could that be I wondered.

The dad was dressed in a suit and tie and looked very CEO except he didn't have on socks with his shoes. I get the no socks with dress shoes thing, but really why? Is it that hard to pull on a pair of socks?

I don't care how cool you think it makes you look. It's not good foot hygiene people and all the sweat is hell on an expensive pair of leather shoes. Besides all that, the no socks with $500 "going to the office" shoes sets off a four alarm, "I am a douche" vibe.

The mom was all high fashion in a dress that was so severe and plain you knew it had to cost a crap ton of money. Her almost mini dress was dirt brown and shiny.

It looked like someone took a paper shopping bag from the grocery store, cut out holes for the head and arms and then headed to the elementary school and had it laminated in the teacher's work room. She finished her bag outfit with some sky-high stilettos and her blonde hair was pin straight and hit her shoulders.

The thing you really noticed was her red lips. You know the clothing spreads you see in *Vogue* magazine and wonder to yourself, "Who the hell wears this stuff and why would anyone wear lipstick that red except at Halloween?" Well, this woman had answered those questions.

There was a kid, sort of, standing near them. I'm pretty sure he was their son because he had on what seemed to be his prep school uniform of khakis, navy blazer, dress shirt and tie. I thought he looked high or was suffering from some severe allergies. Maybe it was both.

As I was debating how best to get these two talking, I noticed the mom was using her phone as a mirror. She seemed mesmerized by her own reflection thus making her easy prey for the likes of me. If there's one thing I know how to do it's get a self-obsessed, forever foraging for the fountain of youth, over forty woman to talk.

I casually sauntered over, gave my still stunning hair a good shake and said, "Excuse me, but you look so familiar. Are you Gwyneth Paltrow?"

Does she look like Gwyneth Paltrow? Maybe if the room was dark and you were suffering from the ravages of macular degeneration. But she was blonde with no discernible body fat, and had a crazed ferret look in her eyes that all women who have been denied refined sugar for weeks-on-end seem to share. It's as if they're not 100% present in the moment. Like a part of their brain is preoccupied with thoughts of eating brownie batter with a soup ladle or something. She's also wearing haute couture Amish edition so yeah; she's pulling a Gwyneth.

The woman was instantly, no longer interested in her reflection. I had her complete attention. "No," she laughed in a haughty ha, ha kind of way. "Although you're not the first to make that mistake."

"Well, you can't be here for the college tour. You're not old enough to have a kid ready for this journey. Are you here in a big sister capacity?"

She laughed again, moved closer to me, and said, "Believe it or not my son is right over there and he's seventeen."

I smiled and commented on what a handsome son she had even though by now he was sitting on the marble floor, with his back up against the pillar and drooling. Forget the allergies he's definitely high on something and I didn't think it was a post-secondary education.

I pointed out my son who had the good manners to still be standing. Never mind that he was scowling directly at me. I've told him a million times to ditch the scowl (which was fast becoming his signature look) because he was going to have premature wrinkling of the forehead if he kept it up.

To keep the conservation moving I asked, "Is this your first college visit?"

"No, it's not. We're on number twenty-six."

My eyes got huge because I can't imagine crisscrossing from the redwood forest to the gulf stream waters to take my kid on that motherlode of college visits.

"Why so many?" I asked.

"Well, you have to do that many. At my son's school everyone does at least thirty college visits. If you don't then it's kind of like your kid's NHCCM."

"What's that? I said hoping it wasn't some kind of disease or acronym for idiot.

"It means *Not Highly Competitive College Material* and according to our college coach it's good for the other schools to know that your child is vigorously scouting other colleges."

"Wait, you have a college coach?"

"Of course, if you're serious about getting your kid in then you must have someone whose job it is to make sure it happens. It's not cheap, but it's worth it."

"I don't mean to be rude, but like how much money are we talking about? If you don't mind me asking."

"It all depends on the school they get you into. If it's a heavy hitter like say Stanford or Harvard, then it's buckets of money. If they help get your kid into a mid-level competitive school like say Vanderbilt or Tulane, it's less. You pay according to the degree of admission difficulty.

By this time I was having a huge problem trying to keep my jaw from hitting the floor and I also picked up on the vibe that the woman was getting bored with my questions. It was time to increase my charm offensive.

"Sorry to be so pushy, but what does buckets of money mean in terms of actual dollars? By the way, did you know your skin is absolutely poreless?"

Pro tip time - I've found that telling any woman that her skin is poreless is akin to casting a magical spell on her. Basically, she'll tell you anything.

Faux Gwyneth touched her face, preened, and then said, "You pay them what the first semester of college costs for the school they get your kid into."

I shouted, "Good God, that's a lot of money!"

She rolled her eyes, took a step back from me and said, "You've gotta pay-to-play. It's the whole in-it-to-win-it thing. In fact, my son's college coach is standing right over there." She points with her phone at the column behind me.

"You mean to tell me she comes with you on these college tour things?"

"Yep, she does everything. The only reason my husband and I are both here is because she got us a meeting with the Dean of the business school. If this was just a tour visit (She says "tour visit" like she's just been condemned to shopping for eternity at Walmart) we wouldn't be here at all."

I turned around and sure enough there's some thirty something woman with a binder talking to a youngish looking man who I'm betting was our "leader" on the tour. Not wanting to miss out on what they're talking about I excused myself from Faux Gwyneth by deftly throwing another compliment her way and walked over.

My first thought after listening to the college coach for about forty-five seconds was that she needed lessons from me on how to work a room. The "coach" was badgering the university admissions dude that I'm pretty sure was low on the old totem pole of who gets in.

The guy was being very polite, but you could tell he was trying to get away. Because I'm perhaps the nicest person in the whole wide world I decided to throw him a bone and intervened.

"Pardon me," I said, "Are you with the University?"

"Yes, I am," He said, looking grateful for the question.

"Umm, there was some guy over there, I think, looking for you."

He gave me a smile and took off.

I then directed my attention to the college coach and asked for her card. Not that I was ever going to use it, but I wanted to see where she was from and if she really called herself something as cutesy as a college coach.

In an efficient and brisk voice, she announced, "I'm not allowed to fraternize with other parents during this tour. All my attention is focused on the Tyler family, so if you will excuse me." And with that she walked away.

Wow, I thought she must have gone to Bitch U, and I know from personal experience that college is not highly selective.

The Sales Pitch

By this time, I was a little hungry. There must be some sort of refreshment table or something. You don't have what looks to be fifty kids and parents showing up at 7:45 in the morning and not have a little nosh for them. At the very least there would be coffee or Capri Suns.

I scoured the foyer and poked my head into the meeting room - nothing - not even water. What the hell?

These yahoos want me to pony up $57,350 a year for my child to have the "privilege" of attending their university and they can't even provide a beverage. I don't care what grand and glorious things might happen on the tour, as far as I was concerned, this place was off the list. A lack of gracious hospitality was a very bad sign, indeed.

As I was walking towards my son to alert him about my decision, I spied a woman in tennis shoes and capri linen pants from J. Jill. I knew this because I had tried on a pair just like it and they were dreadful.

The blame for that was the drawstring waist. It created an unsightly clump around your midsection and from the back there was so much fabric it looked like you had to be wearing multiple Depends or had tucked a beach towel into your backside.

I was mesmerized by the bundle of linen bunching up her butt, but I was even more intrigued with what appeared to be one of those backpack cooler things. Was this lady hauling her own refreshment stand on her back? If so, I wanted in.

I hurried over and without even the slightest bit of shame said, "Hey there, if you've got snacks on you, I'm willing to strike a deal."

She laughed, gave me the once over and asked, "First timer?"

"Yes, what gave me away?"

"Well, for one, you're hungry and two, I've been watching you. (At this point I'm thinking, of course she was watching me. I'm sure she can't remember the last time she's seen hair this fabulous?) "I hate to tell ya this, but you're a little too chatty. The more you go on these college visits you'll notice no one really talks to each other."

"Why not?"

"Everyone likes to play this game close to the vest."

"Okay, I still don't get that." I said hungry and now confused.

"The more competitive the college, the less anyone wants to share anything about themselves. We're all the enemy. Your kid could be keeping my kid out of this school."

"Ohhh," I said while nodding my head. "Now I get it. But don't worry about me, I'm not sending my son to a college that doesn't have the good manners to provide, at the very least, bottled water to its guests."

Linen Capris smiled at me and then ever so slyly asked, "So, what's your family's angle?"

"Huh?" I said confused again and started rambling. "What do you mean what's our angle? Do we need an angle? Our angle is our son. Does he have to have an angle? I mean I know he needs stellar SAT and ACT scores and good grades, but what's with this angle thing?"

She gave me a look that dripped with condescension, and I knew she had to be thinking, "Oh, you poor, pitiful, dumb ass mom."

She then patted my arm and said, "Look you don't know me at all, but I've got three kids. My oldest hit the jackpot - Yale. My middle child had to settle for U.T. and she was lucky to get that. Seven times she had to take the SATs. Seven damn times. Now, all I've got left is my baby girl and I'm praying for a miracle in the form of the world's best admissions essay. I've even conjured up a family drama meets societal crisis to really make her essay sing."

My eyes got huge. Conjuring up a family societal crisis - what does that even mean? But before I had time for a follow up question the university

"Tour Facilitator" announced that everyone needed to proceed into the meeting room.

The group meekly moved into a well-appointed room with large windows, more pillars and enough crown molding to recreate Colonial Williamsburg.

The extended family, of course, took up all the chairs in the entire front row. The Gwyneth family sat in the back, like they were the cool kids or something. And Linen Capris plopped smack dab in the middle. I directed my son to sit towards the back and using a series of dirty looks we fought over who got the aisle seat. I won.

The university representative attempted to be funny but was so not funny. I didn't even think he deserved a polite, pity laugh. He seemed to be in his late 20s and was working some early male pattern baldness.

The whole welcome presentation was pretty boring and warp sped to mind numbing when the PowerPoint got started. Now, I like and respect a good PowerPoint, but this was not just lame but lazy. No good use of color in the fonts, no background and where's the music and photos?

Hello - you're talking to the Instagram generation. They need pictures, lots of pictures. It's like they've reverted back to being babies who loved board books.

I was also getting annoyed because the guy must have sold cars in his previous job. Nowhere in his overview of the college did he mention price. Sure, he talked about financial aid, scholarships, student loans, but gave no hard data on what it was going to cost you to drive the first year of college "off the lot."

Where was the sticker price? That's what I wanted to know. So, I asked. I know I had promised my son I would keep my lips firmly locked, but screw it, I wasn't letting him go here anyway based on the lack of pre-tour snackage.

The university dude acted like he got this question a lot. He smiled and said, "There are just too many variables for me to answer that question." Then he proceeded to brush me off.

Sadly, for him I wasn't brush off material. I'm more of a you have to scrub me off using at the very least a significant amount of Clorox, Comet cleanser, a SOS pad and maybe even a Mr. Clean Magic Eraser.

I quickly replied back, "Why is it so difficult? What is the average number of semester hours a freshman takes.?"

He answered, "Fifteen hours."

"So, why can't you take those fifteen hours of tuition, multiply that by two, add in the cost of books, room and board and auxiliary fees and give me a number? It's not like I'm going to hold you to it, but I need to know what this college costs for not only budgeting reasons but to compare it to the other schools we're going to look at."

Some mom, trying to be helpful, popped up and told me about websites that calculate college costs. I smiled at her and said, "That's all well and good but I think a college meet and greet should include a price tag."

The university dude then admitted that he was "not at liberty to answer my question." The kicker was he said it like I had committed an egregious etiquette faux pas. Like "how dare I mention something as silly and mundane as money."

See, I was right. The whole no snack thing was a red flag. Who wants their kid to go to a school where they don't believe in feeding or hydrating their guests and are too hoity-toity to talk about what something was going to cost?

We are so out of here, I thought to myself. I was about to lean over and whisper to my son that I wanted to skip the walking tour when I saw Linen Capris look over the back of her chair and smile at me.

All of sudden I knew I wasn't ready to leave yet. I still had to find out how "conjuring a family/societal crisis" got your kid into college.

Linen Capris Shares All

Minutes later we were freed from the meeting room and assigned tour guides. The guide we got had a really squeaky voice, so I suggested to my son we ditch her and hook up with the other group.

My real reason to abandon the guide was that I wanted to be with Linen Capris. When she saw me walk over, she took off her backpack cooler and offered me a Smart Water. I eagerly took it and thank God I did, because the tour turned out to be a hot, humidity rich slog through every inch of the campus.

I learned many useful things like dorms still suck and that this particular college we were looking at was a Diet Pepsi school. I discovered this by trekking through one of the cafeterias and noticed that only Pepsi products were served. I told my son there was no way he'd be going to a Pepsi school. Not on my watch, my friends, not on my watch.

He just rolled his eyes and said, "Let's imagine for a moment that by some miracle I get accepted to Stanford and Yale and they're both, as you put it, 'Pepsi schools.' You're saying you would not allow me to attend either of those colleges because of their soda offerings? That could be a first, Mom - kid declines Ivy League because of the lack of Diet Coke on campus."

I had to think hard about that and sighed, "Well no, of course I would let you go, but it's not a good sign. A school needs to have Diet Coke on tap, not freaking Pepsi. It speaks to the overall character."

"Soda speaks to overall character?" He asked in a real smart-ass voice.

"Yes, it does and apparently that's a lesson you're going to have to learn the hard way. In a couple of years from now, don't say I didn't warn you."

He shook his head at me and walked to the front of the group which was perfect because I was overdue for a chit-chat with Linen Capris. I hung back until she was walking with me and inquired, "So, what's up with the whole crisis conjuring you mentioned before the meeting started?"

She smiled at me and said, "It's going to be my angle."

"How is that an angle?"

She took a Nature Valley granola bar out of her backpack cooler, slowly un-wrapped it and right before she took a bite said, "You are familiar with the essays that kids have to write to get into college?"

"Yes, of course. Well, really, I'm not super familiar with the process but my son seems to be on top of all that kind of stuff."

Mid chew she said, "That's a big mistake, you know, leaving it up to your son. If you want your kid to not only get into a school, but to get a little something, something, in terms of financial aid you're going to need a killer essay."

She paused, took another bite of the granola bar and resumed talking, appar-ently totally at ease conversing with food in her mouth.

"The essay needs to hit all the right notes and by that I mean it needs to focus on some sort of personal struggle, where your kid took a stand and was brave. Even better if the focus hits on a current event. That's why I'm going to take the social crisis du jour and manipulate it."

"Still so not getting it," I admitted.

This seemed to aggravate her, but she continued, "I'm thinking right now I want my daughter's essay to be on her personal fight for climate change. Now, in order to give her essay some authenticity I've positioned myself as a climate change denier and that way my kid can write about trying to seek change while living with the problem.

"I know that title sounds weak but consider it a work in progress. I've even joined some militant climate change denier groups online so my daughter will have inside information for her essay. It's going to be epic! Her SATs aren't where they should be and she's going to need something big to get her over the heap."

"Wait, let me see if I have this right. You are currently not a climate change denier, but have become one up to and including joining denier groups to get your kid into college?"

"I'll admit it sounds a little desperate and yes one hundred percent manufactured but trust me these colleges are looking for that kind of real story. What are most kids going to write about? The deep depression they went into when they were banned from TikTok for twenty-four hours."

"Yeah, well, it sounds more like a *Lifetime* movie than a college essay to me, but you've gotten two more kids into college than I have so what do I know."

Linen Capri stopped walking, tucked her granola wrapper into a pocket on her backpack and said, "It's a game, this college thing. You need to remember that. It's just a big game."

"It's something, that's for sure" I said as we each started walking to catch up with our kids. When I reached my son he whispered, "SAT scores."

"What about them?" I asked.

"No, Mom, S-A-T Scores, remember our safe word?"

"Oh yes, of course, SAT scores. Let's go! I'm starving."

We discreetly ditched the tour by turning left as they turned right to go into the library and hauled ass to our car. My son, per my instructions, began looking for the closest restaurants on his iPhone.

We settled on a hamburger place that got awesome Yelp reviews five miles away. As I'm driving, I looked over at my son and blurted out, "You know I would join a militant climate denier group for you."

"What?" he asked, half scared, half confused.

"I mean just what I said, I would go full crazy if that's what it took to get you into your dream school."

"And why would you do this for me?" He said slowly like I've just had a stroke or something.

"That lady back there. The one with that Igloo cooler backpack, well, she told me she's going to become a climate change denier and has joined the most whacked out groups she can so her kid can write an amazing college essay about living with and yet loving the enemy or something like that to get herself into an Ivy League school."

"Mom, that is the stupidest thing I've ever heard and how disingenuous (At this point I am beaming at my son's use of disingenuous, which I knew to be a SAT vocab word.) to pretend that you're something you're not, up to and including infiltrating groups you don't believe in. God Mom, you attract the weirdest people. You're like a welcome mat for anyone who's deranged."

"Whatever, I just wanted you to know I would totally do that for you because I love you that much."

"Mom, stop! That's not love, it's manipulation."

"Is it? I kind of feel like it's also love. And you should know while we're exploring this topic of pretending to be something you're not, your dad, he would never do that. He'd take a bullet for you, but lie, infiltrate a climate change denier group that still believes Earth is square, I don't think he could do it.

"I, on the other hand, would not only do that, but also take a bullet. So, if there ever comes a time when both your father and I need a kidney, remember I would run for climate change denier of the year, but you know only for like a day or something, *and* take a bullet, your dad he's just going for the bullet."

"Okay, okay, you can stop talking now."

"No, I cannot. This is important because very soon you will be leaving me and I need you to know that nothing, no one, not one thing in this whole, wide world is as important to me as you are. File that away. You are going to have some days when knowing that will make you feel better.

"Also don't ever forget that no matter what, I am here for you. Even from the grave I'll be there for you. I don't know how, but I'm sure there is some portal or something that allows mothers to still get to their kids."

"Mom, when was your last Diet Coke? I think you're going through withdrawal and it's affecting your brain. Should I be driving? I really think I should be driving."

"I am fine. I'm just trying to adjust to you being gone."

Don't worry, Mom, you still have one kid left at home to screw up."

That made me smile. "I do, don't I?"

My son patted my arm and said, "Yes, you sure do."

Hmm, what could go wrong when you pair a control freak mom with a group of rowdy kindergarteners who have been given lassoes? Short answer — everything.

Dear Lord Save Me From Vacation Bible School

I'M JUST GOING to come right out and say this and don't go all holier than thou on me people, I speak the truth and I believe that's one of the Ten Commandments. So here goes - most parents view Vacation Bible School, in its purest form, as daycare. Sure, I'll say it's a chance for the kids to bond with the Lord if that makes any of you feel better. But, at the top of the list it's daycare, free church daycare.

Don't even think about arguing that point because even the churches know this. Is VBS offered as soon as school gets out? No. It's offered in the middle of summer. Right when most parents begin hitting the wall of summer. The big, "What are we doing for fun today? I'm sick of the pool. Can I have ten friends over?" wall. My sister-in-law this summer alone has sent her kids to seven Vacation Bible Schools. Which says volumes about my sister-in-law. But those stories are best left for another time.

The calendar placement of Vacation Bible School is perfect. As soon as parents start mentally counting down the days till school starts VBS comes to the rescue providing a brief summer respite.

If VBS is in the morning, then it's three hours for a parent to get some work done. If it's at night, then it's two hours to grab a child-free meal with your favorite adult.

Unless, of course, you have had your arm twisted, guilted into or see it as your gift to the higher power to volunteer to work as a VBS teacher. I'll let you guess which two of those I checked off my list. So, here I was all ready to get my VBS on and "Saddle Up to Ride with Jesus."

Under conditions of my "employment agreement" I was assisting with the kindergarten classes. Please note the emphasis on assist. I was definitely the follower not the leader.

The "teacher" of our group was a delightful woman who I had volunteered with pleasurably at my children's school. She was a little high-strung and very precise and fussy about everything. For example, we had to have three, count 'em three, VBS meetings at her home to go over the curriculum and the arts and crafts.

I had two problems with the meetings. One, no booze. I have a long-standing rule that if you're going to invite someone into your home after 3 p.m. on a Saturday there should be the offer of libations. Especially in the summer when the range of cocktails you can offer really opens up.

I mean who can say no to a watermelon margarita and would I come to a meeting with a smile on my face if I knew there would be watermelon margaritas, why yes, I would. Instead, we were offered water or Crystal Light pink lemonade.

Secondly, the meetings were kid free and on a Saturday. Which both suggest to me that cocktails will be served. Am I wrong about this?

The kid free thing on a Saturday is not that big of a deal but having a meeting on a Saturday is. Most of us have enough meetings Monday thru Friday and I, for one, like to keep my weekend meetings free, if I can help it.

Upon entering Mrs. VBS's home, I was struck by the domestic perfection. It was so clean I was a little bit surprised she didn't require us to shower before entering. As I continued walking through the foyer, I approached the world's most pristine kitchen complete with a massive child chore chart, enrichment activity list, and summer reading log resplendent with "accomplishment" stickers. The whole thing made me a little jealous and I got some pangs of feeling like a parenting failure.

This was because I've tried the chore chart. It lasted maybe two days until I went back to my method of yelling while jumping up and down and threatening my kids. While I'm sure it's not as effective as a chore chart, it is, some days, my only cardio.

It was the summer reading log though that was really killing me. Her girls had read loads of books and we were only halfway through summer. The only reading my daughter had done all summer was *People Magazine's* Harry Styles special edition and as for my son, I was lucky if he read the back of the Honey Nut Cheerios box.

After being offered the no fun drink choice of water or Crystal Light, we got right to work on the craft projects and Bible theme stories that would be the crux of the VBS experience. One of the craft projects was weaving ropes (braiding) to make a lariat so the kids could "lasso Jesus."

It was at this point in the meeting I had to speak up. Being the only mother with a, umm, child who was not an angel, I would be remiss if I didn't mention kindergarten students and lassos are never a good idea. I couldn't even get out my list of reasons before the other moms just glossed right over my well-founded objections.

This, my friends, is what I call the parting of the parenting Red Sea. Done not by Moses, but by well-meaning moms who only have calm, studious, polite offspring with superior impulse control.

Apparently, there are some lucky parents out there that have perfect kids. I call them fairy tale children because they're too good to be true. Years ago, when my son was four, I had a very painful break up with a much-loved friend because she was the mother of three incredible fairy tale girls.

They never yelled, had impeccable manners, could sit still for longer than five minutes and didn't size up every household item for its weapon or flying projectile potential. Her little girls could also color for hours on end and talked in hushed respectful tones to their mother.

I knew we had to break up when during one visit my son (age three at the time) took one of his Thomas the Tank Engine trains (key point here is the Thomas trains have magnets on the front so the trains can hook up with one another) wrapped a Barbie Doll's hair around it and then attached the train with its magnet to a metal stand fan.

The Barbie's hair got tangled up in the fan blades, the fan went all wobbly crazy, tipped over, hit a coffee table, cracked it and sent five cups of grape juice flying off causing an onslaught of screams (me) and tears (everyone else).

The grape juice, by the way, totally proves my point about how well-behaved these girls were. Because what parent gives a kid grape juice in an open container? Not me. We were strictly a clear or white beverage family, and I forced my son to drink from a cup with a lid until about his tenth birthday.

Obviously, this mother and her daughters had never witnessed the awesome powers of a child that loved to be in a constant state of motion and this resulted in the fairy tale family being severely traumatized.

Oh, did I mention this little accident didn't happen at my house. I immediately went into apology mode, called a carpet cleaner, and demanded that my friend let me replace her coffee table and fan. No amount was too high. I then grabbed my son, threw him over my pregnant with another non fairy tale child belly and we made a run for it.

Two days later, I took my friend out to dinner and broke it off. Her girls were too perfect, she was too good of a mother. My son and I clearly frightened her family. There could be no more mommy and kids playdates.

As any mom knows, once you reduce a friendship to just the two of you spending time together, forget about it. It's the death knell in the friendship coffin. When your kids are young there are not enough hours in the day to consistently schedule "dates" with girlfriends.

Now, I told that little story to illustrate not how lucky parents with fairy tale kids are but to show how they can be woefully naive about what happens in the real world. This would prove to be Mrs. VBS's Achilles heel. Not only was she the mother of two perfect fairy tale girls. She was, as previously illustrated, very rigid and keen on structure.

Don't get me wrong, these types of moms are invaluable. They are the backbone of every school's parent organization. Without their skills the gift-wrap sale would never happen. In fact, I doubt any fundraising would happen. The PTA would never have a treasurer that got happy printing out the excel spreadsheets and organization in every endeavor would be slipshod.

These moms are good people and good parents. They just, in this case, at least, should never volunteer to interact with other people's children. They're not prepared for life in the parenting trenches.

Unfortunately for Mrs. VBS our class was full of rowdy kids. I knew we were going to be in for a world of hurt when I saw her outfit. It was a short skirt, a ruffled white short-sleeve blouse and heels.

Yes, heels. WTH? Not exactly what I would call an outfit to get down and dirty in while surrounded by active kids looking to lasso a whole lot of fun.

According to the spreadsheet schedule, posted on the wall and color coded, the first thirty minutes was free play while we waited for all the kids to arrive. Then it was a thirty-minute Bible lesson, followed by arts and crafts, a visit to the sanctuary and then a snack.

Trouble began immediately when a cadre of kids started a Lincoln Log Battle. Lincoln Logs, as any parent knows, are great for building, throwing, and being used as a battering ram to knock down other kids' log cabins. I got down on the floor to act as a referee and corral the log throwing.

Mrs. VBS was dismayed that the boys and a couple of girls would actually throw the logs at each other. Then when two boys put some Lincoln Logs down their shorts and jumped up and down until they fell out, she admitted to being a "little queasy."

The boys thought it was hilarious and if you're five-years-old I can totally get how "pooping logs" would give you a giggle fit.

Mrs. VBS, still looking a little pale, told me, "Her girls would NEVER, EVER do that" and she was freaked out about the now extremely unsanitary logs.

As I put the butt cheek soiled logs in the sink I wanted to shout, "Well, Mrs. VBS let me wish you a warm welcome to the real world. Make yourself right at home because I've saved a seat for you."

After the Lincoln Logs were collected and disinfected it was time for the Bible lesson. Mrs. VBS had no concept of the short attention span theater that is the normal for the soon to be kindergartner. Her Bible lesson was more bible sermon and even I was getting antsy.

The kids were squirming, interrupting, and then started leaving the circle en masse. I whispered to Mrs. VBS that it might be time to deviate from the schedule and perhaps go to arts and crafts.

This freaked her out because we would be hitting arts and crafts a whole fifteen minutes early. I then gently pointed out that since there were no kids even left in the circle, we might want to just call it quits, for now, on the Bible lesson.

The arts and crafts project, in keeping with the western theme, "Saddle Up to Ride with Jesus" involved giving each child a straw cowboy hat to wear then three pieces of rope to make a lariat. The rope was the kind you would use to hang clothes on in your backyard (if people still did that kind of thing). Each kid was given three pieces of the rope so they could braid it for a cool lariat. The three pieces were already tired together so the kids could start braiding.

The first problem was most kids that young can't braid. Almost all of them had yet to master shoe tying. The second problem was the unmitigated disaster of giving very active five-year-olds three pieces of rope connected at the top and the rest dangling.

Hmm, what would a kid do with that rope? Would the child start swinging the ropes and causing a windmill of doom? Why yes. Would a child accidentally start whipping the rope at his closest seatmate? Certainly. Would a rope free-for-all begin? You're darn tootin' it would.

Whap, slap, whip, that was the sound of an arts and craft project going straight to hell. Add in kids crying as they got hit or experienced rope burn and now throw Mrs. VBS screaming at the kids to "stop it, just stop it!" into the mix and it's pretty much like you're there.

I entered the fray and started collecting up the ropes. We immediately executed plan B. I would braid the ropes while the kids colored.

After the ropes were braided, I was given the duty to go into the church kitchen and get the snacks while the kids were going to be taken to the sanctuary for a group prayer with all the VBS students.

Off I went to retrieve carrots, apple slices, and zucchini sticks. This prompted a flashback to my late 1970s cyclamate laden Kool-Aid, Twinkies and Ding Dongs Vacation Bible School experience and I got a little misty eyed. Was there anything better than being eight years old and eating a Ding-Dong and then chasing it with grape Kool-Aid?

As I was carrying the tray of fruit and veggies back to the church classroom, I turned the corner, and my life was forever changed.

There on the ten-foot stone statue of Jesus in the vestibule is the lord and savior with a straw cowboy hat on looking very *Brokeback Mountain*. He has also been lassoed (sort of, ropes are on him but not around him) not once but three times. Apparently, our five-year-old cowboys took the lasso theme to heart.

Mrs. VBS in an attempt to get the hat and ropes had climbed up on Jesus in her short skirt and is straddling the statue. But it's not just a straddle. She is continuing to shimmy up the statue to reach the hat. It's a shimmy, leap, shimmy, leap move. The motion makes it looks like Mrs. VBS is indeed having a "moment" with the Lord.

Now cue the minister with some teen and adult volunteers walking into the vestibule and witnessing this.

Poor Mrs. VBS was so intent on freeing the statue of the hat and ropes she didn't grasp what her shimmy leap dance looked like until one of the teen volunteers blurted out, "Oh my God, she's doing Jesus!"

The poor woman slid off of the Jesus statue, gave her skirt a very lady-like tug and then sobbed her way into the bathroom.

I handed off the veggie tray, took the kids into the sanctuary and prayed. Fervently prayed that the visual of Mrs. VBS and the Jesus statue would be eternally wiped from my memory and that no one would ever ask me to help with Vacation Bible School ever again.

FALL

"Life starts all over again when it gets crisp in the fall."

- F. Scott Fitzgerald

I will enthusiastically admit that I'm not exactly mother-of-the-year material. In fact, I have never felt the need to campaign for that honor. This means I'm still mystified when certain women feel the need to project that they're paragons of parenting.

One of the ways some moms do this is to talk incessantly about how obsessed they are with their progeny. And the bigger the audience for these overshares the better. Which makes the back-to-school parent coffee the perfect setting for some motherhood theatrics.

Note: You'll notice as you read this that I did borrow some of the same techniques that I used to get rid of the spring break braggy mom. Lord forgive me but I do love making up scientific studies.

Back-to-School Boo Hoos

LEAVE IT TO the first day of school to bring out the filthy liars in the motherhood community. I guess the scent of newly sharpened number two pencils, the aroma of brand-new nylon L.L. Bean backpacks and the essence of Johnson & Johnson Strawberry Sensation Detangling spray somehow manifests itself into a chemical cloud that permeates the nasal passages of all moms with school age children.

This potent scent combo platter then must travel to the brain cortex and trigger a nervous system response that manifests itself in grown ass, should know better females, telling great big whopping falsehoods for a twelve-hour period.

We all know what the biggest back-to-school lie is. It's the mother of all fibs when we share to anyone who will listen, but most especially other moms, that our guts are being ripped out, our souls are being shattered, and we're grieving, absolutely wallowing in the deepest, darkest pit of despair because school is starting.

Just the thought of imagining a world in which we cannot spend every waking hour with the magnificent beings that bobsledded their way out of our lady loins is thrusting us into turmoil.

Yeah, I get it. The first day of school is emotional. Every year is a milestone. Your kids are getting older. You're getting older. You're anxious and maybe a little worried because you want your children to have the most wonderful first day. I'm right there with you.

What irritates me is the mompocrisy of women who use this day to over-share that they are "just dying inside" because they'll miss their kids so much.

Please. I'm so not buying it. The self-discipline I have to use to not to tell these boo hoo moms to take the box of Kleenex they are holding and shove it in their pie hole is immense.

I'm not saying people don't miss their kids but when my alarm goes off on the first day of school I spring out of bed and do, at the very least, a sixty second boogie with a few of what I'm going to call rap moves that are so exuberant it scares the dogs and causes the dining room chandelier downstairs to swing violently. I then skip to each child's room and wake them up with this little ditty.

"Get up, Get up, Right Away cause Mommy's happy school starts today.

Hurry, hurry and get dressed cause Lord knows I crave an empty nest.

Don't worry about me, be sure to sign up for loads of free extracurricular activities."

After I see them off to their respective schools. I get back in my mercifully empty car, bow my head in silence and thank the gods of parenting that I made it through another summer with my sanity, somewhat, intact. I then take a deep cleansing breath, roll down all my windows, scream "Yahoo!" while doing multiple air high fives, and toast the new school year by sacrificing a virgin Diet Coke.

Sadly, I have found over the years that I have to hide my joy or at the very least downplay it. It now seems bad form to celebrate your liberation from your children. To do so makes one seem (gasp!) less than mother-of-the-year material.

Nothing highlights this sentiment more than the first day of school Parents' Coffee put on by the PTA in the school cafeteria.

I remember when my eldest son was in kindergarten and the Parents' Coffee was a blast. It was basically a bitch session about everything that had irritated everyone all summer. Bonus – people actually ate the doughnuts.

Nothing says someone's telling a great story like a person dual wielding a Krispy Kreme original glazed in each hand while gesturing widely.

Now it had morphed into a kiss and cry zone with weepy mothers trying to win the "I love my kid more" sweepstakes. When I saw moms posting "crying" videos on social media that left tears trapped on their fake Moxie eyelashes I snapped.

I couldn't take another mother blabbing and using a Kleenex as her must-have back-to-school accessory to emphasize how sad she was that summer was over and her "little munchkins" wouldn't be with her.

Because here's the deal - the mom doing the most award-winning interruption of *"I love my kids more than you because I miss them already"* was a total fake.

Her two kids when not enjoying back-to-back sessions of two-week sleep away summer camps or at their grandparents for an extended stay were at my house so often they even had their own snack cubby in my pantry. Trust me, I'm certain I saw her kids more than she did.

This is when I decided to upstage the weepy mom fibbers with a bigger, better one of my own. I told this group that it was really too bad they were so upset that school had begun because I had seen a recent study, (always my trusty go-to) somewhere, that had shown that moms who are the most sad about school starting are the ones that didn't spend enough quality time in meaningful engagement with their children over the summer and thus their guilt manifests itself into debilitating, chronic back-to-school remorse.

Oops!

Cue the crap storm. Moms got enraged! Kleenex were flung to the floor and women began to defend their summer schedules and suggest "how dare I question their parenting."

"Goodness," I said, (in my best Miss Goodie Two Shoes voice), "calm down I didn't write the study, I just saw it and to be perfectly honest I loved it. It validated my parenting philosophy because every year I'm thrilled when school starts." (And now to toss some hand grenades into the frenzy I added this zinger.) "I'm glad to know it's because according to science I'm doing an incredible job as a parent."

Oh-My-God I committed the cardinal *Mom Sin*. I proclaimed that I was better than all these ticked off moms. Even worse, I credited science for the shout out. And for anyone right now thinking, "Ugh, don't we have enough problems in this country without more people making up stuff in the name of science?" Well, who's to say someone out there isn't really doing a study that focuses on this issue.

Trust me, these weepy women, in no way, wanted someone like me to "out mom" them. In their world I wasn't even a contender. But, thanks to my ability to tell a whopper with a straight face I had yanked their chain - hard.

Score!

Not that I thought I was a better mom. Maybe a mom whose head wasn't up her ass, but better - who really knows?

As I was enjoying their somewhat suppressed fury the "discussion" took a turn for the worse when one mom wanted to know where I saw the study. "I don't remember," I said thoughtfully. "It was some online science journal my husband reads."

Good save, I'm thinking. People will believe my husband reads heavy-duty science stuff, but no one could see me devoting hours to bettering my brain with esoteric journals. To make it sound even more credible I added, "I'll text him and try to find the link for you."

One Rhodes wannabe scholar piped up, "Are you sure it wasn't junk science?"

"No," I quickly replied. "It was in a Pediatric journal."

I knew it was time to make my escape before someone took me up on texting my husband for additional information. So, I grabbed another Krispy Kreme and then went back to the cluster of moms still debating the "study" and said goodbye.

I told them I had to run because I was so busy putting the finishing touches on my family's annual first day of school party which included a summer retrospective that I had made in iMovie.

"It's going to be an amazing evening," I enthusiastically shared.

"Where did you get that movie idea?" one mom asked like I was incapable of thinking it up on my own.

"Oh, didn't you know I'm a parent influencer? Stuff like this is what I'm all about. Hashtag super mom."

And with that I sashayed right out the door, really working it, like I thought I was something. In truth my family would be celebrating the first day of school with pizza and cupcakes and complaining, lots of complaining about the teachers that dared to give homework their first day back, but really was that any of their business?

I think not.

In this story I once again find myself embroiled in some churchy drama. Who knew that following the commandment to "love thy neighborhood" would lead to a very uncomfortable showdown with a pastor?

The Case of the Diaper Dumper

Yesterday morning at approx. 8:47 a.m.

Location: My Neighborhood

I'm walking my two dogs which is an arduous process because one of them is a beagle. He's a combo platter of sniff and no go or all go-go-go with no regard for my preference to keep the arm holding his leash firmly in its socket.

As we meandered through the neighborhood on a beautiful October day, I saw my Bible bunko neighbor Ann Reedy. (And yes, there's a Bible bunko group in my hood. I was invited to play one time and one time only. Which trust me was for the best.) Ann is a sweetheart but, oh my, her personality was like Cream of Wheat original recipe - bland to infinity and beyond.

As I got closer, I noticed she had tears in her eyes and her car had all four doors wide open. I stopped, of course, to ask what was wrong.

But as I waited for an answer, I knew it was probably that she didn't have time to put dinner in the crockpot or something equally boring that led to this episode of watery eyes. Although I was hoping that it was something juicy like she wanted to confess that the HOA board was really a swinger's club.

Unbelievably the response I got from her was even better.

This was because Ann blurted out that she thought a woman she worked with at her church's Mother's Day Out program had hidden six dirty diapers in her car!

Say what????

According to Ann when she went to get in her car this morning to go to, where else, but church, she was almost knocked to the ground by the overwhelming smell of festering feces. She then, through tears, said she opened all her car doors, held her breath and then started digging around in her car for what was causing the odor. Shoved under the rear passenger seats she found not one, not two, but six poopy diapers.

I just stood there with my mouth hanging open. Who would terrorize this very nice, mild-mannered woman by breaking into her car and depositing used diapers? I was intrigued and that left me no other alternative but to offer her my investigative services.

I mean, really, what else could one do? You just don't hear a story like that and go, "Oh, wow, I'm sorry that happened. Why don't you try using some Gain Febreze?"

No, this kind of story demanded action. Anything else would just be un-neighborly and I'm nothing if not neighborly.

Ann seemed confused when I offered to help track down who was doing this to her. She asked me if I used to be in law enforcement. Sadly, I had to answer no. I did though share that I used to be a reporter.

Unfortunately, Ann had passed from her bewildered state to appearing to be scared of me. I'm used to this reaction. Trust me this isn't the first time someone has slowly backed away from me. But using my extensive gifts of persuasion I convinced her that she needed my help.

My moment of brilliance was pointing out that it had to be divine intervention that sent me to her. I almost never go by her house on my morning dog walk. I usually head in another direction. But today for some reason I went towards her home just at the precise minute she was standing in her driveway engulfed in distress.

Praise the Lord, she agreed with that. So, I helped her freshen up her car and told her to not throw away the diapers because they were evidence.

Soon Ann was off to her Bible study, but not before agreeing to meet with me that afternoon at five o'clock.

Yesterday afternoon - 5 p.m.

Ann's House

I suggested we meet at Ann's house to avoid my nosey, tattle-tale kids eavesdropping and texting their dad my latest scheme. (Like I need that kind of hassle.) I showed up with one of my old reporter notebooks which looked just like something I'm sure the F.B.I. would use.

I had already worked out my list of questions because this wasn't my first rodeo. One doesn't grow up reading *Encyclopedia Brown*, Agatha Christie and spending the better part of the early twenty-first century watching every *C.S.I.*, *N.C.I.S.* and all the *Law & Order* episodes without having a serious set of interview skills.

I first asked if she had any idea who would do this to her? She seemed reluctant to answer. This is what happens when you're a very nice person. You don't want to point the finger or think the worst of anyone. I can freely admit I've never had that problem.

Ever so slowly I coaxed Ann to share the name of the woman who "seemed to have an issue" with her at the M.D.O. Then I asked how she thought the woman was getting into her car?

I had already looked for signs of forced entry or any trace evidence on Ann's car and hadn't seen any. I also, with one of my son's drumsticks, had gone through the poppy diapers.

What I found was interesting. There wasn't just one brand of diaper. It was a mix of everything from Pampers to Luvs to generic.

This led to me grilling Ann about the M.D.O diaper changing routine. Primarily I wanted to know when the M.D.O. changed the toddlers' diapers did they use church brought diapers or did each parent leave diapers for their child?

She said when they had to change a toddler, they used diapers bought by the M.D.O. program citing that it was easier than digging through all the different diaper bags. Ann also added that after lunch each child got their diaper changed before naptime.

This proved that if the crime was happening at the M.D.O. it was after the collective diaper change. I then quickly asked if there was any time she left the toddler room for more than, say, five minutes?

She volunteered that right after lunch she took all the food trash to the garbage cans in the custodian's closet. That's also when got a soda from the vending machine and stopped off at the four-year-old room to say hi to her little niece.

My next question was where did she leave her purse? She told me that they all leave their purses in the toddler room, in cubbies. Lastly, I asked who, if anyone, took the dirty diapers out of the room?

From that I extrapolated a timeline. And let me tell you, if I was tested on this kind of math and reasoning skills on the S.A.T. I wouldn't be here toiling away as an amateur sleuth. I'd be on the Harvard alumni website crowing about my newest scientific breakthrough.

Based on my interrogation of Ann, here's how I thought the diaper dump went down: When she left the toddler room at the M.D.O. around noon someone in the room used that opportunity to get her car keys out of her purse. That person then volunteered to take the dirty diapers to the outside dumpster, but instead of the dumpster they went in the backseat of Ann's car.

Then the Diaper Dumper rushed back inside, returned Ann's keys to her purse, and no one was the wiser. Why the person was doing this foul deed to my neighbor was not my first priority. The number one objective was to catch her in the act.

Clearly, I had to do a stakeout. Based on my timeline the Diaper Dumper would strike between 12 and 12:15. At Thursday's M.D.O. I'd planned to be in position in the church parking lot at 11:30 to record the dumper in action.

I instructed Ann to say nothing about finding the gross diapers in her car. She was to act as if her vehicle smelled fresh as a daisy. I wanted to provoke the dumper to strike again.

The Next Day - My House

You can't begin to imagine how excited I was about the stake-out! My enthusiasm was so immense I couldn't help but share my big plan with the fam. My husband, who you would think would be proud of me, walked out the door for work, not with a "I love you" or even a "good luck at your stake-out."

Instead, this is what I got - "Don't get yourself shot" and then he turned and said, "or get us sued."

Ugh. I'm so tired of hearing that. Just because in the past some people, may or may not, have threatened legal action against me was no reason to leave the house every morning with that kind of goodbye. He really needed to let it go.

As for my kids, I think they should be more impressed by me. I'm out there solving crimes - solo. Who else does that? Even the Lone Ranger had Tonto.

I told both of them repeatedly to not bother me with any phone calls or texts of the "I forgot my P.E. shoes, band instrument, or library book" variety because I would be working a stakeout.

As I dropped each of them off at their respective schools, I delighted in bellowing out the window, "Remember, I'll be on a stakeout!"

Both of them just kept on walking. I didn't even get a wave or a thumbs up. Ingrates.

I then rushed home, walked the dogs, unloaded the dishwasher, threw a load of laundry in the dryer and did my stakeout grooming. Really can you go wrong with black Old Navy leggings, a black T-shirt, a C.S.I. baseball hat I got from the Vegas airport ten years ago, my husband's lawn mowing sunglasses because they cover my face more and I think look a little bad ass, tennis shoes, plus a quick dab of my new gift with purchase Philosophy lip balm?

I loaded my supplies in the car which included my fully charged phone, a thirty-two-ounce Diet Coke and the notes from yesterday. Then I gleefully headed to the church. It was on people. It was on!

My first problem was where to park. I didn't want to park too close to my neighbor's car because I thought that would scare the dumper away. But I wanted to be close enough to properly record the crime so there would be no doubt what was going on and who was doing it.

I drove around and tried some spots and tested them with my phone camera to see what angle would take the best picture and be the least conspicuous. Then I waited.

12:07 p.m. Uh, oh, I saw a woman leaving the church with what looked like a white kitchen size trash bag. Was this the Diaper Dumper?

Later That Day

I'm now renaming this *The Case of the Holy Crap Storm*. I would have never volunteered my services if I had known I would have to endure a hostile Q & A by a member of the clergy. But I'm getting ahead of myself, let's back up to 12:07 p.m.

There was a woman walking in the direction of my neighbor's car with a trash bag. She seemed to be in her forties and was very attractive. Jeans, a blonde ponytail, what seems to be a J.Crew cashmere sweater set and from what I could tell some really darling flats.

What in the name of God was this mom doing putting soiled diapers in a co-church member's car? And as a sidebar I was also thinking who wears an outfit that cute to work in the toddler room of a M.D.O. program?

At this point I'm slouched down in my front seat with my phone camera recording. Sweet Jesus, she was unlocking the car and now she was bent over and stuffing diapers not just behind the front seats, but she also had the hatchback open, and it looked like she had at least two in there. Then I froze.

What do I do now? I've got it all on my phone, but do I just show it to my neighbor and be done with it? Do I get out of my car and say something? Do I perp walk her through the parking lot?

Then I thought back to all the detective shows I had spent an inordinate amount of time watching and I knew what I had to do - get out of my surveillance vehicle and confront the "suspect."

I slowly opened my car door, jumped out and yelled as I was walking towards her, "Why are you putting dirty diapers in a car that isn't yours?"

The Diaper Dumper jerked her head out of the rear of the car and stared at me. That was my cue to keep on talking.

In an authoritative voice that I use when playing *Clue* (because you need to sound assertive when you announce that it was Colonel Mustard with a dagger in the conservatory) I said, "I don't know who you are, but I know you must be a member of this church and you work in the Mother's Day Out program. I also know that this is at least the second time you've illegally entered this car and vandalized it."

I then added, "Did you know what you're doing is against the law and qualifies as criminal mischief." (Right about now I was impressing myself - big time. This could be my calling; accosting strangers in parking lots.) She still just stood there, all deer in the headlights. I then quickly added, "Umm, are you okay?"

This was when I saw what the Diaper Dumper was made of. She looked at me, you could tell she was sizing me up, and then she accused me, as in shouted in my face, that I was "trespassing on private church property."

Jesus take the wheel because it's time for review.

One, I've got her on camera entering a car that isn't hers. Two, this woman was stuffing used diapers in said vehicle and now she has the nerve to tell ME I'm trespassing.

Well, now I was ticked off. I replied to her in my best "hey dumb ass" voice and said, "I'm not trespassing on church property if I'm parked here to go inside the church to show my neighbor the video of you vandalizing her car."

This shut her up for a moment. So, I then sprinted into the church while the diaper fiend was in hot pursuit not pleading her case, not throwing herself on my mercy, but bitching to me that it was illegal to tape someone without their permission. God, who is she, Judge Freaking Judy?

Once I got into the church I stopped. I had never been to this church before in my life. I didn't have the slightest idea where to find my neighbor. I thought I would hear kids or at the very least be able to follow the tell-tale smells of M.D.O. - slobber, wet diaper and Play-Doh. But I had nothing.

I noticed that the women's bathroom was right across the hall, and I desperately needed to use it after that thirty-two ouncer. I figured it wouldn't hurt to take a potty break and catch my breath. I also noticed that the Diaper Dumper had disappeared. I guessed that she had grabbed her purse and left the premises.

Unfortunately, that hypothesis was incorrect.

As soon as I exited the bathroom the Diaper Dumper and the minister of the church were waiting for me. The reverend rather rudely asked to see some identification.

Yeah, right, I'm doing a citizen's arrest in the parking lot and the first thing I thought of was to grab my incredible Coach bag that I scored at an outlet mall for $50.00 during my vacation two months ago. That's a big no on that one. All I had on me were my car keys in the back pocket of my leggings and my phone.

I told the minister that my neighbor in the M.D.O. program would vouch for me. He sent his secretary to retrieve her. About a minute later my neighbor was walking up the hall. She gave me a distressed look and I announced to no one and everyone that the lady standing across from me was the Diaper Dumper and I got her in action on my phone.

The pastor asked to see the evidence and I showed him the recording of the Diaper Dumper. He watched, said nothing, went back to his office to get his glasses and watched it again. Then he called his secretary out and they watched it together.

I was thinking, c'mon folks it's not the Zapruder film. It's a pretty high-quality recording with some excellent camera work of one of your M.D.O employees/ church members going all crazy pants or crazy diapers, as the case may be.

He then asked my neighbor and the Diaper Dumper to go into his office while he talked to me.

Huh? Aren't his hands full enough already? Why did he need to talk to me? Unless he's going to thank me but somehow I didn't think that was what was going to happen. He then began to grill me on "my role in this."

I knew I was in the house of the Lord, and I knew this man standing in front of me was allegedly a spiritual person ordained by God. But I don't think it says anywhere in the Bible that I had to take crap off of him.

So, I began talking very slowly because at this point I was doubting his intelligence and ability to process even the simplest monosyllabic words and explained that my poor neighbor, one of his flock, had been terrorized by one of his employees. I, as a citizen of Earth, felt duty bound to offer my assistance. I also pointed out that this was a case of criminal mischief and charges could be filed.

He was silent for a moment and then asked me to erase my recording. I said, "Never going to happen."

He then asked that I "not share this unfortunate incident with anyone."

"Hmm," I said. "That's going to be a problem unless we work out a mutually agreeable solution to this issue."

At this point the minister was getting very angry with a big old dollop of self-righteousness. This made me quickly offer up my solution to the conundrum.

"Here's what you can do for me," I said, trying to sound very holy. "You should be very nice to my neighbor. She loves this church and I respect that. You also must, and as a mother, I mean right now, get the Diaper Dumper off your staff and away from kids. She obviously has some mental health issues that need to be addressed. Who knows, maybe it's as simple as her cholesterol meds messing with her Zoloft, but you have a moral and legal duty to get that figured out."

His response was a very stern and oh so condescending, "I'll pray for you."

You could tell from his tone he didn't mean it in a very reverendly manner. It was an insult wrapped in a Bible. The ecclesiastic equivalent of "F You."

So, I quipped, "Right back at ya." And added, "You should also pay to have my neighbor's car detailed." With that I walked out of that church.

The fact that I didn't get struck by lightning when I exited the building was a sign to me that the big guy/girl way upstairs had my back on this one.

Four hours later I went over to my neighbor's. I was beyond relieved that Ann greeted me with a smile. I eagerly asked her what happened, and she shared that the Diaper Dumper decided to take some "extended personal time" away from her M.D.O. duties and my friend was promoted to head of the toddler room.

I said, "That's great but did the woman ever give a reason for putting the diapers in your car?"

She quickly responded, "She was jealous of me. Can you believe that?"

"Of course, I can," I said. "You're sane and she's crazy. She was jealous of your sanity."

I kept on prodding and finally in bits and pieces a story came out about envy, misplaced rage, coveting and revenge. A whole Ten Commandment/Golden Rule saga. Who knew a church Mother's Day Out program could be such a hotbed of seething emotions?

It seemed Ann was becoming a rising star in the M.D.O. program. She started working in the toddler room right after Labor Day and the little kids loved her, all the moms thought she was wonderful and the director of M.D.O. told everyone who would listen that Ann was "quite possibly that best M.D.O. worker she had ever had."

Apparently, Diaper Dumper, last year's M.D.O. Queen Bee got jealous and was attempting to make my neighbor quit by freaking her out with the dirty diapers in her car.

Got a headache yet? I know I do.

While you may think the moral of this story is to approach any Mother's Day Out program with extreme caution and to beware of clergy that ask for I.D. you'd be wrong.

The moral was I should really, seriously, consider opening up a detective agency. I think I kind of rock at this.

I recently walked into a Michaels craft store and had a post-traumatic stress episode so intense I had to grab on to a shopping cart for support. Trust me, I don't have anything against Michaels but when I saw a row of tri-fold project boards I got light-headed.

This was because those boards brought back a motherlode of panic inducing memories about the dreaded Invention Convention and science fair projects. Here's a riddle for you. You know what sucks more than a science fair project? A science fair project that includes a diorama.

I loved (most days) being an elementary school parent, but I do not miss the school projects. I especially don't miss all the hyper competitive parents.

This is Why I'll Never Judge a Science Fair Again

WHO KNEW THAT by agreeing to judge an elementary school science fair I would be putting myself in harm's way?

I think back now to just one day ago when I was an innocent, naive to the cruel, harsh ways of the world and how as a trusting, kind-hearted person I was eagerly looking forward to helping my neighbor, an elementary school assistant principal, by being a judge at her school's science fair. In my wide-eyed ignorance I even thought it sounded like fun.

Although I did question my neighbor if I had the necessary educational and work background to qualify as a judge. She assured me that I would be "perfect, just perfect." They already had two retired college science teachers, a local high-tech wizard, and a woman who writes science textbooks.

So, what was I there for, I joked, to collectively lower the group's IQ? Oh no, I was told my area of expertise would be in the "Did a kid really do this?" category.

Excellent. I had plenty of experience in that department. With a total of eight science fairs and invention conventions under my belt I could definitely serve as the "how much of this did a parent do" translator.

Yesterday, I arrived at the elementary school ready to spend an intellectual day looking over the fourth and fifth grade students' science projects. I even brought my lunch. I had no problem giving up my day to volunteer, but I wasn't woman enough to make the ultimate sacrifice of eating the school's cafeteria food. It was an action-packed morning.

The kids were excited hauling their project boards into the gym and setting up their experiments. Most of them had at least one parent hovering or helping get everything rigged up.

After the teachers shooed the parents out of the gym (It started as a polite "parents please exit the gym" announcement and turned into a "parents if you don't leave the gym your child's experiment will be disqualified from medal consideration") and the kids went back to class that we began evaluating the projects.

Our morning was spent looking at each experiment, rating their project board and their "spirit of scientific inquiry and creativity." During lunch we compared notes and did a preliminary ranking.

There were many experiments that I had serious doubts ever breached the brain of a nine or ten-year-old. Hell, I couldn't even understand the data or concepts. But I reserved my judgment until we had a chance to talk with the budding scientists.

This happened in the afternoon when, in teams of two, we visited with each child and asked them questions about their experiment. This was where things got interesting.

There were some really impressive experiments. At least a dozen were "borrowed" from the "Amazing Science Fair" website that I have visited so many times I felt like I could be in a long-term relationship with the URL. Then you had your classic science fair projects - volcano, potato batteries, plant growth with and without fertilizer. Pretty much the ones you and I did in school.

It was the incredible ones that had me concerned. The retired college science professors were enthralled with one fifth grader's experiment that, are you ready for this, "examined the use of peptide nucleic acid in combination with DNA to create unique double-crossover structures to serve as scaffolding upon which to create molecular size electronic circuits."

Yes, it sounds amazing, even if I don't know what the heck it means, but truly did a ten-year old do this? I know fifth grade geniuses walk among us, but this had all the tell-tale signs of "mommy and/or daddy did this for me."

The giveaways were a theme that was way too complicated for a child even one gifted with an extra-large hippocampus. Now add in a project board that had no signs of ever being touched by a child's hands. There were no glue drips, no smearing, no uneven paper placement or scissor cuts that were just a teeny bit off.

Another red flag was that the experiment would require equipment that you'd find in a research hospital, not the toolbox of a crap that most families have in their garage.

It looked like the work of an anal retentive forty-five-year-old with a Ph.D. Not a ten-year-old who still believed in Santa Claus.

When the child was asked to explain the experiment, she, God bless her, had memorized her entire project board written report, but she couldn't answer any questions that weren't "board" related.

Inquiries like "how did you think up your experiment" and "what did you like best about it?" produced a deer in the headlight's response. But it was when I asked what was the most fun part of her science fair project that the truth serum was released.

That question broke her. She confessed that, "none of it was fun" because her mom "did all of it" and once she got warmed up, she began to express her moral outrage that her mom "wouldn't even let me glue anything!"

After our afternoon visits with the kids, we went to the school library and began tabulating our results. The high-tech guru and I were in agreement that the "Lego kid" should get first place.

A fourth-grade boy had done an experiment that focused on the quality of the official Lego versus the generic version. The child had gotten the idea after his mother kept on insisting that it wasn't worth the money to buy Lego when the off brand was "just as good."

The Lego kid had done a series of tests/experiments that would have done *Consumer Reports* proud. I liked it because you could tell the kid knew his Lego, was passionate about the experiment and had, through science, definitely proven that Lego has no equal.

We eventually, after an official ruling (Sigh. We had to bring in the assistant principal who once again stressed the prime directive that the experiments had to be, without a doubt, the work of a child) got the two college professors on our side that the Lego kid was the winner.

The lone holdout was the text-book writer. She was all about pure science and it seemed to me she had an unhealthy dislike of Lego and kids and not necessarily in that order.

Fortunately, it didn't have to be unanimous to decide first place. Lego Kid was declared the winner. After thirty more minutes we had nailed down second thru sixth place, picked most creative, most environmental, most unusual etc, etc.

Every kid got a ribbon, and they were the super fancy kind like people received at horse shows. I honestly didn't blame the school for going the "ribbon for all" route.

The science fair was at a private Christian elementary school where parents pay about $2,000 a month in tuition. For that kind of coin, I'm sure mom and dad demand and receive a ribbon rich environment.

At seven that evening all the kids (and their parents) came back up to school to see what ribbon they had won and to wait for the official award ceremony where first through sixth place would be announced. It was these winners that would proceed on to the city science fair.

All the judges were there for the awards ceremony. I was circulating through the crowd enjoying listening to the kids talk about their experiments, but as I approached the peptide nucleic acid girl, I sensed danger.

The girl's mother was crowing about her child's experiment (while her daughter played with her iPhone) to anyone who was within a fifty-foot hearing radius.

The poor kid who had been deprived of doing anything on her project had won a ribbon for "Most Intriguing." Based on that the mom was in high spirits. I guess she thought intriguing was code for first place. I very quickly bypassed the mother and went to the other side of the gym.

At eight p.m. sharp the awards ceremony began. The principal sang the praises of the kids, the parents, the exceptional staff and then introduced the judges. One by one the awards were called out.

I had my eye on the Peptide Mom. Yikes. The closer we got to first place the more excited the mom was getting. She thought she had it in the bag. When first place was announced, and it was the Lego Kid the crowd clapped and the Lego Kid went wild.

It was beyond obvious that he and his parents were stunned. Lego Kid was definitely not one of the usual suspects, who won the science fair, the spelling and geography bees and the mathlympics, which I think made his victory sweeter.

After Lego Kid accepted his medal the Tech Guru and I went and congratulated him, but as we were talking, I felt a disturbance in the force.

The Peptide Mom was headed straight towards us with the assistant principal in tow and she looked super pissed. She did a rude, pushy "pardon me" to the Lego Kid's parents and demanded to speak to us about our judging criteria.

"Okay," I said, "Why don't we move over to the corner."

My main goal at this point was to relocate the mother before she had a chance for her sore loser attitude to take away from the Lego Kid's moment.

As we walked, I made eye contact with my neighbor, the assistant principal, and she looked worried. As soon as we were out of earshot of the Lego Kid, I asked the Peptide Mom what exactly she wanted to know?

"What I want," she hissed, "is for you first to tell me what your qualifications are to judge a science fair?"

"Well," I responded, "I was asked by the assistant principal. I didn't actually apply for the job."

"No, no," she choked out, "I want to know your curriculum vitae?"

I looked at my neighbor and gave her the "help me I did this as a favor to you" look and you know what I get back?

NOTHING.

Holy crap, my neighbor was afraid of the Peptide Mom and then I saw the Tech Guru whose new name is now the Dickless Wonder leaving the science fair. When the Peptide Mom was hissing at me, he skulked off.

"Look," I told the Peptide Mom in a super rah, rah got spirit, let's hear it, voice, "I'm sorry your child's evening didn't go as you planned but everyone was a winner here tonight. It was a great day for science."

Apparently, that was not the right thing to say because ladies and gentlemen put your tray tables in the upright position and brace for impact because the shit hit the fan.

The woman started booing me. Yeah, that's right booing me as in "boo, boo" to my face. "Um, okay," I said, "I'm going now."

As I turned around, so she's now booing my back, Peptide Mom ran in front of me and growled, "You wouldn't know science if it fucked you up the ass."

Whoa!

My first response to this was to take my purse and cover my backside. Then after I was sure I was protected from an unlawful rear entry search and seizure I started some evasive maneuvers which all failed. I couldn't shake this mom. What she lacked in sanity she made up for in stalking.

This meant I really had no other choice but to start lying as a means of escape.

I told her, in the dulcet tones I save for when I'm dealing with people who scare me, to give me just a few minutes and I would see what I could do to perhaps have the results reconsidered.

After placating her with that ruse I fled the school out of a side door that set off an alarm that only increased my panic. Running faster than I thought possible in a suede clog with a sizeable wedge heel I sprinted to the safety of my car. My solitary thought was hauling ass to my house.

Finally, I was close enough to my car to hit the unlock sensor and as I was about to open the door Peptide Mom caught up to me. "Why are you leaving?" she demanded, "Did you get the results changed?"

"Oh, I did better than that," I said, trying not to freak out. "I got you just what you wanted."

"What, what?" she chanted excitedly.

I grabbed the ribbon I got for judging (It was a big blue ribbon with a gold center that said judge. Sparkly, yet still classy.) and tried not to shove it in her face while I said, "This is for you!"

"Why do I get a ribbon?" she asked confused yet with a death grip on it.

"Well," I chirped, and by now I had my car door open, and I was sliding into the front seat, "Isn't that what you wanted all along - a ribbon just for you and all your hard work? It's your special ribbon for Best Parent Participation. You earned it for doing your child's entire science fair project. That's why she didn't win, because she didn't do the experiment or the project board - you did. So, congrats."

I then quickly closed my door, threw my car in reverse, hit the accelerator, ran over a curb (which really ticked me off because I just had my car aligned at Discount Tire) and prayed that she didn't follow me as I drove home.

Good God, who knew judging a science fair could be hazardous to your health. There really needs to be warning signs posted.

Thanksgiving is one of my favorite holidays. Primarily because it's all about the food and there's pies, lots of pies. But a part of me believes that since there's not the distraction of presents sometimes all that family togetherness can lead to drama or in this case a throwdown.

Thanksgiving Throwdown

THANKSGIVING AT MY parent's house is what my husband and I liked to call the "indigestion express." It wasn't my parents' fault. They were wonderful. It was my three older siblings. They're all loud, exceedingly annoying, opinionated, and full of themselves. In other words, nothing like me. I'm shy, reserved, and thoughtful.

Okay, I'm none of those, but I like to think that I'm the least annoying member of my family. Not exactly, high praise, I know. One Thanksgiving many years ago, in the B.C. era (Before Children) my sister and I got into it at the dinner table. It all started with the mashed potatoes.

There I was, oh so innocently, scooping myself a second heaping helping of mashed taters when the dinner conversation turned, like I'm sure it does at most families Thanksgiving dinners, to world annihilation.

My eldest brother posed the question: If the world was under attack by aliens and you could pick only two family members to help you fight the horde of space invaders who would choose?

Talk about getting my feelings hurt, none of my siblings picked me. I got a little ticked off and asked why no one would want me on their team. My little brother said my smart mouth would result in instant death if we were captured and then my sister uttered the phrase that kicked me right in my overly full stomach.

She announced, "You couldn't handle the physical exertion it would take to defeat the aliens."

I stared at her, my mashed potato mouth wide open in shock, and choked out, "Are you kidding me? I could so take you."

She smirked and then shoveled a spoonful of green bean casserole in her mouth.

Let's pause the tale here for a second so I can fill you in on the back story and by that, I mean a brief history of my "sister relationship."

My sister is a scant seventeen months older than me. We're polar opposites in every way. She's super smart and I'm, to be kind, let's say not so super smart. To follow behind her in school was misery. Teachers, dismayed by my lack of upper cranium brain matter, would actually say to me, "Are you sure you're Valerie's sister?"

She burns. I tan. She has black hair; I have light brown. The most glaring difference is she's skinny. I'm well, to be kind again, not so skinny. I don't begrudge my sister anything, not even her naturally thin body. The only part I'm beyond envious of is her legs. Her shapely, thin legs that are one hundred percent cankle free.

Many of you know that I'm a longtime cankle sufferer and to say I covet my sister's lovely lower calves and trim, petite ankles is a gross understatement. Also, my sister is not just skinny. She's a delicate skinny where I'm more hearty, curvy, peasant stock. Growing up she always had to buy her clothes in super slim sizes. At age eleven I was wearing women's clothes and a women's size ten shoe. Talk about life not being fair.

Now, back to my Thanksgiving tale. We left off with my sister smirking at me. I wasn't going to let that go without a comment. "Valerie," I said authoritatively, "who had your back all through school when kids on the bus would tease you about being four eyes or a nerd? That would be moi. I was like your mafia bodyguard. Trust me, you wouldn't have made it through elementary school unscathed if it weren't for me."

She shot back, "I didn't say you weren't big and... scary."

Oh no she didn't! Those were fighting words. I didn't even care if she was joking. I was ready to pick up a turkey leg and indulge in an extreme case of poultry assault. That's if I could get to the turkey before my husband. He looked mad enough to slap her with or without the aid of a domesticated game bird.

My second brother, Connor, always up for a good time said, "Why don't you two have a contest to see who's in better shape?"

I didn't care if it was a triathlon to hell, I was going to do it. I eagerly said, "I'm in because you, Valerie are skinny/fat whereas I am fat/skinny."

"What's skinny/fat mean, you freak?" she asked. Before I could answer my mom butted in and said we were all acting juvenile, and she was ashamed of all of us. My dad added that our behavior was "very uncivilized."

I pointed at my sister and said in a very mature tone, "She started it." Then I explained to her that skinny/fat meant she may be thin because of her freakish metabolism, but she sure as hell wasn't in shape. Then I dropped this bomb in front of my parents, "And you, Valerie, smoke!"

My parents in unison gasped and stared at my sister. They were horrified that she smoked. In my head, I'm saying, "Ha, ha, you're in trouble now." But then my sister explained to my parents that she "rarely smoked" and only touched a cigarette when she was stressed from doing an audit.

For the love of all that is holy she was a tax accountant. She was always doing audits which pretty much meant she smoked all the time.

After my parents had been calmed down with false assurances that my sister was quitting smoking for good after tax season, we continued with the contest discussion. My brother proposed that the contest should take place the next morning and feature five events. The Pumpkin Pitch, the Pool Freeze, the Wood Stacker, the Turkey Trot and the All of the Above Obstacle Course.

The winner got bragging rights to her sister superiority. The loser had to clean up the Thanksgiving kitchen, which would sit overnight, waiting for the loser to do their duty. My mom didn't like the idea of the kitchen not being cleaned right away. It took a lot of cajoling from us to convince her that the world would not end if she went to bed with dirty dishes in the sink.

The next morning, I woke up ready to take my sister down a peg or two. After a hearty breakfast of pumpkin and pecan pie, I couldn't wait to get started. My brothers in an effort to make the contest "more interesting" decided it would be fun to place bets on their sisters.

Everyone had their money on my sister, except my husband. He bet all he had, twenty bucks, on me. My parents declined to take part in our "childish pursuits," although they did watch the action.

The contest began with the Pumpkin Pitch. We went to my parents' backyard where each of us got six pumpkins to throw. Whoever threw the pumpkins the farthest won.

My sister, skinny/fat, went first. She totally sucked. I gleefully taunted her by saying, "I guess all those hours sitting at a desk and "rarely smoking" have really hurt your upper body strength." She managed to flip me the bird without my parents seeing.

I was confident I could not only beat her at throwing pumpkins but shame her. A little-known fact about being a TV reporter is that you have to carry heavy equipment. Those camera tripods are not light (especially back in the day) and not only did I lug around heavy equipment, but I also got to drag it up and down the steps of the Texas State Capitol building - in heels.

You also on a fairly regular basis had to chase politicians and other assorted state officials around the capitol all while jumping over camera cables and sprinting towards elevators to shove microphones in their faces. It was an aerobic, strength training/conditioning workout every damn day.

Now, I could use my work workout to best my sister and I was psyched. I picked up my first pumpkin and it soared into the neighbor's yard, same with pumpkin two thru six. The winner, hands down, was me! That potato smirk my sister gave me at Thanksgiving was wiped off her face.

I was even more excited about the next event, the Pool Freeze. We had to jump in my parents' pool, current temperature sixty-one degrees, and see who could swim the most laps in ten minutes. I knew I had this one in the bag. My sister was a big wuss about cold water, and I was more of the polar bear persuasion. Yes, body fat can come in handy while braving cold water.

Ready, set, go and off we jumped into the water. My sister hit the pool and began screaming about the water temperature. "It's freezing. I can't swim in this. I'll get an upper respiratory infection," she wailed.

I shot back, "Shut up and swim!" and began to do laps with flip turns just in case I got bonus points for finesse. Once again, I'm victorious.

It was two to nothing when we started the Wood Stacker event. The goal was to see how much wood (from my dad's woodpile) we could fill up a wheelbarrow with, then race with the wheelbarrow to the other end of the yard, dump the wood and race back to get more wood. The sister who had the most wood on the other side of the yard in ten minutes won. The pressure was on.

If I won this event it's o-v-e-r. I'd be up three to nothing and my sister would be kaput.

My hearty peasant stock worked to my advantage. I grabbed wood and flung it into that wheelbarrow like my life depended on it and then hauled down the yard balancing the weight of the wheelbarrow with my sturdy arms. My cankles were on fire, but I didn't care I was going for the W!

Yippee ten minutes was up, and I was the winner! My woodpile was twice the size of my sister's. I wiped wood bark off of me and got ready to accept my award for awesome when my skinny/fat sister shouted, "It's not fair, it's not fair!"

I yelled back, "What's not fair, sore loser?"

She started pleading her case that the first three events played to my strengths because I have "man hands and shoulders." (Is it a crime that women's gloves don't fit me?) No one said anything. Her unkind, but perhaps accurate statement sucked the air right out of the backyard.

The silence was so eerie neighbors outside hanging their Christmas lights came over to see what was going on. It was my mom shouting "Valerie, shame on you!" that broke the silence.

I then had to put my dude size arm out to stop my husband from delivering what I'm sure was going to be a not so gentle rebuke of my sister. (God, I love that man.) After that crisis was averted, I yelled, "Okay, you immature little troll let's combine the next two events - the Turkey Trot and the All of the Above Obstacle Course into a finale and it will be winner takes all. Plus, the loser has to do the Thanksgiving dishes for the next freaking decade."

The skinny/fat crybaby was all over it. We waited as my brothers set up the final challenge.

I, after getting a pep talk from my husband, was feeling confident, but a little scared. We had a one-mile turkey trot through the neighborhood, then we had to swim ten laps, after which we would dive to the bottom of the pool, grab six pumpkins, chuck them out, then pick them up, put them in a wheelbarrow and race to the back of the yard.

My biggest problem was running. I don't like to run. I enjoyed walking, skipping, dancing, but not running. To beat my sister though I could endure it.

The starting line was my parent's driveway. My brother honked his car horn, and we were off. Damn it if my skinny/fat, "rarely smoking" sister didn't take off like the mighty wind. Crap. I had hoped to pace myself, but now I had to run full-out to stay even with her.

Thank goodness, I had put not one, but two jog bras on because my girls were taking a beating. I figured I could let her stay a little ahead of me because I would make up time in the pool. But then my pride kicked into overdrive. I couldn't let her win the race. I would vanquish her in every event.

It was as if I was being fueled by my less than perfect childhood memories. All of a sudden my man hands and shoulders, my strong/large thighs and cankles, my now size eleven feet all worked in unison to make me into some kind of Wonder Woman. My body moved faster than it ever had before or since.

I was flying. I zoomed past my sister and dove into the pool fully clothed, came up for air, took off my shoes, burned through ten laps, tossed out the pumpkins, grabbed that wheelbarrow and hauled ass to the back of the yard. I not only won, I won big! My sister hadn't even finished her laps in the pool. My family was cheering, the neighbors were cheering, and my husband was pumping his fist in the air. It was a magical moment.

I stood there soaked, cold and with a chest that felt like it was going to explode yet I had never felt better in my life. My brothers rushed over to announce me as the winner and gave me my award - last night's greasy gravy ladle.

My husband started chanting, speech, speech - so I raised the ladle high and said, "This family, neighbors and friends is for big girls everywhere - never, ever underestimate the power of the cankle!"

More cheers erupted. I then gave my sister the ladle and suggested, very kindly, of course, that she get to work cleaning the kitchen for the next ten years.

When I depart to the great Snarky beyond, I want two things in my obit. One, is that I survived a three-hour middle school combined band, choir and orchestra concert while sitting on metal gym bleachers that were off gassing a noxious foot funk. The second is that I was kicked out of the Junior League. It's not that I'm proud of the fact. It's just that it sums up so perfectly who I am.

Dropped Kicked Out of the Junior League

TECHNICALLY SPEAKING I wasn't officially kicked out. Let's just say I was strongly encouraged to surrender my volunteer badge, Junior League apron, cookbook, exclusive not to be shared with the general and lesser public JL phone directory and any claims and/or connections to the organization up to and including attendance at Junior League events and charity galas.

So, it was really more like I was banned for life, which is not like being kicked out - right?

Okay, maybe it's worse than simply being kicked out. In my defense there was never any hard evidence to justify my expulsion. The whole incident that got me ousted can best be described as a work-related technical error.

I'd also like to say that I have nothing, but the highest regard for all the charitable work the Junior League does across the country. This is just one woman's story, not a condemnation of any national volunteer organizations so please no emails telling me I suck.

My Junior League saga took place years ago when I was a mere twenty-three years old, newly married, (with almost all my wedding gift thank you notes written) and had just started a new job in a brand-new city.

Life was good until the phone rang. It was my mother and she told me she had exciting news to share. Breathlessly she cooed that I had been invited to join the Junior League.

Ugh. I was less than thrilled. It had been only a year ago when I had completed my four-year sorority tour of duty and I was still suffering from a Post Dramatic Stress Disorder from that high-octane "sisterhood" experience.

I thought I would get some time off for good behavior before I had to join another organization. But no, my mother had other plans for me, and it included carrying on her vast legion of volunteer work.

At first, I refused straight out. I didn't have the time. I really didn't have the money. I knew there would be dues and other fees. I wanted to focus on my career etc. etc.

My mom took my, "thanks, but no thanks" with grace, which should have been a clue that she wasn't finished with the topic, just yet.

Then no more than three hours later my dad called and informed me that my mom was very "put out" with me and then he plunged the guilt knife in my heart and twisted it hard by saying, "Would it be too much to do something that would make your mother happy?"

Not finished with that knife just yet, he added, "Besides it would be good for your job. The Junior League would be an excellent place to network and learn more about the city."

Of course, I gave in (cause I'm a sucker) and told my mother to mail me the letter and paperwork and I would join the Junior League in my new hometown.

One month later I was officially a Junior League Provisional which was very much like being a pledge in a sorority. You have one year to learn about the Junior League while doing a series of volunteer or pre-placement rotations, going to weekly meetings, working long hours sorting through used clothing donations in the JL thrift store and doing grunt work on all their fundraisers.

You even have a provisional leader (much like a sorority pledge captain) except my sorority pledge captain was like the good witch in the *Wizard of Oz* and my provisional leader was an angry, aggressive, princess of darkness with a chin length bob.

Her stuck in the air nose was supremely out of joint because over the years the Junior League had apparently dropped its stringent requirements for membership. According to this snob since family background and breeding were no longer de rigueur "just about anybody was being let in these days."

One meeting she even pointed at several of us and said, "old money, new money and no money." I'll let you guess who her exquisitely manicured bejeweled finger landed on for "no money."

She also mentioned several times that we were the first provisional group that didn't include one debutante, Jewel Ball princess or a duchess of some kind of flower, food, plant or grain. Excuse me that I didn't know the pinnacle of a woman's existence was being able to wear a sleeveless wedding gown, yank on some long white gloves that hit your elbows, very unflattering, I might add, and master a bow where your nostrils grazed the floor.

I don't know why but she hated me from the start. It could have been because I stuck out like a sore thumb. In the provisional meetings if you asked someone, "What's wrong with this picture?" they would have pointed at me - repeatedly and with vigor.

Was it my fault I was the only one in my provisional group that seemed to really need to work so I could, you know, eat and have a roof over my head?

I was outclassed starting in the parking lot. This was the decade where everyone drove either a boxy BMW or the boxier Volvo. I was driving a "vintage" (crappy) Karmann Ghia that had seen better days. Yeah, that's right, I'm the person that had to open my car door to retrieve my fast-food drive-thru order because my window had stopped rolling down two years ago.

Then there was the fact that I would come to meetings sometimes with that not so fresh feeling. I was a reporter for a local TV station which meant that, on occasions, due to time constraints, I would be forced to rush to my provisional meetings right after I had done a story on, say, a pipe failure at a wastewater treatment plant.

No doubt I was packing some serious funk that day, but you got "fined" when you missed a meeting, so I had no recourse but to go reeking of well-seasoned sewage. I would show up in my Gap clearance khakis, rumpled blazer and shoes that had traipsed through wastewater muck or God knows what else that day and walk into a sea of well-groomed, shiny haired, mani-pedi women.

I'm almost certain they usually would smell me before they actually saw me. Their heads would turn and give me the bitch diss.

You know what I'm talking about - first they did a barely audible deep sigh, then slowly their head completed a one eighth rotation, accompanied by one arched eyebrow, and then the two-part eye movement that consists of part one:

laser stare to get your attention followed by part two: the "you are so beneath me" slow eye roll and finished with an exhaling breathe.

I get it. I'm the freaky, unclean person who, depending on the news of the day, has to work in a non-climate-controlled environment. I did, to the best of my ability, attempt to fulfill all my provisional requirements. Although, I felt I was volunteering in a hostile non-profit environment and my misery was, of course, all my mother's fault.

I tried though not to feel too sorry for myself because at least I wasn't in the Junior League back in my hometown where the Provisionals had to do something incredibly frightening.

At the JL Charity Ball they had to wear goofy, if not at times, risqué, costumes to the event. Everyone else showed up in an evening gown and the Provisionals were dressed as cartoon characters or worse.

Then, and it's a big then, the Provisionals were required to do a song and dance number! There, up on stage, were a group of women - attorneys, physicians, stockbrokers, teachers, mothers, etc. dancing and in some cases going into a full straddle (aka an eager beaver) in front of an audience that was composed of their clients, patients, clergy, and neighbors.

I'm relieved to share with you that not only does my hometown JL no longer make their Provisionals shake their groove thing, but the charity ball is also ka-put. Coincidence? I think not. I consoled myself with that thought and it helped me make it through months one, two and three.

It also helped that our merry band of leaguers included a woman who was a scepter of death. This chick intrigued the hell out of me. Here was a woman who happily gabbed about which wealthy relative was going to die soon and leave her a boatload of cash.

Miss Death was so gleefully ghoulish that I couldn't help, but look forward, a teeny bit, to the meetings. I never greeted her with a "hello," but instead would ask, "So, have you attended any good funerals lately?"

One time, she brought house remodeling plans A and B to our provisional meeting. Plan A was based on no imminent death of a relative. Plan B was relative deceased, will probated, and inheritance in her bank account. There was no doubt that she was rooting for Plan B.

Things didn't get really bad until late November.

It was all hands-on deck for the Junior League's biggest fundraiser - The Christmas Festival. This was where for three days a convention center would be turned into a holiday market for shoppers. For the Provisionals it meant we had to work like peasants before the French Revolution.

It started with decorating the convention center. My hands were bloodied from wiring wreaths, hanging garland and decorating Christmas tree after Christmas tree. It didn't help that sometimes I felt like I was the only one given the yucky jobs, like hauling trash to the dumpster and doing anything that involved a twelve-foot ladder.

You know how sometimes you think that maybe you're imagining things, that someone actually doesn't dislike you and you're just being overly sensitive. Well, I had given myself that pep talk aplenty about the provisional leader, but on hour ten of my thirteen-hour shift during day one of the Christmas Festival my fears were proven well founded.

I had been making yet another trash run and was bent over, my hands on my thighs, recovering from my jump shot that landed a gigantic bag of garbage into the dumpster, when I heard two women make their way outside for a very un-Junior League smoke break. I had no plans to eavesdrop until I heard my name and then I cuddled close to the dumpster and perked up my ears.

The provisional leader was talking about me so much I doubted she had time to inhale on her cigarette. According to her I was "N.J.L.M." (Not Junior League Material). This was based on her theory that my family lineage was "suspect" which led to me "not having a pot to piss in." She also had a big snorty laugh when she said my car was "tragic." (Well, duh, on that one.) Her list continued with my "lackluster grooming" and "questionable leather goods."

Oh, and on top of all those insults she admitted that while not trying to actually kill me, (I knew all those ladder assignments were harbingers of doom.) she was doing her "best to get me to drop out." Not just me, but several other women she felt were undeserving of the Junior League.

Because I was still young and yet to develop the emotional hide of a rhinoceros, I stayed in my dumpster huddle, nursed extreme hurt feelings, and waited for her and her smoking buddy to go back inside. If that had happened today, I would have shown my face and called her out. But my lack of courage right then and there didn't mean I wasn't going to seek a little revenge.

⋯═◉ ◉═⋯

Day Two of the Christmas Festival I was scheduled to "volunteer" during the 3 p.m. to 9 p.m. shift. At noon I showed up to do my real job. I had talked to my assignment editor at the T.V. station where I worked, into allowing me to do a little VO/SOT on the Christmas Festival.

VO/SOT stands for voice over/sound on tape which means the anchor reads a little ditty about the event over video of the festival. Next there's a jump cut to a quick interview and then back to the anchor saying something like, "The Junior League Christmas Festival is open today and Saturday blah, blah."

I had arrived with my favorite photographer, shot some video of the convention center, and then went in search of an interview. Now, if I was being a good little reporter, we would have interviewed the Junior League President about all the largesse the Christmas Festival does for the community. But no, I was being a scheming reporter, up to no good and so I grabbed the provisional leader/bitch for an interview.

She, in a surprise to no one, eagerly agreed to have her smug face grace the airwaves. I clipped a wireless microphone on her, asked her a couple of questions, barely listened to her, thanked her, made a big deal about taking off her microphone and gave my photographer ten bucks and told him to get a muffin and something to drink in the Holiday Tea Room. He asked, "What about the gear?"

I told him not to worry about it. "I'll turn everything off, pack up and meet you at the van, in say, twenty minutes."

He hauled off to find the tea room, and I asked the provisional pain in the ass if I could talk with her for just a second? She seemed put off, like now that the interview was over, she was too good to be within ten feet of me. I stood beside the camera and informed her that I heard the less than flattering comments she made about me yesterday. "That's right," I told her, "I was right by the dumpster during your whole witch tirade."

"What did you hear?" she asked.

"I heard what you said about my family. What makes you think you're any better than me? I mean you're older than me, but that doesn't make you better."

As planned, hoped and prayed for that set her off. She began gutting my family tree, told me my college degree didn't hide my "bumpkin background" and then made fun of my car - again.

Oh, goodie, she was on a roll. To get her steamed up more I said, "The Junior League is for any woman who wants to learn how best to give back to her community. It's all about service not social standing."

She huffed, puffed, called me a "naive ass," and then said it was people like me that were ruining the Junior League. After that insult dump, she strode away like she was Queen of the Universe. I got the camera off the tripod, packed everything up and made my slow gear laden trudge to the news van.

When I got back to the station, I wrote up the VO/SOT and then went to edit her interview. Oops and then double oops because it seems although I had taken the microphone off the provisional leader, the camera and its microphone were still on and yikes it picked up everything she said.

I guess catching that "interview" on camera made me a little distracted because I accidentally edited the soundbite of the provisional leader ripping me a new one for being déclassé and not the interview where she's talking about how "crucial community service was to grow a strong, vibrant city."

You can't imagine what a stir it made on the ten o'clock newscast when her interview hit the air!

I was in a lot of trouble - kind of. Our news director had to go through the motions of reprimanding me. But I could tell he was pumped up over all the phone calls. Phone calls mean viewers and viewers mean ratings! Most, if not all, expressed outrage at that "bitch who doesn't think her shit stinks."

I, personally, couldn't have been more apologetic about my technical error. I also pointed out to my boss that it might have been the edit system's fault. We had been having some problems with it and maybe the machine locked on the wrong edit entry point. Although, I did take full blame for not double checking the tape.

The Junior League, on the other hand, was not amused, at all, or so easily placated. They had, to put it nicely, taken a momentary image hit. I was summoned to the JL headquarters for a meeting where I was very politely and firmly asked to "reconsider my League commitment." It seems I really wasn't Junior League material after all, and I couldn't have been more okay with that.

CHRISTMAS
The Bonus Season

A balanced diet is a Christmas cookie in each hand.

(I don't know who wrote this but I love them.)

The Cookie Caper

THERE WAS A thief in my family, a low-down, sneaky thief. A bandit without morals with zero regard for loyalty. This family member had stolen something so precious, so irreplaceable, that things were about to get real - 1970s style (which is kind of like Gangnam style, but in Earth Shoes).

The thief in question was Susan. She wasn't even blood kin. The girl had married a second cousin, (maybe third) once removed, and this, sort of, family member had run off with my great-aunt Shirley's recipe book.

Oh, don't you dare poo poo the recipe book. Aunt Shirley's was priceless. Shirley had no children of her own. Her recipes were her children. She could cook like no other and bake like an angel working a Viking range for Jesus. She was also very protective of her recipes. She shared them with no one - not a family member, not her Bible study besties or even her preacher.

Whenever you would ask her for a recipe she would smirk and croak out in a southern drawl that was made frog like from her couple of packs a day unfiltered Camel habit, "You can find out when I die."

Now, as a kid in elementary school, hearing that was downright creepy. I was a little afraid of her. I think all the kids were, but we were in love with her cooking. The holy grail of her recipe repertoire was a sugar cookie. Yep, a simple sugar cookie that was so sublime two of my cousins got in a fight, that drew blood over who would get the last one. (P.S. While they were fighting, I ate it.)

The thing that made the sugar cookie worthy of a wrestling match was that it was an enigma. The sugar cookie can easily go south. It can be too sweet, too puffy, too plain, too flat, or too crisp. Most people see the sugar cookie as just a conduit for icing or sprinkles. But Shirley's cookie was the rare breed. It was perfection. Putting icing on it would be like painting over the Mona Lisa.

For years family members debated what the secret ingredient was in the recipe. Some thought it was lime juice, others cream of tartar and then there was the seriously misguided camp that thought Shirley mixed in some vegetable shortening to the butter component.

Whatever it was, every single woman in the family wanted that recipe - badly. In 1977 they thought they would finally get it. Shirley died and the talk at the funeral wasn't about how they'd miss their aunt. It was about when the family would get the recipe book. Shirley told everyone that her recipes were stored in a safe deposit box at the bank. It turns out she lied.

After all the will rigmarole was sorted out no one could locate the recipe book. Until Christmas of 1978 when Susan, a woman my grandmother said didn't know how to spell oven much less turn one on, showed up at a family holiday function with, you guessed it, the world's best sugar cookie.

Hell hath no fury like a band of women, all tipsy on gin and tonics, dressed in un-ironic ugly Christmas sweaters, who have been recipe robbed. At first, I didn't know what was going on. I was too busy stuffing my face with cookies. It wasn't until I went into the kitchen to get some milk that I discovered some mighty harsh accusations were being whispered about Susan.

The kitchen clique was one hundred percent certain Susan was a recipe rustler. I remember my mother being the most irked. "How can a woman who pours Cheez Whiz over Fritos and calls it a King Ranch casserole suddenly make the exact duplicate of Aunt Shirley's sugar cookie?"

Her sister joined in by proclaiming like an evangelical preacher getting testy about a Bible verse interpretation, "Does she or does she not bring store-bought to every family reunion?"

There was a rowdy round of agreement and then from the mouth of babes (which would be me in case you were confused) came the question, "So how do you think she got the recipe book and what are you going to do about it?"

My mother shot me a look that said, "I hope you weren't aiming for sassy because that's what I'm hearing young lady" and I'm certain she would have scolded me, but my aunt piped in with a "Yeah, how did she get it?"

After that it was an hour of conjecture and conspiracy theories. It took my mother who devoured mystery novels at such a rapid pace that our local librarian called her Agatha Christie to come up with a plan. The best part was it involved me. I was thanking my lucky stars I had walked into the kitchen when I did.

My grandma and mom, the brains of the operation, had theorized that Susan had never set out to steal the recipe book, but had stumbled upon it.

Because Susan wasn't "really family" the day of Shirley's funeral she had been assigned the task of staying at the deceased's home and standing guard over all the aluminum foil wrapped food offerings for the after funeral meet and greet. They both thought that as Susan was digging around in the kitchen for Saran Wrap or, more likely, booze, she found the book and kept it for her own nefarious needs.

All of this made sense to my young mind because I never understood why you would keep a recipe book in a bank vault. Wouldn't it be a huge hassle to go back and forth to the bank every time you wanted to cook something? So, of course, Shirley would have kept the book in her kitchen. Duh.

The big issue was where did Susan hide the recipe book and how to get it back. Some of the women thought that the book was, for sure, in Susan's double-wide. (Yes, Susan and my cousin adjacent lived in a trailer, but it was on a bunch of acreage so according to my grandma they were a "little uppity about being land rich".) But my mom had another thought. She was certain Susan had the recipe book on her.

"Think about it," my mom said. "If she's bold enough to bring those cookies to a family party and just rub our face in it that she knows the recipe then I would bet dollars to donuts that she's got the book on her."

This is where it gets fun, at least for me. I was assigned the very Nancy Drew-ish task of rummaging through Susan's, very large, handbag. My aunt was going to spill a drink on Susan and haul her off to the bathroom to help in drying her clothes off while I got the purse and went through it. The thinking was that a kid getting caught being nosey was more acceptable than an adult being seen pawing through another woman's personal belongings.

It took me approximately ten seconds to find the recipe book, which was sharing space in the cavernous bag with, you guessed it, a Bible. I grabbed it and ran like the wind to my mother who then team swaggered with my grandma into the bathroom brandishing the book. They both gave Susan an earful. It got so loud in there that the men were complaining they couldn't hear the Cowboys game.

After buckets of tears from Susan and a prayer all was fake forgiven and by that I mean everyone pretended that it was "all good." But, for years if anyone thought you were doing something sneaky, they would say, "Don't go pulling a Susan" or "This family doesn't need another Susan."

As for the recipe book everyone got to pick his or her favorite one and write it down. The sugar cookie recipe, as agreed upon via an unanimous vote, was shared with everyone.

I'd love to give you a holiday shout out and tell you the secret behind the world's best cookie, but on that fateful day the family had to swear a solemn oath that we would all follow our Great Aunt Shirley's lead and take the recipe with us to the grave.

It's not that I'm big on following pledges made when I was a mere child, but if there's one thing I've learned in my multiple decades - I don't ever want to take even the smallest of chances of ticking off the women in my family.

I like to think I'm a pretty good baker. I even have moments of fantasizing about competing on the Food Network's Holiday Baking Championship. But since I can't decorate a cake to save my life and have yet to master macarons, I don't think it's ever going to happen.

Although, if I did get on the show, I'd like to believe I could really bring it in the quips and comments department. So, maybe that would pull me through to at least the second round. Because nobody wants to do the walk of shame of being the first baker booted out of the kitchen.

Anyhoo my dreams of baking grandeur was why I got my feelings hurt at a cookie exchange party. How could I let a bar cookie made with Fruity Pebbles best me?

Oh, No You Don't Fruity Pebbles

ONE OF MY favorite things about the holidays is baking. It gives me an excuse to feast on cookie dough. Yeah, I know you're not supposed to because of the whole "raw egg can kill you" thing, but God bless Betty Crocker. If that's what sends me to the great beyond so be it.

I'm one of those people who thinks that sometimes the dough is better than the finished product. I also have a theory, well more of an ongoing research project, that the prettier the cookie the worse it tastes.

Take the elaborately decorated sugar cookie - that artistic treat is all for show. One bite and your taste buds are severely underwhelmed. My decorated sugar cookie rule is if you can actually tell what it is then it's going to suck.

I know that didn't exactly make sense so hear me out. Of course, you can tell that it's a cookie. But what I mean is if you can look at a decorated sugar cookie and it actually resembles Santa's sleigh because the frosting doesn't overwhelm the shape then it's probably going to taste icky.

Why? Because it means the frosting on the cookie is not buttercream. It's the demon spawn of buttercream - royal icing.

Royal icing in the cookie world is like a beauty contestant - all style, no substance. And by substance, I mean no rich, buttery, melt in your mouth, goodness. Do you know what's in royal icing? Things like water and meringue powder.

Does that sound delicious to you? Absolutely not, but people use it because it does nifty things like "harden," maintains a "high gloss" and works like "cement." Based on those descriptions you might as well spray your cookies with Extra Hold Aqua Net. I'm sure the taste would be about the same.

This is why I'm for the less attractive sugar cookie or the cookie that would win Miss Congeniality (robust personality, but not that cute) in the baked goods beauty pageant. Because a cookie that has you wondering if it's supposed to be shaped like a Christmas stocking or a vacuum cleaner usually means it's got a delicious, overlay and overload of buttercream frosting.

And I'm talking about American buttercream. It's frosting made with confectioners' sugar, butter and milk. Not that fancy ass Swiss Meringue buttercream made with egg whites because eggs *do not* belong in frosting. I'm USA all the way baby!

Okay sorry for the detour into the land of yummy buttercream but seriously just know that if you make the mistake, like I did, of taking Miss Congeniality sugar cookies to a cookie exchange your feelings could get hurt.

What's up with cookie exchanges? I swear it's like sorority rush or the NFL draft. (Having been in a sorority and having watched the NFL draft I'm here to tell you both of these institutions have way more in common than you would think). You go into the party with your platters of cookies and then people select, maybe bid, on the ones they want to take home.

Well, at this exchange my Miss Congeniality cookie was the lonely girl sitting solo in the middle school cafeteria. There wasn't one single taker. There they were perched on a marble kitchen countertop that probably cost more than my first car, all by themselves - lost and all alone. (Give me a second. Just reliving that moment got me a little teary-eyed.)

The real taste bud taser was that a woman who brought multi-colored "cookie presents" was acting like she had just won *Top Chef*. Guests were oohing and ahhing over her tray of desserts.

How many Mistletoe Mojitos had these women consumed? Couldn't they tell these squares were made out of Fruity Pebbles cereal and melted marshmallows?

Seriously, who over the age of four gets that freaking excited over a jacked-up Rice Krispy Treat? Sure, Mrs. Top Chef had decorated each square to look like a present with a fondant bow. (Just yuck on fondant. It's like eating flavored tile grout.) But bow or no bow that still didn't excuse this woman's hubris. She kept talking about the "flavor profile" of her cookies. Really? Fruity Pebbles cereal has a flavor profile? What was it red dye and palm oil?

At this point I started to panic a little. I felt sorry for my cookies, and I wanted them to find a good home. So, I thought WWPDD - What Would the Pillsbury Doughboy Do?

I'll tell you what Mr. Poppin' Fresh would do. It would be to not let a mighty fine sugar cookie made with the finest of ingredients (I'm talking Kerrygold butter and expensive vanilla from Williams Sonoma) get bested by freaking Fruity Pebbles (and honestly, I think this woman even went generic and used Fruity Dyno-Bites because the shape and color of the rice cereal seemed just a tad off). So, I went for the soft spot of any cookie exchange – caloric content.

The cookie exchange is quite the dichotomy. You have a bunch of women wearing Spanx, who work out twice a day and have either just finished a juice cleanse or are about to start one surrounded by their mortal enemies – carbohydrates and sucrose. So, I shared that my cookies were more energy bars than desserts. (People will eat an energy bar that has as many calories as a Snickers as long as they think it's full of "good carbs.")

Then I backed up that claim with more fabrications. I might have casually mentioned that protein powder was mixed in with almond flour and that a flax and sesame seed oil reduction replaced most of the butter.

Before you could say Merry Christmas, women were putting down those Fruity Pebbles squares and going for my Miss Congeniality cookies.

Was it wrong of me to umm, let's call it overhype my cookies? Of course, but it was the holidays and my gift to everyone was guilt-free eating.

Sorry, but I won't feel bad about that - ever.

How fitting that we're ending where it all began with none other than Barbara Gray. Oh yes, the battle for freedom from her neighborhood tyranny continues even during the holidays. So, I decided to give Barbara a one-of-a-kind present she won't soon forget.

A Very Snarky Christmas

YOU KNOW YOUR life has hit a new low or perhaps taken a much different, darker path then you ever imagined when you find yourself at a Goodwill haggling over the price of Christmas decorations.

I had gone to Goodwill to drop off two large Hefty garbage bags filled with clothes my kids had either outgrown or had "never liked" and only wore because they didn't want "to make me mad."

Some people would choose to go through the Goodwill drive thru lane. That, my friends, would be a mistake. You should always go into the Goodwill because you never know what treasures are waiting for you.

I went in and discovered the motherlode of the crappiest Christmas decor you've ever seen. What caught my eyes first was the collection of torn and faded yard blow ups. I had found the Island of Misfit Inflatables.

There was a Frosty with no eyes and a corn cob nose that looked like it had been disfigured in a knife fight with Jack Frost. Poor inflatable Santa Claus had an outfit that had faded to a light pink, and it appeared that at one point Jolly Old St. Nick's head must have been ripped and reattached with duct tape giving him a tracheotomy Santa vibe.

There was a Mickey Mouse with no tail and one ear and a Rudolph that some disturbed individual had drawn a life size target on. If this wasn't ghastly enough, I turned around and what to my wondering eyes should appear but a "mooning Santa."

When the inflatable was new, I believe it had some kind of motorized action that pulled Santa's pants up and down. Now, Santa pants just hung there at full moon like there was no way he could hold it till he got back to the North Pole. It was the "Santa's going to take a dump in your yard" inflatable.

I almost wept with joy. I must have these inflatables. God forgive me, but I had a plan. I found the manager of the store and began the bargaining process.

He informed me, in what I thought was a very superior tone, that, "Goodwill doesn't negotiate on their prices." I explained to him that I really only wanted to borrow the decorations and I would return them or re-donate them in less than a week. So, what I was basically asking for was a lease agreement.

Now, you may be thinking that I'm a deluxe cheapskate trying to rip off a charity, at Christmas, no less. This couldn't be further from the truth. I wish I could pay full price. Sadly, I don't have any kind of budget for schemes or mischief. So, this money would be coming out of my sacred hair highlight funds. Lucky, the Goodwill manager, in I'm sure an attempt to get me out of his store, agreed on a flat price.

I happily skipped out of Goodwill, folded down the seats of my minivan, loaded up the inflatables and their accessories and headed home. It was time for me to marshal my troops and call a meeting.

Later that day

In my kitchen I had assembled the suburban equivalent of the Navy's SEAL Team Six. This highly skilled group consisted of myself, my three best friends and my son who would be providing the tech support. Our mission was to "enhance" the snootiest, biggest pain in the ass neighbor's holiday party. Oh yes, you guessed it Barbara Gray was going to be gifted with a tacky, trashy, tawdry Christmas.

In case you've forgotten (And really how could you?), Barbara is the worst neighbor ever who thinks she wrote the book on good taste and graceful living. Then there's the issue that she lives to tell me I suck.

She's called me out on my yard maintenance, my holiday decor, my parking (She seriously bitches at me that I don't put my car into the garage during the afternoon. Excuse me, I'm home in fifteen-minute increments dropping one kid off and hauling another kid to some kind of practice. I'm not putting my car into the garage to spare her having to gaze upon the beauty that is my Sienna minivan) my children, my pets and my love of Target. You can insult my home, my kids and my pets, but when you start dissing Target you've crossed a line lady and you will pay.

I probably would hate her less if she was unattractive with a hook nose or chunky. But nooo - Barbara is exceedingly well groomed with the dewy skin of the affluent. You just know she devotes a hefty portion of her day to a nine-step skin care regimen. The whole exfoliant, cleanser, toner, tonic, serum, primer, hydrate extravaganza with the glands of virgin sea urchins.

Meanwhile, I'm in the shower hoping the Suave Damage Care conditioner with moisturizing properties will take a detour from my hair to my face and hitch a ride on my pores thus completing my skin care routine.

She's also very fashionable. Her winter outfit is tight black pants stuffed into black boots that look like the ones the S.S. officers wore in Hitler's Imperial March and I'm sure they cover her cloven hoofs. Then there's her collection of designer ponchos that could double as a cloak for her coven.

Barbara is also so very proud that she's so very busy doing important volunteer work. The Symphony, the Lyric Opera have all, according to Barbara, been "blessed by her dedication." Every December Barbara and her husband, Mr. "No Balls" host a party for her fancy friends. This gives her a chance to play Lady of the Manor in a neighborhood devoid of manors. (Or even mini-manors which I guess is like a McMansion with a faux English countryside vibe.)

Two weeks before the party Barbara goes door-to-door and distributes letters to all the neighbors requesting that we "strive for immaculate yards, use a less is more philosophy when it comes to holiday decorating and to "please house our cars in our garages during the evening of her party."

Hey Barbara, I have two letters for you F & U.

Barbara's party was three days away and using my kitchen island as command central I mapped out my plan on two Brawny paper towels with a Sharpie. Directly across the street from Barbara's house was a lovely home that was currently unoccupied.

The owner, a very nice man, was somewhere in Eastern Europe working on a telecommunications project or as the neighborhood gossip went, collecting his mail order bride. All I needed to know was that the gentleman wasn't coming home anytime soon.

We would be using his house, or more specifically his front yard, as ground zero for our caper. The goal was to take all the inflatables I had "rented," eleven in total, (including an Easter bunny that due to the unfortunate stretching properties of a portion of the nylon looked like he had male genitalia) and get them in the yard.

Next up we needed to add in other "not so gently used" pieces I had picked up like broken candy cane yard stakes. A layer of loud holiday music and a light show would be the piece de la resistance.

The very big catch, as in the most important thing, is that Her Royal Highness of the Cul-de-sac couldn't see us doing any of the set up. This meant we had to get the whole yard rigged an hour before her party and we would need at least an additional hour undetected by HRH to do some electrical work in the backyard. We had to lay out all the extension cords (Just in case you're curious it took twenty-three super long outdoor extension cords.) and get them hooked up on my home's exterior outlets.

All these covert maneuvers required the assistance of my friend Kelly. She would have to use her clout as the Homeowners Association Treasurer to get Barbara out of her home. Oh, yes, the old HOA ploy. It worked so well in the spring I decided to use it again.

Barbara, as I'm sure you remember, is the HOA recording secretary. (Yep, she got the Yard of the Month death penalty in April, but she still got to keep her position on the HOA board.) I suggested/told Kelly that on the afternoon of the party she needed to call an emergency meeting at Starbucks to discuss something sure to get Barbara's attention like some kind of juicy financial malfeasance or unauthorized shrubbery installation. Kelly, who really needs to work on her fibbing skills, was afraid she wouldn't be able to pull off.

This was when I had to tell Kelly to put on her big girl granny panties and then reminded her of all the things I had done for her up to and including my August smoke bombing (left over from July 4th - waste not want not) of a car. It was my way of helping Kelly get her twin daughters into kindergarten

Yes, I know that sounds extremely odd and a little unsettling. So, here's the quick backstory.

There are only eighteen, very valued, morning kindergarten slots at the school our kids attend. (Yes, it's a public school but the morning slots go fast, and you have to sign up in person to get them.) This past summer a group of moms formed a little team to make sure their kids would get those slots and be in the same kindergarten class.

On the morning of the kindergarten sign up Kelly called me in a panic. There was a mother who was standing in the sign-up line holding spaces for herself and eight other mothers thus totally blocking Kelly from getting her twin daughters enrolled into an a.m. kindergarten program.

Kelly, who had been standing in line since five a.m., called me for help. She had figured out by eavesdropping on the line hogs phone conversations that ten minutes before the school opened the other moms would haul ass up to the school and take their "rightful" places.

I, on the spur of the moment, awakened from a deep slumber, came up with the brilliant idea of a smoke bomb. I asked Kelly to find out which car was the line hog's and then leave the rest to me.

Still wearing my sleep T-shirt, I snuck up to the school, did the stop, drop and roll, chucked a harmless smoke bomb and yelled, "Oh my God, who's Range Rover is on fire!"

The mom who was the human space holder started screaming, left her place in line and ran to her SUV thus enabling Kelly to move up and grab two slots for her twins.

My little reminder did the trick and Kelly assured me she'd be able to pull off the HOA subterfuge. Our goal was to get Barbara out of her house no later than two in the afternoon on Friday. We would use that time to rig all the electrical and lay the inflatables out making it easier for us to drag them into the front of the house right before the party.

The electrical part would require me springing my son early from school. I told him I would need speakers for the yard, preferably surround sound and some kind of computer-generated light show. He was also given a budget of $10 to purchase the most obnoxious Christmas songs ever produced and put them on a continuous loop. I suggested anything with *Kidz Bop* in the title.

Once everybody was clear on their responsibilities, we kicked my son out of the kitchen, and toasted our plan with some Jingle Juice.

Friday

It was party time, and I was pumped. I went through my to-do list and checked it twice. All was good. At 2:30 I got my son out of school and gave him the "it's best not to bother your dad with this information" speech.

Yes, that's right, I keep secrets from my husband. It's called a marriage not truth serum. Besides what man wants to be updated constantly on the day-to-day minutiae of his wife's life? The answer to that question is a guy you never want to marry.

We met up with the rest of the crew (minus Kelly who had successfully managed to get Barbara to attend the emergency HOA meeting) at the rendezvous point (the out of the country neighbor's backyard) and began attaching extension cords to the inflatables, setting up speakers in the front yard shrubs and positioning two spotlights.

Kelly texted us when she was leaving Starbucks which gave us just enough time to clear out. As we were getting back into our cars, I shouted something I had always wanted to say, "We ride at dusk ladies! We ride at dusk!"

Barbara's fancy pants cocktail party started at 6 p.m. I had planned for us to be in position in the backyard at 5:55. I wanted to ensure that a few party guests had already arrived before we went into full triple T mode (trashy, tacky and tawdry).

My feeling was it was best to plug in the lights and inflatables with a few guests in the house thus keeping Barbara busy from peering out any of her front windows. After we saw three cars pull up and the guests welcomed into Chateau Snooty I gave the signal to begin.

Dressed in black, of course, my friends and our older kids dragged the deflated inflatables into the front yard. Then we jammed all the falling apart signs into the lawn, put up the broken candy cane yard art and threw piles of Christmas lights on the grass. (You didn't think I would actually take the effort to string lights, did you?)

When all that was done, we ran to the backyard and texted my son to plug everything into Mission Control which was my garage with about thirteen large power strips. He was also in charge of starting the music and a computer-generated light show that was so intense I was afraid it would induce seizures in squirrels.

Like magic, all the hideous inflatables began to come to life, hunks of Christmas lights shone brightly and *Grandma Got Run Over by a Reindeer* began blaring from the speakers as green and red strobes hit the house like army artillery in an elf domination saga. It was a sight to behold, and it got even better.

At around 6:15 car after car began cruising down the street creating a wee bit of a traffic situation. This was because earlier in the day I had gone on Craigslist and under events listed a "Ho, Ho, Ho House" as a "don't want to miss holiday drive by" with candy canes for the kids.

The bounty of cars, the lights, the music, and the abundance of less than classy decorations had Barbara so livid that she called the cops.

No worries on that front because I had it covered. I find for any scheme to be successful you need to work backwards from a worst-case scenario objective. And in this case the worst that could happen was someone calling the cops.

Since we're talking about Barbara, a monument to worst case scenarios, I knew, without a doubt, that a police officer would most likely be visiting us. This is why I also mentioned in the "event" announcement that we would also be collecting canned goods for the local food bank.

I was surprised by how generous people were. In under an hour, we already had a sizable number of donations. This was very good for several reasons, one of which was because when two police officers arrived, I was ready to extol the virtues of the Ho, Ho, Ho, House.

When I explained to them that our children, in the spirit of the season, had decorated the house, for one night only, in an effort to bring holiday cheer to the community while collecting canned goods, they thought the "woman who called in the complaint" was being a "real Scrooge."

I smiled as I agreed with them and then offered each of the officers a candy cane. They told us to "keep up the good work," and left.

I'm pretty sure Barbara had been watching my interaction with the police. I could see some of her party guests were transfixed to her living room window viewing the merriment of the common folk. As soon as the officers drove off, she ran over wearing what can best be described as a fur monstrosity, and screeched, "Why are you still here?"

I gave her a confused look and said, "What are you talking about? Those delightful police officers came over to admire our handiwork. They think it's great. Don't you like it?"

She bellowed, "I'm not done yet. I'm calling the sheriff!" and scurried back to her yard."

It was right about then that my daughter started yelling to people in their cars to "Honk if they love Santa!" What a beautiful sound that made, like angels trapped in a traffic jam.

I was so happy and overflowing with the spirit of the season that I hugged my friends and paraphrased Dr. Seuss, just a bit and said, "Tonight maybe Christmas, doesn't come from a store. Maybe Christmas, perhaps means a little bit more! Like showing our horrible neighbor that we've now declared war."

With that we all laughed, and I realized one of the greatest gifts of all was friendship and of course, revenge.

Thank You!

I'm sending you much love for reading *Four Seasons of Snarky*. I hope this book made you laugh. I absolutely live for that. If you have a moment, I would greatly appreciate you reviewing *Four Seasons of Snarky* on Amazon. And for news on upcoming books, social media and current blog posts please go to www.snarky-inthesuburbs.com

If you missed out on the first two books in the Snarky in the Suburbs book series here's a peek at the book that started it all – *Snarky and the Suburbs Back to School*.

Chapter One -New School Year's Eve

The real "New Year" for any mother is not January first but the day school starts. This is when we have our rebirth. We make goals and to-do lists and attempt to implement new and improved habits and routines like an actual bedtime for our children. Today is my New Year's Eve. It's the day before school starts and it's being kicked off with the annual Spring Creek Elementary School PTA Parent Coffee.

Don't be misled by the "Parent Coffee" label. No self-respecting dad has ever shown up for it. This is a pity because the coffee is a harbinger of all the delicious drama the new school year holds.

I'm a woman who relishes drama. To me, drama is the buttercream frosting of life. Sure, you could live without it, but who would want to? Oh, I know it's unseemly to admit you enjoy drama, but drama is so much more than the over-blown theatrics of attention-seeking females.

Mom drama tells a story. By closely watching the nuances, you can learn so much from who's possibly cheating on their husband to which mom is making a calculated move to climb the ladder of the PTA hierarchy. All of this information is invaluable, especially to someone like me.

I find it impossible to mind my own business. You may call this an immense character flaw. I call it the makings of a great humanitarian. Hi, I'm Wynn Butler, wife, mother, and professional pot stirrer.

If you think pot stirring is a bad thing, you couldn't be more wrong. I only stir the pot of people who, quite frankly, need their icky pot stirred. I'd like to think I've taken this skill to a new almost superhero-ish level.

I'm a mom with cellulite and spider veins that resemble the Mississippi River on a Rand McNally map of the forty-eight contiguous states, fighting for truth, justice, and revenge. Including, but not limited to, schemes, payback scenarios and much-needed comeuppances.

I believe I've always had this talent seared into my genetic code, but I didn't reach my full pot stirring potential until I became a mother. Blame it on the estrogen surge, but you know how before you had kids you would take people's crap more? I did. I would suck it up, tell myself to let it go, and move on.

Motherhood (and maybe being middle-aged) changes that. It's one thing for someone to be mean spirited to you. It's another thing altogether for that same person to exact their character flaws on your child (or really any children).

I'm all about prevention as in not letting this kind of thing happen and if that doesn't work, I move on to my specialty – remediation: the act of correcting an error, a fault or an evil.

This PTA shin dig screams remediate!

The coffee typically is held at a house inhabited by a family in the higher socioeconomic strata of the school district. This year Jacardia (Jeh-car-de-ah) Monroe, my arch nemesis, is the hostess.

Jacardia resembles an upside-down broom, with the face of a really not-aging-well Taylor Swift and hair that would put Goldilocks, Rapunzel, or any Disney Princess to shame. (Think excessively long blonde ringlets.)

She looks rather like one of those Dollar Store off-brand Barbie dolls that have been left out in the sun to cure, kind of like a strip of beef jerky that's been soaked in chlorine and then rode shotgun on a pool float for an entire summer.

I can sum Jacardia up with one sentence: She's the sort of woman who still, two plus decades after leaving college, insists on putting a sorority sticker on her Range Rover.

Every time I see her in her car, I want to roll down my window and yell "Move on! There's not a SAE formal in your future!"

She's also number three on my list of moms I'd like to Botox in the jugular with an epidural needle.

My first problem with her is I know for damn sure her real name isn't Jacardia. That's because women who have blown out forty candles on a birthday cake weren't given that kind of name when they entered the world, headfirst with a firm forceps yank, in the late seventies.

Here's what fortyish year-old women are called: Jennifer, Melissa, Amanda, and Jessica. No mom in 1978 named her kid "Jacardia." To turn my hunch into solid fact last year I asked Aleexiah, Jacardia's eight-year-old daughter, what her mom's real name is. "You know," I said, "what does your grandmother call her?"

She quickly replied, "Oh, my nana calls my mom Janet."

Bingo!

My other problem with Janet/Jacardia is that she brings back repressed memories from junior high. No, I didn't go to school with her, but she represents everything I used to fear.

Here's the deal: I'm a big girl, and by that I mean I'm working a size 12 pant (on a good day), a size 11 shoe and my shoulders are just a little bit broader than my husband's. I'm okay with that. I mean really, who cares? We grow up. We go to college. We have careers, marriages, kids. All that junior high angst is but a distant memory, right?

Hell no.

This is what happens. Your kids go to school, and it's like you've time traveled back a couple of decades. It's been eight years, but I remember my son's first day of kindergarten like it was an hour ago. There I was clutching his hand and feeling more vulnerable than I ever had in my life. I was about to voluntarily surrender him over to another woman.

As I was fighting back tears, I had my first Jacardia sighting. You could tell she was the lead dog in a pack of moms with perfectly blown out hair and breasts that in no way were in accordance with their body mass index yet defied gravity and, quite possibly, the speed of light and sound as well.

They were whisper dissing about the other kindergarten moms and here's the good manner's deal breaker – the other kids. Who disses five-year-olds, except other five-year-olds. Certainly not other moms!

My son Clay was getting dissed because of his haircut. The day before kindergarten he decided to give himself a trim. Suffice it to say, based on what he did to his hair, I don't see a future for him in the beauty industry.

I did get my stylist to do her best to fix it, but he was still sporting some very short hair, which, I thought, by the way, he was totally pulling off.

The whole scene was making me break out in a cold sweat. There I was surrounded by older versions of the girls who taunted me in junior high school. They weren't the same exact girls that terrorized me, but they were the same type.

A posse of bitchy, one-upper, judgey females were back in my life as mothers and now they're weaponized. They've spawned. Creating smaller and possibly, but not always, more evil versions of themselves as ammunition.

Right then and there is when I decided I had no choice, but to declare war on these toned armed, collagen enhanced, cliquey, cruel, haughty moms. It was one thing for me to endure (or worse hide from) these types of females in junior high, but now the stakes were so much higher. I had kids and no way was I going to let these women mess with mine or anyone else's children. It was time to stand strong.

It took me a while to work up the courage. At first, I tried the kill them with kindness routine which lasted till Christmas and was a disaster. All it did was make me their doormat. Then I went to Plan B – ignoring them which took me through spring break. After that, I mustered up my courage and declared war.

You may be thinking a declaration of war is a little over the top or even that I should have tried more earnestly to make friends with the Hot Mom Herd. The problem with the whole "friend" thing is I'm so not HMH material.

Primarily, because I don't have a PhD in Evil or hold dual positions on the PTA and HOA boards wielding power like Mrs. Darth Vadar on her period (which is a really, really bad thing because Mrs. Vadar's cycles are based on the Endor moon which means every fourteen days it's a go).

Then there's the other stuff. I don't have the single-digit body mass index. My breasts are original to owner and aren't inflated, hoisted, and cantilevered to the point of creating a bookshelf for my chin. There is no closet in my house just for my Lululemon yoga pant collection. Shopping isn't my avocation, and I don't worship the holy trinity of acid-based fillers – Restylane, Juvederm and Radiesse.

I know this sounds harsh, with excessively bitter overtones flavored with a smattering of jealousy. All things my mother told me were very unattractive qualities and I freely admit that I might be suffering from the smallest sliver of envy.

I'm a mom who buys clothes in the double digits, suffers from a debilitating case of ankle calf hypertrophy (cankles) and my shirts are a nice and roomy L to XL. I wouldn't be human if I didn't harbor resentment for women who can wear butt crack leggings. By the way thanks TikTok for that trend.

I can't even wear corduroy pants because my thighs rub together so furiously when I walk that it sounds like someone is running a terry cloth towel over a cheese grater. Plus, with all that friction I'm afraid my pants might spontaneously combust.

But besides coveting their trim thighs and pert backsides I'm really, I swear, not that envious. I like that I'm okay with dropping my kids off at school without the benefit of concealer and lip plumping, high impact gloss.

I know I have a lot to be grateful for. I'm in love (most days) with my husband Sam. He's the city attorney and the boy next door all grown up. We started dating in high school and got married the day we both graduated from college.

Beyond brilliant move on my part. I know a good thing when I see it. Sam had everything I wanted in a man. He thinks I'm funny, *does not* think I have cankles, is kind and meets my strict IQ demands.

My genetic code needed a pretty significant upgrade. I had to marry a man with optimum brain power who could help dilute the dumbass gene that's been running rampant in my family for generations. No way did I want to pass that on to my kids. It's too soon to tell, but I dare to dream that my thirteen-year-old son Clay and my eight-year-old daughter Grace will be dumbass-free.

Because I'm entering year eight of fighting the mean mom wars, I'm battle ready when I get to Jacardia's huge ass home after running the gated community gauntlet. By that I mean entering the damned security code four times before the protective portal to "The Land of the Second Mortgages" decides to slowly creak open.

I'm so sick of these stupid coded entry gates that allegedly keep middle-class riffraff like me from entering freely. I told my two kids last month, "No more friends who live in gated neighborhoods. If I can't drive non-stop to your friend's house, then forget about it."

After I find a place to park (which is outside of the gates and requires me to leap over some impressive shrubbery that spells out the name of the subdivision) I re-apply my Lancôme gift with purchase lipstick, notice my teeth look really yellow. (Damn you Crest Whitestripes why don't you work?!) suck in my gut and get ready to see all of the moms I hadn't missed, at all, all summer.

Now about this Mom Coffee – it's serious business. Oh sure, it's presented like it's a chance for everyone to be welcomed back into the warm embrace of the PTA (Yeah, right.) and, as migraine inducing as it is, almost every mom attends out of sheer fear because if you don't, well, the chances are you'll be gossiped about with vigorous enthusiasm. I'm talking work schedules are shifted and babysitters are called in because it's a no kids allowed affair.

I'd like to say that I don't participate in the Mom Coffee game and show up in my "day pajamas" (baggy leggings), a T-shirt, my brown, chemically enhanced with sun-kissed highlights, hair in a ponytail and tennis shoes. But I was raised in the South and an invitation demands that I put some effort into my appearance.

I enter Jacardia's seven thousand square foot French Chateau in my wide leg Gap pants, which were an end of the season steal for just $12.00. I was so excited. My heart was racing as I pulled them over my thighs and behold, they fit AND I didn't have to do the turbo gut suck in! You know, when you suck in your stomach so hard you get dizzy and start seeing spots. I've paired them with my Ann Taylor Loft blouse and my Kohl's sandals, which I got with Kohl's cash – score!

The major faux pas with my outfit besides the fact that it proudly screams, "clearance rack!" is that I'm headed into the Mom Coffee without the must-have designer handbag of the season.

Here's the deal. I don't worship on the altar of Gucci because the day I spend four figures on a purse is the day that my husband will dual schedule divorce proceedings and my competency hearing.

This means I've infiltrated this coven of shrews totally purse-less (it's my way of saying "I surrender") with my car keys in my pants pocket adding a little extra thigh bulk I really don't need.

As one of the only mothers who eat at the Mom Coffee, I head straight for the dining room table and begin to engage in a merry little carbfest. I'm just a girl who can't say "no" to coffee cake.

After very adroitly piling a double-decker of baked goods on my plate and politely stuffing my face I survey the room for friends. First though I have to say howdy to the hostess, Janet/Jacardia. She's not hard to find. All I need to do is look for that mass of blonde hair.

It takes me about three seconds to spot her and it's as if I've been blinded by a disco ball.

Janet/Jacardia is wearing a metallic glitter halter top by Alice + Olivia that is searing my corneas. It doesn't help that the top highlights her terminal torpedo nipples that look like they're trying to drill their way through the Earth's core and as a bonus she's also working some significant side boob.

But wait there's more. Jacardia just happens to be wearing, of course, white butt crack ribbed leggings. She's topped off her outfit by layering on probably a dozen David Yurman necklaces and is flip flopping around in ivory Tory Burch monogrammed sport slide sandals.

"Janet," I say, just to tick her off, "great turnout and this coffee cake is the bomb."

She corrects me with a drawn-out sigh. "You know it's Jacardia and I'm not acquainted with coffee cake. I haven't had a carb since 2007. Keto is as Keto does."

Her loss because the coffee cake is incredible. I take another bite and continue to make my version of small talk with Jacardia by inquiring about the woman she has answering her door wearing a black dress with a white, frilly apron.

"What's up with the maid costume?" I innocently inquire. "Did you get it from the Halloween superstore that just opened up in the abandoned Walmart?"

She looks at me, attempts to frown, but is thwarted by her Botox, so she resorts to pouting her Juvéderm enhanced lips and says, in a bored, breathy voice, "Are you serious?"

I respond, "Well, I saw an outfit just like it there and thought maybe you were giving it a trial run before you wore it for trick-or-treat."

As I'm talking, I'm walking backwards to seek refuge at the dining room table with all the baked goods. I know Jacardia won't follow me. She's a diet vampire and being in a four-foot proximity to carbohydrates is akin to throwing holy water on Dracula.

While I'm getting more coffee cake – sorry, not sorry it's delicious – I'm pondering why all the somewhat sane mothers don't join forces and boycott this ridiculousness. I've even tried to organize a protest movement but, so far, no takers.

It could be because the Mom Coffee is fairly decent entertainment. It's equal parts "Show and Tell" and "Look What I Did This Summer." You've even got a little bit of "Fashion" Week thrown in.

By that I mean there's always a handful of hotties who show up ready to walk that "Mom Runway." In this case, the runway is the path from the crystal-chandelier foyer to the marble-floor-cathedral-ceiling living room, to the Sub-Zero-see through-fridge-eight-burner-Viking-range kitchen.

Once you arrive in the kitchen the "runway" loops through the lodge inspired family room where the fashionista moms can strike a relaxed, yet pretentious final pose. Quite a few mothers get all Spanxed up for this event. I don't know about you, but I think wearing triple Spanx at 8:15 in the morning is a little distasteful.

The Mom Coffee is also where ladies entertain themselves by counting the summer cosmetic surgery procedures. It usually goes something like this: boob job, boob job, Botox, yikes, too much Botox, eye lift (Hmm, wasn't she a little young for that?) Restylane, Restydon't and so on.

Let's just say there are enough chemical fillers in Jacardia's living room that it probably qualifies for its own E.P.A. landfill designation.

You also need sunglasses to protect your optic nerves from the glare of the recently bleached teethed moms. Here's a safety tip: In case of an emergency, if you can't find a flashlight, grab one of these women. Their glow-in-the-dark, UVA-emitting, L.E.D. teeth could serve as spotlights or even create landing beacons for first responders.

The highlight of the soiree is the purse parade. Anyone who has scored a designer handbag is all ready to show it off. It's easy to tell who has a new, thousand-dollar plus purse because they never set it down. The handbag stays securely gripped in their well-manicured hands or dangling off their shoulder. All the better for them to fondle with and for you to see.

Before I even make it back to the dining room for round three (Or is it four?) at the baked goods table, the PTA president Elizabeth "Queen Liz" Derby, rings a sterling silver bell (of course) to quiet the crowd so she can say a few welcoming words.

Liz, draped head to toe in that Burberry plaid stuff that looks like placemats from World Market or a Catholic girls' school field hockey uniform, suffers from an acute case of "Regal Fever." She seriously thinks she's descended from English royalty Don't ever ask her about her family crest. You'll be time traveling back to William the Conqueror. Her hobby is correcting other people's behavior.

The "Queen" is a graduate of the National Academy of Protocol and Etiquette, which she believes has given her the right to tell you that your family is precariously close to being one rung below heathen and that you really need to step it up.

I, on numerous occasions, have pointed out to her it's atrocious etiquette to tell someone r-e-p-e-a-t-e-d-l-y they have bad manners, but she just sticks her nose up in the air and walks away.

Right when Queen Liz gets to the part where she begins hitting everybody up to donate to the Spring Creek PTA Education Fund someone shrieks, "It's a fake! A great big fake!" from the back of the living room.

I'm thinking this is awesome. The extra effort I took to apply lash booster before my mascara is now worth the grooming effort because I'll look fabulous while watching, what I'm hoping will be, a middle-aged chick fight.

I follow the fracas and attempt to work my phone's video camera with one hand, while holding a slice of coffee cake with the other. Oh dear, alert Milan, one mom has accused another mom of trying to pass off a fake Prada as the real deal.

I quickly discover "Murchy" (Mom+Churchy) has started the argument. Murchy (real name Jen Weaver) has the distinction of having more plastic surgery than anyone I've known, and that's saying a lot because I lived in L.A. for three years.

From her reddish-gold hair extensions to dermal injections in her feet to give her more substantial toe cleavage she's one big artificial preservative, kind of like a Rice Krispy treat. Of course, she won't admit to any of her procedures and offers up "living a life of faith" as the reason she looks so "fresh."

I don't care how many Bible study groups she chairs and organizes (which I'm sure focus more on the worshipping of recent advancements in cosmetic surgery then looking deep into the meaning of the Pauline Epistles) Murchy is a bully with a Bible.

To prove my point, she is, right now, accusing the hardest working mother at Spring Creek Elementary, Kathy Ferguson, "Croc Mom," of passing off her purse as a Prada.

Kathy is known for two things. One is her love of Crocs. Winter, spring, summer and fall she's always wearing a rubber shoe. Kathy even has a collection of fleece-lined Crocs for the colder months, and I've seen her break out a gold Croc for more formal occasions.

Her Croc fetish is superseded by her dedication to education and her ten-year-old triplets (two boys, one girl) who are scary smart. I know one of them will find the cure for cancer and the other two will probably colonize the rings of Saturn.

I can see how Croc Mom carrying a Prada handbag has confused Murchy. The two don't really go together, but who cares. Murchy needs to chill the hell out and not be attacking Kathy.

"Your Crocs may be real, but that bag of yours is an *el fako*," Murchy announces. "Anyone can see it's lacking the characteristics of a true Prada bag. The logo plate is way too big and the leather, or should I say pleather is soooo not designer."

Kathy is a lovely, sweet woman who has sacrificed herself on the altar of motherhood. By that I mean she does nothing for herself. All her effort is expended nurturing the brains of her exceptional children.

Most days it doesn't even look like she's thoroughly brushed her hair which is usually in a ponytail with a scrunchie. I think the only makeup I've ever seen her wear is Burt's Bees tinted lip balm.

She's usually very timid so I'm surprised when she gently, but firmly replies, "My purse is vintage, and I do believe the logo plates were bigger back in the day."

Murchy blurts out, "Vintage, as in outlet mall, maybe."

Jacardia and Liz, step into the fray to try to restore some order to the meeting. Liz says she's an expert on Prada and volunteers to judge the authenticity of the purse. She adjusts the Burberry headband on her black severe bob haircut and executes superior posture as she walks over to examine the purse.

There's not a sound in the room. (Except for me eating the coffee cake I grabbed on my way to the throwdown – I couldn't help myself. It has an incredible brown sugar crumble topping.) Liz takes the purse and begins her analysis. She's really getting into her verification duties, even going over the stitching inside the lining. Who knew designer handbag authenticator was in the PTA president's job description?

I look away from the fashion C.S.I. team and see my very young, sweet, beautiful, teaches Pilates and has perhaps the best backside I've ever seen on a human being, got-knocked-up-at-nineteen-and-is-twenty-five-with-a-son-in-first-grade friend, Nikki Sakowski across the room looking distressed.

She mouths "do something" to me. Of course, I'm going to do something. I like Croc Mom and Murchy is number five on that epidural list I've already told you about.

I wink at Nikki and then walk over and interrupt the handbag forensics, "Ah, excuse me, you can quit your quest for the handbag's origin of birth. I know for a fact the purse is a vintage Prada. It's from the 80s. You know big hair, big shoulder pads, big Prada logo."

Jacardia looks over her shoulder at me and in a condescending voice asks, "How would you know what a vintage Prada purse looks like?"

"Well, of course," I say, "I'm no authority on designer leather goods, but my mother-in-law has one just like it and it's so valuable she's left it to my sister-in-law in her will."

The mother-in-law line is the perfect fib. If I had said my mother no one, taking one look at me, would believe that I had grown up in a household with a woman who took a Prada to Target. My mother-in-law on the other hand lives (thank you higher power) two thousand miles away and no one has ever met her. It's conceivable that I could have married "above my station" and have a MIL who's a handbag connoisseur.

In reality, her idea of being all fancy pants is T.J Maxx and I totally love that about her. The genius is my line about leaving it to my sister-in-law. Everyone in the room can see my mother-in-law leaving me her vintage Tupperware, but a Prada, not so much.

I use my declaration of authenticity as a chance to reach in and yank the purse out of Queen Liz's clutches so I can give it back to Croc Mom. As I'm returning the handbag to its rightful owner, I look at Murchy with her immense breasts (Seriously, they're so huge it looks like she must be lactating to feed quintuplets.) pushing out of her hot pink top and ask, "What's wrong, jealous?"

Murchy sneers, "Not of you or her, e-v-e-r. Yuck."

Croc Mom quickly and quietly exits Jacardia's McMansion swinging her purse as she walks out as a kind of F you to Murchy. The good news is that the purse squabble broke up the meeting. As hard as Liz tries, no one wants to get "down to business." We're all spared the boring agenda and introduction of new PTA officers.

Best of all, no one gets a chance to do the Education Fund shakedown. There is one thing I did notice while finishing up the last of the coffee cake – something's up with Jacardia. There isn't anything specific I can point to, but I've got a bad feeling, and I don't think it's from eating half a coffee cake. Jacardia's acting extra full of herself, and she seems sneaky, like she's planning something. This can't be good.

Printed in Dunstable, United Kingdom